Doc's madness-inflected tones cut through the howling wind

"Unhand me! I shall not go softly and gently. Unhand me, I say!" The sounds of scuffling increased. There was a shout of pain, and Doc's voice, raging incoherently, retreated into the distance, buried by the wailing wind.

Jak looked to Ryan. In the dim light, the one-eyed man could see the tension in the albino teen's face. He nodded.

"Who's next, love?" Krysty asked as Jak opened the wag door a sliver and squeezed through. "You or me?" She couldn't believe that they seemed to be breaking all their rules.

"Mebbe both—whatever it takes. Sometimes we've just gotta stand or fall as one."

Other titles in the Deathlands saga:

JAMES AXLER

DEATH LANDS®
Prophecy

A GOLD EAGLE BOOK FROM
WORLDWIDE®

TORONTO • NEW YORK • LONDON
AMSTERDAM • PARIS • SYDNEY • HAMBURG
STOCKHOLM • ATHENS • TOKYO • MILAN
MADRID • WARSAW • BUDAPEST • AUCKLAND

Recycling programs
for this product may
not exist in your area.

First edition January 2010

ISBN-13: 978-0-373-62600-7

PROPHECY

Printed in U.S.A.

The quest for certainty blocks the search for meaning. Uncertainty is the very condition to impel man to unfold his powers.

—Erich Fromm
1900–1980

THE DEATHLANDS SAGA

This world is their legacy, a world born in the violent nuclear spasm of 2001 that was the bitter outcome of a struggle for global dominance.

There is no real escape from this shockscape where life always hangs in the balance, vulnerable to newly demonic nature, barbarism, lawlessness.

But they are the warrior survivalists, and they endure—in the way of the lion, the hawk and the tiger, true to nature's heart despite its ruination.

Ryan Cawdor: The privileged son of an East Coast baron. Acquainted with betrayal from a tender age, he is a master of the hard realities.

Krysty Wroth: Harmony ville's own Titian-haired beauty, a woman with the strength of tempered steel. Her premonitions and Gaia powers have been fostered by her Mother Sonja.

J. B. Dix, the Armorer: Weapons master and Ryan's close ally, he, too, honed his skills traversing the Deathlands with the legendary Trader.

Doctor Theophilus Tanner: Torn from his family and a gentler life in 1896, Doc has been thrown into a future he couldn't have imagined.

Dr. Mildred Wyeth: Her father was killed by the Ku Klux Klan, but her fate is not much lighter. Restored from predark cryogenic suspension, she brings twentieth-century healing skills to a nightmare.

Jak Lauren: A true child of the wastelands, reared on adversity, loss and danger, the albino teenager is a fierce fighter and loyal friend.

Dean Cawdor: Ryan's young son by Sharona accepts the only world he knows, and yet he is the seedling bearing the promise of tomorrow.

In a world where all was lost, they are humanity's last hope....

Chapter One

The sky was a dark blue bleeding into an umbra of purple. It lurched, turned, then spun through 180 degrees. Sickening pain jarred in Jak's elbow, making him bite back the curse that welled up in his throat as bile sought to join it. The Colt Python .357, never a light blaster at the best of times, felt like a deadweight in a hand momentarily numbed. He spit out a lump of bitter phlegm and turned his head.

"Fuck's sake, Ryan, can't fire like this."

The one-eyed man grunted by way of reply as he pulled hard on the wheel of the wag, seeking to avoid another rut in the dry, hard-packed surface. There was no time for words.

Jak cursed again as he slid across the seat in the back of the wag, careening into Mildred, jolting her arm as she took aim at their pursuers.

"Damn it," she snapped as the shot from her revolver sailed high and wide of its intended target.

As soon as they had left the blacktop, each of the companions had known that any attempt at a perfect aim was little more than a hope; but none of them had realized quite how deceptive the surface they had chosen would prove to be.

And their pursuers were more familiar with the territory.

"EASY, BOY. WON'T BE long 'fore we have 'em exactly where we want them."

Jase Demetriou, the driver of the pursuing wag, chuckled. High, with a keening edge, it was the sound of someone who had a high regard for pain and suffering, and who would enjoy inflicting it before the merciful release of a chilling.

"Less laughing and more driving," the speaker cautioned.

Jase nodded with a manic precision. Unhinged he may have been, but Jase was the finest wag driver to come out of Brisbane ville. He looked like he'd barely hit adolescence, but was pushing twenty-five. The sweet, boyish looks that made him a hit with all the gaudies were betrayed by the glint in his eyes. Corden had covered for him many a time. The sights he had seen sickened him, but without Jase his band of coldhearts could never catch their prey.

Like they were doing right now. The stupes were trying to fire on Corden's boys, but the graying brigand knew the land around well enough to feel assured that they would never find their target. The plains that spread between what had once been northern Kansas, Iowa and Nebraska were still—in many ways—the same as they had been since thousands of years before skydark.

The only difference was that after the nukecaust the crust of the earth had seemed to ripple along this flat expanse. Just a little. Just enough to be invisible to the naked eye, but like a never-ending corrugation when you hit it with a wag. Especially a wag in which you were putting pedal to metal. Speed and poor suspension would jolt you, bounce you around the inside of the wag like a pea in a can.

Jase knew the land like it was a part of him. He'd driven it since he was tall enough to get in a seat and have his foot touch the pedal. It was still rough, but he could ride it. And Corden's men knew better than to waste ammo while the wags were in motion.

It was real easy: wait until the stupe driver of the wag they were chasing tipped himself over, then go and pick at the carcass like vultures. There was little real danger. Anyone who put up resistance was usually too dazed by the crash to shoot straight. It was simple to pick them off.

Corden smiled slow as Jase skirted another ripple in the earth. This was one easy way to make jack.

In the rear of the old four-by-four they used, the other two coldhearts who rode with Corden waited their call to action. Thornton yawned and scratched at the ginger stubble on his sharp chin. Nothing excited him until the moment he was called upon to act. Chambers ran a hand over his shaved skull repeatedly, a nervous action. Unlike the others, the dark-skinned coldheart always felt a gnawing in the pit of his stomach until the moment of action. Only then could he really relax.

"We ain't gonna catch 'em in time," he murmured.

"We will," Corden drawled. "Jase ain't let no fucker get away yet."

"Always a first time," Thornton muttered. "Just not today, Jase, just not today."

Corden's smile broadened. "You got some more gambling debts to pay?"

"Win some, lose some." Thornton shrugged.

"Lose some, lose some." Chambers added. "This guy's good. Knew this 'un would be hard."

"Nothing beats Jase for pace," Corden chuckled.

"Never has, never will," the wag driver said softly.

RYAN COULDN'T SEE the ruts before he was on them. The land ahead looked smooth; that was why he had opted to leave the blacktop behind to try to outrun the wag on their tail. Outrun enough to circle and take the offensive. Except it wasn't quite working out as he had hoped. It was all he could do to keep the wag from tipping. The scrub—dark browns with a glimmer of green and some purple and blue to echo the sky—went by them in a blur, both near and in the distance. Over to the horizon, depending on which way he spun the wheel to try to ride another rut, there were the low outlines of hills leading to a plateau. Good cover, but too far away.

They were exposed. Ryan couldn't see behind him, but from the terse epithets dripping from the lips of his companions, he was in no uncertain mind that their pursuers were gaining, with little hope of effective fire to push them back.

Their wag was powerful, with a tuned engine that

was only now beginning to whine at the strain he was putting on it; a solid body with roll bars; no windows— bar the windshield—to either obstruct firing out, or to injure with flying glass from incoming fire; no roof; not armored, but a good, thickly steeled body and a four-wheel drive system. So, it was a wag made for endurance and a driver who knew how to pilot the vehicle. Ryan had escaped from too many similar situations to be caught easily. By the same token, he also knew that his pursuer was a wag jockey who was far, far superior. More importantly, he knew the territory too well.

"Gaining," J.B. said shortly. "Mebbe a few more minutes, then they're on us."

"Can't get a decent shot at them," Krysty gasped, her breath coming short after a swerve had flung her against the wag's central column.

"I would venture that perhaps these coldhearts are so per…sistent because they know what we carry," Doc stammered between jolts, his frame flung around the interior of the wag.

"That's not rocket science," Mildred breathed. "I'd just like to get my hands on the bastard who talked."

IF ONLY SHE KNEW IT, Mildred Wyeth would have been too late to extract revenge on their betrayer. Tilson was chilled, his sightless eyes staring into the sky as his corpse lay behind the bar he had, until a few short hours before, tended, the bar where he kept his eyes and ears open for any information he could sell.

Ling and Smith had been the inadvertent source of

his tale. The two sec men for Big Bal Hearne, baron of Brisbane, had been admiring of the people they had so recently worked alongside. Too admiring, and too mired in brew.

"Still don't see why Bal didn't trust us with the job," Smith had muttered.

"Specialist job needs specialist worker," Ling slurred. "Look at it like this. We know these people. Mebbe Bal figured we were too close to things, couldn't see what was going on under our own noses."

"Fuck off. We're good sec. Best there is. Wouldn't keep jobs otherwise."

Ling shook his head so hard he nearly fell off his stool. "Shit," he muttered, grabbing the bar for support and looking around before he said anything else. He beckoned Smith nearer. Neither of them noticed Tilson. No one did. That was the secret of being a good bartender. And the secret of learning secrets.

"Doesn't matter what we are. Mebbe Bal was right. How would we know? Point is that he got to be the baron he is by being careful. Eyes in his ass. Eyes on everything. Suspects every fucker. Trusts none of 'em, either. That includes us."

"So why does he trust them?" Smith asked, his brow furrowing as he tried to make sense of Ling's words through the fog of alcohol.

"Reputation. Word spreads by trader. Traders live or get chilled by how they run their convoys. Coldheart cheating bastards don't last long. These guys rode too many convoys. Simple." He shrugged and nearly fell off his stool. Righting himself again, he added, "Besides, they got it right, didn't they? I wouldn't have thought Alex had it in him to sell us out like that. Too stupe, for a start. 'Cept we were the stupes not to see what he was doing."

Smith sighed heavily. "Sure could have done with that jack as bonus."

Ling barked a short laugh that turned to a cough. He hawked, then said, "That ain't all. Good wag and supplies for the six of them, too."

"Fuck's sake, why they get that?" Smith questioned, his eyes wide.

Ling shrugged. "Dunno. Guess it's 'cause they missed the convoy out of town. Figure Bal would want them to go rather than wait for the next one." He grinned when he saw the puzzled look on Smith's face. "Know too much. Know Bal's weak spot. Know the whole story. We don't. Would you want them still around, knowing what they do?"

Smith's puzzled frown grew more intent. "That's a fuckload of knowing," he muttered.

One thing Tilson knew: neither man would remember what they knew come the morning. Neither would, in all likelihood, remember a word of what they had discussed this night. The pair had drunk far too much. Tilson knew them well: not as men, but as customers. He knew their limits, had added shine to their brew when he realized their tongues were loosening. Knowledge was power. That was what "knowing" really meant.

It was late. The bar was quiet now. Only a few solitary drinkers and the two sec men remained. Tilson cast an eye over the dingy interior. He could slip out for a few moments and not be missed. Big Bal Hearne made his people work hard, in return for which they had a reasonably secure life. There was little else in this territory. Few people stayed out late when they had backbreaking work come sunrise.

Tilson left the drinkers and made his way to a rooming house down the sidewalk. It was a pretty fair bet he wouldn't be seen, but he still maintained a level of caution.

The main door to the rooming house was unlocked. The hall was dark, but he knew his way along it by feel. His boots greeted each sagging floorboard and splintered crack like an old friend. On the steps, he knew which ones were liable to creak, and which ones he could tread securely.

Second floor. Third door on the left. As he reached it, he could hear the low murmur of voice within. Softly, he tapped on the door. Two quick, pause, two slow. The door opened a crack, the face in shadow from the dim glow of the oil lamp within. But the high-pitched giggle was unmistakable.

DEMETRIOU GIGGLED again. "On 'em soon enough."

Corden looked over his shoulder and into the rear of the four-by-four. Chambers was wide-eyed, intense concentration on his face. He was cradling a blaster in one arm, the hand of the other unconsciously stroking the barrel. Thornton looked almost asleep, heavy-lidded eyes masking his expression. A remade Glock and an old PPK .38 were lying loosely in his lap, his hands barely touching them.

Corden's weathered skin creased as he looked from one to the other. 'Get ready, boys. Showtime.'

Thornton sat forward, his eyes barely opening any farther. "'Bout time. I've got a hot date with some craps, and this is taking way too long."

Chambers shook his head. "Man, you're gonna lose that before it's even dented your pocket. Might not get a payday like this for some time to come. You should be more careful."

"Like you, eh?" Thornton murmured with a sly grin. Chambers looked uncomfortable. He thought that his little jolt habit was a secret. He should have realized that a person couldn't keep such secrets in a small ville like Brisbane.

Corden, seeing his expression, barked a harsh, loud laugh and reached across, clapping Chambers on the shoulder.

"Who gives a fuck, as long as you do the job. Just keep that in mind, boy." With which, he turned back to the plain unfolding in front of them. There was less distance between the wags than before. With each turn the vehicle ahead made, it lost a little. With each spin of the wheel Demetriou made, they gained a little more.

It wouldn't be long now. And while the four cold-hearts rode every bump and dip in the plain, knowing from long experience where Demetriou's driving could not avoid disturbance, Corden knew that the six people in the wag ahead would be bounced like a pig in a barrel, until their heads were ringing and they couldn't see straight.

Easy meat.

"GAINING," JAK SAID simply.

"How much?" Ryan snapped over his shoulder.

"Too much," Krysty replied. She was in the front, next to Ryan, and had wedged herself—as much as was possible—between the seat and the dash. Her head was against the roof at an angle. She risked her neck, but at least she had some stability and her bastard ribs didn't hurt so much. It also gave her a view that was the equal of the others, and another pair of eyes for the driver, who could not risk a backward glance.

"No way we're gonna outrun them, lover. This is their land. We're gonna have to stand and fight."

"Always assuming, my dear, that we can work out which of them we should fire upon," Doc said softly. "I fear that I will be seeing double, at the very least."

"If we didn't jump so much on this bastard surface, then at least we could get off some fire at them," J.B. muttered as much to himself as to anyone else.

He knew what Mildred was about to say before the words came out of her mouth. It was the natural repost: "They know we can't. That's why they were so keen to follow us out here."

Ryan's mind whirred. That was the key: their pursuers' knowledge of the territory had allowed them to bide their time. Just keep driving, and the land wasn't going to get any flatter. Sooner or later someone would get injured—already had, if he was any judge of how Krysty had positioned herself—and if it was him then the wag crashed. They were making it easy for the cold-heart bastards.

So give them something they wouldn't expect.

"Stay frosty. This is gonna hurt," the one-eyed man yelled as he threw the wag into a spin.

TILSON HAD NO INTIMATION of what would happen to him when Demetriou admitted him to the darkened room. He had some good information. Corden paid him well. In the wake of a convoy there was always someone who wanted to get out of the ville. They headed off, and no one knew if they ever reached their destination. No one cared. It was that simple. This time, there was more jack involved than usual. He should get paid well.

Not that this was the only kind of information he ped-dled. You fade into the background, keep alert and you hear all sorts of shit. Tilson knew that Corden would do anything to rake in the jack. And there were always things going down that Big Bal Hearne wouldn't like, things that could be kept secret at a cost.

"So what brings you here when you should be tend-ing bar?" Corden asked from where he sat on the room's only chair. "Something good, I hope."

Tilson told him as concisely as possible. He knew he had to get back to the bar.

Corden nodded, then shrugged. "Sounds good. We'll

keep an eye for them. The usual arrangement, right?"
Tilson nodded. "Okay. Fuck off."

Tilson had hurried out, closing the door behind him.

DEMETRIOU YELLED incoherently, throwing the wag into
a spin and throwing Chambers and Thornton into each
other, their blasters clattering to the floor of the vehicle, the noise mingling with their shouts of incompre-
hension and fury.

Corden, on the other hand, just smiled. Softly he
said, "Well, well, they got balls, I'll give 'em that. Even
the bitches."

Demetriou slewed the vehicle counter to the grain of
the land, bucking as he hit a rise that he would otherwise have avoided. Corden braced himself, looked over
his shoulder at the coldhearts in the rear.

"Ready to rumble, boys. Looks like they want some
action."

JUST AS CHAMBERS and Thornton had been taken by
surprise, so, too, had the companions in the wag ahead.
It was only the fact that there were four of them
squeezed tighter in the rear of the vehicle that saved a
greater injury.

"Ryan, what—"

"I get it. Take the fight to them." J.B. grinned.
"Why not?"

Ryan's jaw was set tight in concentration, but still the
ghost of a smile flickered across his lips. "Attack is the
best form of defense."

He was headed straight for the wag that had been pursuing them. For the first time, he got a clear look at his opponents. Two in front, two in back. The wag jockey had an intense, focused look about him. The man next to him—older, more battle-scarred—had a little more insouciance. A veteran. He didn't get a clear look at the two in the back before the wag slewed to one side, trying to flank them. With their knowledge of the territory, he couldn't let them do that. Ignoring the jolting, bone-rattling impact of each rut in the plain, he altered his own course so that he could stay head-on.

Krysty had maneuvered herself around so that she was facing front. Impact on one rut lifted her from her seat and slammed her against the dash, eliciting a yelp as her ribs felt like they were turning in and spearing her, driving the breath from her body.

Dust clouds from the two wags as they crossed paths and tried to circle back rose in swathes around the vehicles. The choking blanket obscured vision and trapped in throats and noses as it billowed into the glassless windows. Even in an attempt to counter the attack, Ryan might have miscalculated his play. The other wag had glass to keep the dust clouds at bay. They might not be able to see, but at least they weren't choking.

Ryan tried to guide the wag over the treacherous terrain, but now even his visual guide was gone. In the yellow-ochre dust cloud he could see little more than a yard or two ahead.

Over the whine of their own engine, he could hear a

keening note, growing louder, as the coldhearts' wag bore down on them.

But from where?

TILSON DIDN'T EVEN KNOW what had hit him until it was too late. He'd made it back to the bar, where Ling and Smith were still deep in incoherent discussion, still half badmouthing their baron, and half holding back lest they be overheard and reported. The other drinkers stayed apart and kept their heads down, lost in their own private hells.

Tilson didn't have to serve another drink between getting back and closing up. These guys didn't really want to drink anymore, they just didn't want to go home because of what awaited them, either awake or sleeping.

As he locked up, Tilson was kind of scared about what waited for him when he closed his eyes. Visions of Corden and Demetriou. Maybe of what they might do to him, which made him think a little more of how he felt about the two men: the way they had greeted his information, the way he had been dismissed…. It was not like usual. He couldn't exactly say what it was that got under his skin, crawling like a roach up and down his spine, making him want to piss with fear. Just a feeling.

It should have made him careful. It should have made him look over his shoulder. But it didn't. It just wrapped itself around him, making him look inward rather than out. The slightest noise should have made him start.

He didn't notice Demetriou, waiting in the shadows for him. The young man was going to step out and take him before he had a chance to yell. Seeing how distracted he was, grinning to himself all the while, Demetriou decided to let him pass. Would Tilson spot him? Would he realize? That would make it more fun, like chasing rabbits.

Tilson was oblivious. Demetriou slipped out of the shadow, fell into step behind him. Nothing. He wasn't even going to jump, turn around in fright, give Demetriou a chance to show how quick he was by cutting him before he could yell. This was boring. He needed to get it done with.

Demetriou quickened his pace and was on Tilson in three steps. One hand snaked around to cover his mouth. The other, holding a sharp blade, slipped up under the ribs at the back, piercing and twisting.

Tilson's eyes bugged as the pain hit. Any sound was deadened by Demetriou's hand and the blood that welled in his throat, filling his lungs. Already dark, the night slipped away to black.

Demetriou let Tilson fall back against him. Twisting the blade to break the vacuum of suction, the young man eased it out. He let Tilson slump, his face up, and looked into his eyes. Demetriou laughed softly before he melted back into the shadows, leaving the corpse alone in the alley, barely aware before its chilling that life had been snuffed like a candle.

Chapter Two

Ryan didn't even get a chance to curse his shock as they were broadsided by the four-wheel-drive wag. Sky that was visible through the thinning clouds of dust as they rose now became perpendicular to the ground, the lurch of the vehicle as it reached its optimum tilt making their guts spin and churn.

The dust raised by the pursuit had served their opponents well. It had allowed them to flank and corner, to take their prey sideways-on and attempt to halt their progress by simply tipping them over.

But the dust also hindered Ryan's aim.

Inside the wildly shuddering wag, Mildred and J.B. were thrown against each other and into Jak, who felt his ribs creak at the impact. Sandwiched between the two older companions and the side door of the wag, the albino teen felt breath squeezed from his body, saw flashing lights and stars in his head as he cracked it on the metal of the wag.

Doc was flung over the seats at an obtuse angle, his spine twisting in a way that he wouldn't have thought possible. The back of his skull cracked on Krysty's knee, and for a moment all went black before the rising bile in his gullet brought him back to wakefulness. He retched the thin strings over Krysty's boots, and over the LeMat he had dropped in the shock of impact.

Ryan gripped the wheel. He could do nothing to right the vehicle, but an instinct—perhaps a finely tuned sense of balance—told him that the vehicle could not tip onto its side. There was something about the way in which it slowed and came to a halt, if only momentarily, that told him there was not enough momentum to tip them.

If they landed upright, there was still a chance. He tried to speak, to yell, to tell the others to ready their blasters. But with no breath in his body, and dust choking his lungs, all that emerged was a strangled, hoarse croaking.

The wag engine died. Outside, he could hear the engine of the other wag, purring and ticking over. It was still. Why?

Inside his wag, Ryan could hear the others painfully rasping and coughing as they sucked in breath and dust, trying to break past the pain caused by the collision. He forced himself to move, even though every muscle seemed to have lost its strength and solidity. He felt as if he was moving through quicksand, the dust in the air echoing the effect by his seemingly breathing the same way.

At the back of his mind he felt the urge to give in to the blackness that wanted to enfold him.

He knew he couldn't do it, even though it seemed so inviting.

"Woo! Jase, what the fuck are you—"

Thornton, raised from his torpor by the impact,

yelled at the driver of the coldhearts' wag, slapping him on the back of the head. Demetriou turned in his seat and glared at Thornton, his eyes dead and cold, looking through his very being as they sized up how he could chill him, slowly and agonizingly. Chambers, eyebrow raised, watched Thornton shrink back.

Corden put a hand on Demetriou's shoulder, turning him back to the wheel.

"Not now, Jase. He can keep, if you want. We got more important hunting."

He spoke softly, and with no apparent urgency, even though he felt a quickening pulse in his chest. He knew from experience the way to deal with the young hothead. Jase was the best wag jockey he'd ever known. He was also a stone chiller, with no thought for any consequence. Fearless. Thornton was lucky not to have had his throat slit already.

They were wasting precious seconds while this continued. Corden looked out of the windshield. The dust raised by the close pursuit and stalk was now beginning to settle. Both wags had stopped moving. Closed windows let in little of the dust, but outside it was like looking at a wall. The purple-and-ochre-tinged blue of the sky was forming a larger slice of the picture framed by the windshield, but at ground level it was a wall of swirling brown hues.

Demetriou wasn't sure of the other wag's location. Then there was a break in the wall, the chance to hit the wag when they couldn't see from where the strike would come. Corden didn't have to tell the wag jockey what to do. Demetriou acted on instinct. He knew that the constant circling was losing his orientation, and thus his advantage. He knew that it evened the odds. And that was something none of them wanted. So he took his chance.

Only thing was, he didn't bother to tell anyone of his plan. Corden had a split second of warning as the wag appeared from the swirling dust. Chambers was always braced for any dangers. His natural caution and nervousness served him well in this instance. Only Thornton had been blindsided.

And now they stared at the wag in front of them as the dust settled. Now, without the churning of the wags to stir it up, the dust fell rapidly to the ground.

"Shit, thought I'd put 'em on their side," Demetriou whispered.

"Figured you had, too," Corden agreed. "Still, gotta work with what we've got. Tell you something, that was one hell of a hit they took. Must've scrambled their brains a little."

"Sure hope so," Chambers murmured.

"Only one way to find out," Thornton added. His hand had reached for the wag door before Corden had a chance to speak. Corden's jaw tightened. He was supposed to be the chief here. He couldn't have Thornton getting uppity and above himself.

"Wait, Sean," Corden said mildly. The fact that he was so mild was a threat in itself. Thornton and Chambers had run with Corden long enough to know that he was at his quietest before he struck.

Thornton's hand froze. Corden looked from Thornton to the windshield, taking in what was happening in front of them. As the dust began to lay flat back to the earth, he could see that the figures in the other wag were hardly stirring.

"Yeah. Let's go, then. But take it slow. We know they're good. Just a matter of how fucked up Jase got 'em."

Demetriou giggled. "Fuck 'em up some more."

KRYSTY GROPED for her blaster where it had fallen beneath the dash, then pulled herself upright. She hawked out a glob of dust-heavy phlegm and blinked heavily. Her eyes were running with tears, and her sight was blurry, but at least the grit was shifting. A wag stood about fifty yards from them. Four doors were opening, and a man was getting out of each, blaster in hand.

She could hear Ryan's raw, painful breath behind her shoulder. She could sense when he was in trouble, when he was struggling. Now was such a time. Even though Krysty's ribs felt like knives, her head was clear, and she could feel that he was struggling to clear his own.

She knew without looking in back that the others were beginning to stir. Jak, Mildred, J.B.—they were all moving, but they were slow. As fogged as Ryan.

Doc was an easier proposition. He was at her feet, coughing up the last of the bile jolted from him by impact. With a final spit, he picked up the LeMat and dusted it off with the tail of his frock coat, rising steadily to her level. Clear eyes on the wag a short distance away, he spoke without looking at her.

"My dear, when one's mind is as apt to wander as mine, it is surprising what concussion can do to focus and center oneself."

"Glad one of us is," she murmured.

"Two, I think," he replied. "We need time. Can we purchase such a commodity?"

"Only one way to find out," she said, raising her blaster.

"Admirable," Doc whispered, raising his own.

"THEY MAY BE POSSUM." Corden gestured to his own blaster. "Shoot first."

"Takes the fun out of it," Demetriou snarled with a vulpine grin.

"Ain't s'posed to be fun. S'posed to be business," Chambers said from behind.

"Mix 'em up," Thornton said with a snigger.

"Easy now," Corden muttered as he stepped forward from the cover of the wag door. It was as much to himself as to any of the others. As soon as the coldheart broke cover, a shot from the wag ahead kicked up dust at his feet.

He fired a volley in reply as he stumbled back to the cover of the wag door. It whined as it hit metal and ricocheted into the blue sky.

"Possum it is," Chambers said. "Gren?"

"Right, and whoever throws it is an open target, even with covering fire. 'Sides which, we blast that fucker and we lose what we've come out for in the first place."

"So what do we do, then?" Thornton asked.

Demetriou smiled slyly.

"How we doing?" Krysty rasped as soon as she had snapped off a round.

"Fucked, but not chilled yet," Jak replied. He had disentangled himself from Mildred and J.B., who were still struggling to clear concussed heads. Like Ryan, whose soft moans bespoke of his attempts to break through the concussive fog, they were temporarily out of action. It was down to the three who had clear enough minds.

"We can keep them at bay, but that's about it for now," Krysty said. "Reckon Ryan can get this wag going again?"

"Not likely," Jak said shortly.

"So we can't move, but they can," Krysty whispered. "Big advantage."

"A predictable one," Doc countered, "as, I think, we are about to see."

Sure enough, even as he spoke, the engine of the wag facing them sprang to life.

"You can't be serious," Chambers breathed.

"Why not?" Corden countered. "We don't want them, we just want what they're carrying."

"But what if the wag goes up?"

"Won't hit near the tanks," Demetriou told him. "Side-on, near the tail. Spin 'em and scramble 'em. They ain't got the firepower to stop us. Play with 'em a little."

Chambers sat back, sighing softly. Crazies. Demetriou and Corden. Running with these stupes was doing nothing for his nerves. He felt his stomach lurch in agreement. Stealing and chilling was something he wanted to do because it was easier than breaking your back for Big Bal. Doing it with Corden's crew wasn't easier—no way.

Demetriou gunned the wag engine until it roared, put the wag into gear and released the brake.

Chambers closed his eyes as the wag shot forward.

"STUPE CRAZY bastards," Krysty cursed. There was every chance that the idiots coming for them could total their own wag as much as they could overturn the wag— now a seemingly too flimsy shelter—in which she and her companions were clustered. It was as if these cold-hearts didn't care. Maybe their wag was the stronger. Maybe the front bars on the wag had been put to a test like this before.

It didn't much matter. They had some firepower, but would it be enough to stop the oncoming wag, or at least to deflect it from its course?

"I think this may be one for me," Doc said in her ear. He was whispering, but it still sounded loud and clear. Using the frame of the glassless window as a rest for the barrel of the LeMat, Doc took aim for the windshield of the oncoming wag.

If the coldhearts were crazies, then maybe they had met their match in Doc. The prematurely aged Tanner grinned, his strong white teeth reflective of the mad glint in his eye. This was a challenge he could relish. Only a fool would accept it. Doc was that fool. When you had seen all that he had seen, experienced three different eras and still been left alive, isolated and marooned, there was little else left but to accept the insane as the sane, and to rise to any challenge presented.

If the windshield was shatterproof, then the fire would harmlessly strike and be deflected. If the grille on the front of the wag was open enough to allow the inclusion of fire…

Squeeze that trigger soon enough, and maybe you could hit both targets.

All of that swept through the tangled and darkened skeins of Doc's mind in the few moments it took him to rest the LeMat and squeeze. He didn't worry too much about aim. Keep it straight, and the onrushing target would be hard to miss.

The impact of the shot charge held within the percussion pistol sounded loud and deafening in the confines of the wag. A cone of silence followed it as traumatized eardrums adjusted to the sudden concussion.

A single moment stretched to infinity and back as the grape shot of the pistol spread in the molten air, close enough to take all impact, distant enough to allow it to spread across the windshield and fender. By accident or design, Doc had picked the optimum moment.

The wag slewed away from its stationary adversary, throwing up a cloud of choking dust that obscured its path.

DEMETRIOU DIDN'T FEEL the shot and the glass shards that rained over his chest, face and thorax. All were hit head-on. Nervous jerks of a traumatized system made him spin the wheel, taking them off a collision course.

Corden had seen the raised and steadied barrel, had thrown himself down, yelling a blurted and incoherent warning, a noise that made no sense in syllables but said everything in tone. It was enough to make Chambers and Thornton dive to the ground.

Corden screamed in pain as he felt shards score his back. His head connected with the edge of door frame and dash, blurring those lines of pain. For a moment he almost lost the light, but his survival instinct kicked in. If this was going wrong and they had to fight back, then he needed to stay alert to stay alive.

Demetriou's life snuffed as he fell heavily on the wheel. His foot hit the accelerator and the wag shot across the uneven plain. The jolting made it hard for the other three coldhearts to regain any kind of control, but that very lack of guidance saved them. One rut too many, and Demetriou's corpse shifted in his seat, his foot sliding from the pedal.

The wag slowed.

THE DUST CLOUD SETTLED and Doc could see that his volley had met with some success.

"Even playing field, I think," he murmured. "Level, the term might be."

"Shut up, Doc," Krysty replied. "Let's see what they do next. How are we doing?" she questioned a little louder.

"Okay," Jak stated.

"Not okay," Ryan breathed in her ear. "Seeing bastard double. Stupe thing with one eye."

"Watch our tails, then, lover," she said gently. "No way are you going front line until that's fixed. Mildred? J.B.?"

"Feel like a mule kicked me, but at least I can see straight," the Armorer said wryly.

"Second that," Mildred added. She looked beyond the confines of the wag to where their enemy had come to rest. "Real question is, how are they doing?"

"Badly, I hope." Krysty looked over her battered but unbowed friends. "At least," she added, "a lot worse than us. Because it's going to get up close and personal, if I'm not mistaken."

Chapter Three

Thornton and Chambers wasted no time with words. Before the dust settled, Thornton kicked open the door on his side of the wag, which faced away from their now revitalized opponents. He scuttled out onto the dusty, hard-packed earth, scrambling to the front wing of the vehicle. Chambers followed in his wake, opting to cover the rear end. It would leave him a little more exposed when he chose to take a shot, but safer in the meantime. Chambers was a believer in caution.

Corden, meanwhile, had opened the door against which his bloodied shoulder was wedged and slid out, face-first. He rolled over, grimacing as the dust and grit from the ground bit into the exposed flesh. Tears of pain ran down his face. Eyes up to the sky, he could see that the blue, bending to purple and ochre, remained unchanged. For him, though, things were far from the same. Now, he was driven by more than just greed. The need to take from them what they had taken from him—a life—was a burning desire.

"Wayne, you with us?" Thornton queried, concerned at Corden's expression, the like of which he had never seen.

"Yeah…oh, yeah…" Galvanized into action, Corden pulled himself to his feet and joined Thornton in his long-range recce over the cover of the wag's hood. "They can't move, and if we go to them, then we expose ourselves. Right?"

Thornton agreed. Corden glanced down the length of the wag at Chambers, who nodded.

"Right. Then we need to take ourselves to them. I'll replace Jase. Just get as much firepower as you can and start blasting when we get in range."

"What if we—"

Corden's hard-eyed, ice-cold stare choked Thornton's query in his throat. Corden's voice was low, deep in his own throat, and had an edge that would brook no argument. "We chill those fuckers. I don't care if it's quick or slow. Slow's better. But they buy the farm. If we get Hearne's jack, then even better. But that don't really matter now. They got one of ours. That's what matters."

With that, Corden pulled open the door of the wag and climbed in, keeping his head low. Thornton looked back at Chambers. The dark coldheart shrugged, gesturing helplessly. There was little they could do except go along with it. Corden was boss, and they were used to following without question.

Inside the wag, Corden gently closed Demetriou's eyes. The young coldheart had slumped so that his torso had fallen into the well between the seats. Corden cradled his head.

"They won't get away with this," he whispered to the

chilled man. Heaving the deadweight body upright, he reached across the bloodied lap and flicked the catch on the driver's door. Pushing it open, he heaved the body so that it fell toward the gap, pitching off the seat and into a heap on the ground.

The engine was still ticking over, the gear preventing it from moving. Corden closed the driver's door, then called to Chambers and Thornton.

Chambers entered the rear of the wag once more, while Thornton took Corden's old post. Now he was riding shotgun, and would have a clear arc of fire through the shattered windshield.

"You know what we should do," Corden said in a toneless, dead voice. "I'll set her rolling, and then we just start blasting. Don't give them a chance to fire back."

"Wait—"

Corden looked back at Chambers. "Lost your nerve? If you have, then I'll—"

"No need for us to do anything, Wayne," Chambers interrupted him. "Stop a second... Can't you feel it?"

Corden frowned. What was Chambers talking about? But wait... His grim visage cracked into a grin wreathed in malice.

"Yeah, I can, now. Looks like we won't have to worry about anything. The spirits are gonna take care of 'em, right?"

Chambers nodded. "Spirits, nuke shit, call it what you want, Wayne. But it's coming. And they ain't been around these parts long enough to know anything about it. They won't survive it."

"Neither will we. Not if we don't get the fuck out of here soon," Thornton added, looking through the blasted windshield and up at the skies. There was no sign above them, but the air around was charged, like static electricity. The previously airless plains had the slightest of breezes, carrying that charge across the empty expanse.

Corden looked out of the wag, down at Demetriou's corpse. Maybe a proper burial would have been good. Stop the mutie critters getting him, using him for carrion. But what the hell. Jase was gone. That piece of chilled flesh wasn't him. Not anymore.

Corden smiled as he looked across at the wag that held their erstwhile opponents. "They'll be expecting us to attack. Won't know what the fuck to think when we hightail it outta here. Makes it kinda sweeter, doesn't it?"

"Guess it does, Wayne," Chambers agreed. He would have agreed to anything at that moment, as long as it got Corden turning the wag and headed back toward Brisbane.

Corden put the wag into gear and spun it almost 360, so that they headed away from the stranded wag and back toward the blacktop they had seemingly left so long ago.

"WHAT—" MILDRED FOLLOWED the progress of their one-time pursuers with a rising sense of bewilderment.

"That no way attack. Something wrong," Jak commented tersely.

"Sure as shit is," J.B. muttered. "Why come all this way, push it this far, and then…"

"Unless, my dear John Barrymore, there is a greater

danger in the offing than perhaps they would wish to deal with?" Doc mused.

Krysty scanned the land around. There was nothing visible except the receding dust trail of the retreating wag. "Can't see a thing. But…" She was aware of how tightly her hair was clinging to her neck, snaking down her back as though searching for cover.

"But?" Mildred queried.

"Feel it," Jak whispered. "Not coldheart trouble. Something worse."

A distant hum in the air, like the thrumming of a taut wire, was all the indication they had of anything amiss. There seemed to be no account for the coldhearts' sudden withdrawal. Yet still that gnawing at the pit of the companions' stomachs said that there was something very bad on the way.

Without a word, both Jak and Krysty got out of the wag, stiff, sore limbs protesting at the movement. Krysty winced as she could feel her ribs creak and tighten with every breath. Both she and Jak stood still and silent on the plain, looking slowly around. The air was moving more than previously. There was no reason why there shouldn't be a breeze, so why did it feel uncomfortable and unnerving? It took both of them only a few minutes to realize that there seemed to be no direction from which the air moved. One second it seemed to be westerly, the next it was from the east. Or else it seemed to come from the north, only to switch south when confirmation was sought. Even more so, there was no pattern to these changes. They seemed to be either random or in such an extended sequence that it was difficult to follow the pattern.

Jak and Krysty exchanged puzzled looks. The albino teen's normally impassive face was twisted into a questioning look.

Before either could say anything, sounds from behind them indicated that the others had come out into the open. Krysty turned to see Doc stretching, black-clad limbs twisted against the empty backdrop of the sky. J.B. stared, puzzled, at the sun as the breezes plucked at the folds of material on the backpack that held his ordnance stash. Mildred was making Ryan lean forward so that she could check his good eye for any signs of concussion.

"How you feeling, lover?" Krysty asked.

Ryan grunted. "Like shit."

"But not concussed shit," Mildred added dryly. "You'll be okay. What's with the coldhearts?" she added, indicating the direction in which their attackers had fled.

"That's what I'd like to know," Krysty murmured. "Doesn't feel like it's good, though." She looked around, aware that even as she spoke, the winds had begun to pick up. There were no clouds in the sky, yet the air was becoming charged with the kind of energy that preceded a storm.

"We find cover, quick," Jak said matter-of-factly. Ryan looked around. Apart from the battered wag, there was precious little else that could provide cover. The black-and-green dappled hills of the plains were distant. The scrub within a radius of about five hundred yards was sparse. A few clusters of rock dotted the spaces between, but these were low to the ground and of little substance.

The wag had a windshield, but no other glass to provide protection from the elements. But they had tarps covering the supplies. Just maybe… If it was an electrical storm, the frame should conduct any lightning hits. If it was strong enough to blow the wag across the plains, well, it could do that, and it could buffet them wherever else they sought shelter out here.

Even as those thoughts raced rapidly through his mind, he was aware that tracers and eddies of dust were beginning to swirl around his feet, reaching up past his ankles.

Looking up, he could see that J.B. had reached the same conclusion and was already heading back to the wag. Ryan indicated that the others should follow suit. It was only when he saw that Doc had stopped that he turned to face where the old man stared.

"Fireblast," the one-eyed man whistled softly.

"By the Three Kennedys!" Doc murmured.

In the distance, a column of dust had risen into the air. As they watched, it grew in height and width from a zephyr to a tornado, then shrank again before rising once more. It seemed to pulse, as though with a life of its own. It was moving toward them at speed. The dust eddies around their ankles had now risen almost to their knees. The breezes that had raised the dust plucked at their calves.

The others were already in the wag. The window openings facing the oncoming storm had already been blocked out by the heavy, dark tarp. J.B. was covering the rear opening. Krysty looked at Ryan and Doc.

"Come on—what are you waiting for?" she yelled.

Ryan was shaken from his reverie and moved toward the wag. The dust eddies were now bigger, stronger. He blinked and coughed as dust began to clog his nose and throat.

Then it hit him. Rain he would have expected, perhaps a rock or stone picked up in the force of the zephyrs that crossed and recrossed to make the approaching maelstrom. But while the object was not as hard or as sharp, it still dealt a heavy blow to his shoulder, but not enough to cause pain. Another of the objects hit him on the side of the head, thrown sideways and kept aloft by the counterflows of the air currents. As it slapped against his head, Ryan was shocked to hear it make a noise.

He stumbled forward, hit time and again by these objects, sure that at times they made deep noises that seemed familiar. Ryan felt soft squelching underfoot, the hard-packed surface of the plain now a shifting, uneasy and uneven mass that seemed to move, give, then be uneven again. As he reached the wag, the one-eyed man looked down, and through the murk of the dust motes, he was sure he saw...

Frogs?

Momentarily he faltered, unsure if that blow on the head had affected his senses in some way. Then he heard Krysty and Mildred calling to him through the thickening swirls of dust, and he pressed forward. Already, any sense of depth or distance was rendered a matter more of luck than judgment, and he almost ran into the wag before he saw it. Hands clutched at him, pulling him into the wag's quieter, less dust-riddled interior, as the heavy rain of frogs splattered around him. Inside, they sounded loud and booming on the roof, a constant tattoo against which it was almost impossible to make yourself heard.

J.B. and Jak had secured every window opening except that on the door through which he had been dragged. Tendrils of dust snaked around the barely secured tarp, which the two men now held over the opening while Mildred helped Ryan into the rear of the wag. It was possible to breathe in the wag's interior, and he took several deep breaths, his head swimming. It was dark, as J.B. had secured a tarp over the windshield, too, as a precaution against the storm shattering it and showering them with glass. But even in the gloom, Ryan could see Mildred's amused expression, her eyes torn between trepidation and amusement.

"I know. It's raining of frogs. Go figure. They used to have myths about that when I was a kid, but I didn't think I'd have to wait until I'd been frozen, defrosted and seen the future before I'd witness it. Now I really have seen everything."

"But how—"

"I don't know. Maybe the crosswinds have whipped them up from some river running across the plains. Let's face it, it's so weird out there it could have brought them from anywhere." She shrugged.

Ryan looked around. "Doc?"

"Stupe bastard still out there," Jak said shortly. "Quick recce."

J.B. nodded, and the two men let the tarp drop for a second before slamming it back into place as frogs and dirt slewed through the gap.

As the darkness came down once more, they were all left with one image searing their collective retinas. Through a swirl of dust and dirt that made him seem as though he were painted on parchment, Doc was whirling in the winds, moving with the currents, laughing maniacally as he was bombarded by frogs. It seemed as though he didn't even notice the impact.

"Crazy old buzzard's going to get himself killed," Mildred muttered. "I'm going after him—"

"If anyone does it, it should be me," Ryan said, preparing to move out before being stayed by a hand from the Armorer.

"I'll go with Millie," he said. "You're still not up to speed, and it'll take two of us to get that mad bastard in here."

Before Ryan had a chance to protest, J.B. had flung open the wag door, and both he and Mildred were swallowed up by the maelstrom. Jak struggled to pull it shut, needing Krysty's assistance to secure the tarp once more, and let the dust and frogs that had blown in settle on the floor of the vehicle. The frogs that had survived the buffeting of the storm croaked contentedly in their new haven, at odds with the emotions of the three humans with whom they shared shelter.

Time seemed to slow to a drip as they waited for a signal that J.B. and Mildred were returning with the errant Doc. There was nothing.

"Have to risk another look," Ryan said.

Jak agreed, and indicated to Krysty that she be ready to let the tarp fall for a second. When it had been returned, and they had coughed up the dust that had swirled in, they were also aware of a new problem: insects buzzing around the interior of the wag. Slapping them down, Ryan could see that they were locusts.

If these scavengers had been added to the swirl outside, then there was no knowing what they could do to Doc, or Mildred and J.B. They could eat anything in their path, living or chilled: they had all seen evidence of this in the past.

"They not back soon, go after," Jak said. He looked at Ryan in a way that forbade any argument. Ryan simply nodded. He understood.

And yet, for a moment, it seemed that this wouldn't be necessary. Cutting through the howling winds were the sounds of approaching footsteps and Doc's keening, madness-inflected tones.

"I tell you… You know your scriptures better than any of us here in this place forsaken by the good Lord, my good doctor. You know what they foretell—plagues that will rain down upon those who are the unjust and the unrighteous. Locusts that will sweep through the land, stripping it back to the bare, glistening bones so that the way is paved for the fresh and the good to rise from the remains. This is what it is. At last, this could be the salvation for which I have so often prayed. This nightmare could at last be ending."

There was the mumble of J.B.'s voice.

"Unhand me! I shall not go softly and gently. Unhand me, I say."

The scuffling increased, there was a yell of pain, and Doc's voice, raging incoherently, retreated into the distance, buried by the wailing of the winds. It was followed by the shouts of Mildred and J.B. as they followed.

Jak looked to Ryan. In the dim light, the one-eyed man could see the tension written in Jak's scarred and weathered visage. He nodded, almost imperceptibly.

The albino youth needed no second bidding. Before Krysty had a chance to realize what was going on, Jak had opened the wag door a sliver and squeezed through. Ryan reached out and closed it behind him.

"Who's next, you or me, lover?" she questioned, her voice dripping disbelief at the way in which they seemed to be breaking all their own rules.

"Whatever it takes. Sometimes we've just gotta stand or fall as one."

Chapter Four

"Doc, Doc…" Mildred's tone was half imprecation, half resignation. Her words were choked and strangled by the dust that swirled around her, frogs battering her head and shoulders, locusts buzzing and swarming around her, singing in her ears as she batted them away. She could feel the occasional plucking of a locust as it came close to her, experimentally prodding and poking to see if she should be a good source of food.

Why the hell had she and J.B. left the shelter of the wag to come out here after the crazy old buzzard? If he wanted to act like some fire-and-brimstone preacher and wander into the wilderness to meet his maker, then what business was it of theirs? Too many times he had endangered the group; too many times he had—

Even as the angry thoughts passed through her mind she knew that she already had the answer. Doc was like her: cast adrift on the choppy currents of time and fate, with no options as to when and where he would finally hit land. Hell, there were times when she had envied him his insanity. Sometimes it seemed a much more pleasant place to live than where they had actually come to rest. Like all of the people she traveled with, Doc was an outcast who had sought some sort of sanctuary among those who also sought survival with some kind of moral boundary.

When was the last time she had consciously thought of morality? She guessed that it was something that had informed her actions in the time since she had awoken, but to stop and consider would be madness. She became all too aware that these thoughts were a symptom of the terrible weariness that now swept over her, enveloping her like a blanket. It was warm, fuzzy, and she wanted to lie in the sand…

It felt soft and yielding beneath her, like something that rippled pleasantly. She remembered a water bed that Ed Stasium had. She was at college then, so that had to have been the late 1980s? She wondered what Ed was doing now. Yeah, he'd be chilled. Like everyone she knew….

Mildred realized that her mind was beginning to wander, and at the very back of her brain a survival in-stinct was screaming at her to get the hell up, shake her head clear and find shelter. Or Doc. Preferably both. But her body didn't want to obey.

Why the hell did the plains feel like a water bed? Through her clogged nostrils there was a dank, earthy smell. Then one of the frogs croaked, loud and sonorous as it lay near her ear.

Mildred cursed and, still feeling like she was in a strange dreamworld, tried to scramble herself to her feet. The frogs were slippery, moving under the grip of her boots. The palms of her hands felt the cold skins slip and slide as those frogs that survived the fall from the sky sought to move from under the weight of her hands. Every time she thought she had purchase, she found herself slipping and falling once more to the ground.

And then she felt a hand grip her upper arm, an iron band around her biceps that squeezed tight as it pulled her up. She winced at the pain but appreciated the assistance. She had a scarf wrapped around her face, as much as was possible, so that she could keep out the worst of the flying grit. Still she had to squint. Was that Doc?

No, it couldn't be. The grip was too firm, the momentum of the lift too strong. She could see J.B. standing beside her. His glasses were almost entirely obscured by dirt, although areas of his face had remained clean, protected by the brim of his battered fedora. In that way the dazed and confused had of putting inconsequence before all else, she wondered how it was that he had managed to keep the hat secured to his head. She opened her mouth to ask and somehow—by bizarre chance—a locust managed to penetrate the mask of her scarf and fly into her mouth. She choked and bit down hard. The buzzing, which she had felt amplified in the cavern of her jaws, ceased suddenly as she clamped down and bit the insect in two. A foul, bitter taste filled her mouth, and she spit it out. Part of the insect became trapped in the scarf, and she pawed frantically to pry it loose.

J.B. pulled the scarf away, shaking the partial insect remains loose, and then he slapped her sharply across the face.

Instinct told her to hit him back, yet as she made to raise her arm another part of her kicked in—that which had remained alert and yet trapped at the back of her mind, screaming, now burst through the barriers.

"Doc," she said simply.

J.B. shrugged and indicated in the direction from which she assumed he had appeared.

"Gone," he said simply. "Too much shit. Shelter."

She nodded. It had been misguided to try to find Doc, no matter what their motives. All they could do now was to try to find somewhere to sit out the rest of the storm. To try to work out direction right now would be pointless. In this world of dust, frogs and locusts there was little indication of what was up or down, let alone east, west, north and south. Doc could be anywhere. So, for that matter, could be the wag in which the others were waiting for them.

The only thing they could really hope for right now was that this bastard storm would soon abate.

Still clinging to J.B., her own limbs jellied and refusing to respond to her command, Mildred moved through the whipping storm. It occurred to some part of her that the locusts were nowhere near as destructive as she would have expected. She recalled stories from her predark days of fields stripped within minutes. From more recent times, she could remember animals and people stripped to the bone by postskydark mutie locusts. If these, too, were muties, then thank God that the mutation had made them seemingly less vicious and harmful. Although it did seem so contrary to the way of the world as to be remarkable.

The frogs still rained down on them, enough to form

a slithering cover across the ground, yet not enough to drive Mildred and J.B. down with sheer weight of numbers. Still, the battering was enough to make shoulders and necks sore, to hit with such force as to occasionally make them stumble. Balance was also disrupted by attempts to swat away the locusts that still buzzed in and out. And there was the dust and dirt, still moving in crosscurrents. That was another puzzle: surely the weight of dust that clogged nostrils and throats should have suffocated them by now? Yet still they were able to breathe, labored though it was.

By now, they had no idea of direction. J.B. was leading her blindly, she realized, just hoping that, by sheer blind instinct—and maybe luck—they could find something or somewhere in which they could find shelter.

They almost stumbled over it. The swirling, dark brown to black atmosphere made it impossible to see more than a yard or two in front of them, if that. Distance was something for which they now had no yardstick. Under their feet, the carpet of amphibians ceased, replaced by a ledge of something hard and jagged.

Remembering what she had observed shortly before the storm came down on them, she realized that if they had reached the scant cover of small rock outcrops, then they had to have strayed some distance from the wag. Could they have really trudged that far, in this kind of storm?

Guided by J.B.'s hand, hardly able to even see him as the winds howled around them and the dust whipped and scoured at their skin, Mildred found herself being laid down in the shallow shelter of the outcropping.

Even lying flat, feeling the jagged edges of rock bite through her clothing, she was barely below the parapet formed by the uppermost points of the rock. She felt J.B. lay down beside her, pulling some kind of sheet over them. Following the lead of his touch, she tucked the edges of the material under her body, as some kind of attempt at anchoring it in place. She felt the material go taut as he did the same.

Like a tightened drum skin, the material reverberated as frogs bounced off it. Beneath, although it was dark and hot in the enclosed space, it was a little easier to breathe. The absence of dust and dirt in the air was a welcome respite. Mildred felt her chest ease, and her raw throat found some relief. She still had the sour taste of the locust in her mouth. Right now, she would give anything for water. Her canteen was pinned beneath her; she could feel it pressing beneath her ribs. To try to get at it, to pry it free and find the room to move her arms and drink from it, would demand that their shelter be moved. There was the risk that it would be whipped away by the wind.

Mildred could wait.

Her right arm was raised, her hand by her face. Numbness spread through it as the blood supply was staunched by her own body weight. To try to keep it alive, to stop the pins and needles that began to irritate under the skin, she prodded experimentally at her face.

She was shocked. Even with the scarf, there had been enough of the swirling dust and dirt to scour away the top layer of her skin. Numb from the cold of the winds, she had figured that this was why her face did not pain her. And yet, to her surprise, the skin still felt smooth and unblemished. No warm, wet blood. No grazing or roughness. No sudden, sharp tingling of pain when the exposed flesh was touched.

There was something here that made no sense, that indicated a strangeness that she would have to master to ensure survival. Whatever it was, she knew that it was vital she keep it at the forefront of her mind.

But it was so hard. Weariness crept over her, the numbness in her arm spreading throughout her body, sleep beckoning to her.

She could feel J.B.'s body heat against her, and it lulled her weary mind all the more. Fighting it became harder and harder.

Consciousness slipped away.

"REVELATIONS. THE time of the beast is upon us, and we shall face up to the consequence of all the actions that have led us to this point. The plagues have been sent to teach us the error of our ways and we shall atone. We shall be forced to face up to that which we have perpetrated.

"And why not, I ask of you? By the Three Kennedys, mankind shall speak to Mother Earth and be forced to account for the way in which she has been raped and violated. She has struck back, at the behest of her—and our—Father, and we shall perish in the flames of her wrath."

Doc's ranting voice, already lost to all hearing in the maelstrom around him, tailed off into a cackle of manic laughter that degenerated into a hawking, coughing fit as dust and locusts clogged his nose and throat. He retched and spit phlegm onto the ground, spattering a frog that strayed too close to his range.

Rubbing his eyes and looking down, Doc saw the frogs that moved around the toes of his boots, obscuring the ground in a carpet of crawling, leathery skin. Remembering, somewhere in the fevered depths of his imaginings, something he had once read about the hallucinogenic properties of the mucus that oiled the backs of a particular species of frog or toad—he could not recall which, and did not at that moment care to differentiate—he bent to the winds that holed around him and picked up an amphibian from the floor of the plains.

He lifted the creature and turned it to face him, so that the impassive, dark eyes of the frog met his own.

"So, my friend," he said softly, "we find ourselves, both, little more than pawns at the mercy of an unseeing, unfeeling hand. Our destinies are preordained for us as, at this moment, we are witnesses to the greater powers seeking to flex their metaphysical muscles. But why am I bothering to explain this to you, little friend, as you are nothing more than a frog. I wonder what I shall see if I lick your back…by God, it is some time since I was able to say that to anybody, let alone to anything."

With which, Doc turned the frog and raised it to his lips. Flicking his tongue out in a manner that was, in itself, reptilian, he licked the back of the creature. It tasted foul. He grimaced, threw the frog to the ground and spit the resulting sputum from his mouth with haste.

"So much for that," he muttered. Then he laughed once more and threw his arms wide, beginning to spin in a circle. He threw his head back and began to cackle wildly as he spun, trying to catch the insects, dirt and frogs in his mouth. He wished to drown in the excrescence of the storm. It had come to them as a punishment, so let it punish him. He wished to be claimed by the elements, to be negated and wiped from the earth. If the end times were here, then let him welcome them with these open arms.

And yet the insects that buzzed around him did not attack, did not fly into his gaping maw. The frogs missed, hitting him on the shoulders and outstretched arms, yet not in the face. The dirt that swirled in the crosscurrents of the storm whipped across his skin, yet did not block his air passages nor settle on his tongue. He wished to be claimed, yet the elements refused.

Tears of frustration replaced the manic laughter. They coursed down his cheeks, making runnels in the dirt that covered his face. The constant whirling began to make him dizzy, the ground uncertain beneath his feet as his inner ear became confused and his balance became unsteady. The circles he proscribed on the floor of the plain became wider, more elliptic and erratic. He stumbled sideways, felt the ground seemingly move beneath his feet. His outstretched arms windmilled wildly as he tried to keep his balance.

But it was of little use. One eccentric circle too far, and he found the ground shift beneath his boots just a little too much for him to compensate. Momentum pulled him over, and he found himself falling to the ground, his head still spinning as though he were whirling. Nausea pitched in the pit of his stomach, and he thought that he might vomit.

It was his last thought before his head cracked against the hard ground, squashing unsuspecting amphibians beneath him, their flimsy skeletons providing no cushion against the hard-packed earth.

Doc, like Mildred in another place, also lost consciousness.

JAK WAS LOST—physically, and also inside his head. The former was nothing: a temporary loss of bearings had happened many times before, and all it took was time, and the chance to stop and take bearings. In a situation like this, where it was now impossible to see anything—up, down, forward, backward—because of the clouds of dirt that swirled around in the crosscurrents, it was a matter of shelter, rest and wait until such time as it was clear. Even the frogs and the locusts didn't bother him. The way they buzzed and bounced around him was irritating, sure, but Jak had experienced a whole lot worse over his life. This was nothing. Find shelter, hunker down, wait.

No, it wasn't any of that that caused him to feel the dark clouds of fear edging into his consciousness. It was something else. Something that was, for the most part, alien to him. A feeling that he had only rarely experienced, and then only in the relative safety of dreams.

Dark doubts began to assail him. He had left the

shelter of the wag to find J.B. and Mildred; and, in turn, to help them get Doc to safety. But now he was wandering in a storm, with no sign of shelter and no sign of those he had set out to find. Tracking, hunting, finding people and animals: that was Jak. He was a hunter. A good one. Without that he was nothing.

And he was failing. Had failed. He was alone.

Failure.

Jak stopped walking. He stood simply, with no defensive or offensive posture. There was no point. He could sense no danger: in truth, he could sense nothing. The hearing, smell and sight that served him so well had been reduced to nothing. He was nothing.

Looking slowly around, trying to focus those senses that had served him so well, he became aware that he had no notion of anything living that was near to him. He had no idea of where his friends might be, where the shelter of the wag may be, or even if they were alive or chilled.

He had no idea of where he was. It was as though the storm had formed a cocoon of dust and dirt around him. He was contained within it, and had no idea of what may exist outside the immediate area that was all he could see, hear or feel. Even the locusts that buzzed around him, and the frogs that fell at his feet, seemed to have no real substance. His awareness of them had become reduced so that they were little more than the vaguest of distractions. He could no longer smell the earthy scent of the amphibians, nor feel the flutterings of the insects as they passed his face, ears and eyes.

Such a complete negation of his being made Jak feel empty and alone. Alone was not such a new feeling: Jak had never been a person who was close to anyone—at least, not for so long—but this was more than that. This was a complete desolation.

And if there was nothing—not even himself—then what was the point of continuing to exist?

Jak sank to his knees. For what was possibly the only time in his life, Jak paid no heed to anything around him. There was no need to keep triple red. No need to be aware of any dangers. No need for anything other than to just give in to the darkness that was beginning to envelop him.

Without any resistance, Jak allowed it to take him.

"ANY SIGN?" Ryan asked as he rubbed the aching area over his good eye. Zigzag lines in white crossed his vision, each line accompanied by a searing pain in his skull.

Krysty risked another look beyond the tarp at the swirls of dirt that now seemed to constitute the very air.

"Nothing. Can't see or hear a thing. Sweet Gaia, I've never seen anything quite like this."

She was finding it hard to think. Those few locusts that had penetrated the tarps were buzzing annoyingly around the inside of the wag. Each time she smacked one down, it seemed that there were two more to take its place. The rain of frogs beat an insistent and arrhythmic tattoo on the roof and hood of the wag. And always, in the back of everything, there was the moaning of the winds that drove dust and dirt at them.

In the midst of all that, how the hell did Ryan expect her to hear the cries of Jak, J.B., Mildred and Doc? Maybe they had found one another. Maybe they were all wandering around, close to one another yet unable to see or hear in the confusion. Maybe they'd all bought the farm… This latter she did not wish to consider, yet it still prodded at her consciousness.

Why had it happened this way? Not the storm: that was just one of those things, the kind of hazard that they encountered almost every day of their lives. No, what she wondered was why, when Doc had wandered off, Mildred and J.B. had been so quick to get after him. Why Jak had followed seemingly without any thought or consideration. Why Ryan had let them. Why she had let them, come to that.

Ryan was concussed, not thinking clearly. Confused at the very least. As she looked at him, she could almost see the struggle manifest itself physically as he moved uneasily, rubbing his head and grimacing in pain.

None of them had acted totally as themselves—even herself—and it was getting worse. Both Ryan and she were trapped in this wag as surely as if it had been a locked room. Unable to move, caught in an agony of indecision.

They would sit it out until the storm abated. Not because that was the best course of action, but because they could think of nothing else to do. While, outside, their friends may be facing the farm on their own.

Krysty tried to move. Nothing. Her limbs were heavy, almost paralyzed. Yet it was a paralysis in which there was still feeling. A heavy torpor washed over her. She had no strength

It was such an alien feeling that it should have terrified her. Yet even this capacity was now beyond her grasp.

She felt all awareness begin to recede into an infinite distance.

Chapter Five

Mildred was aware, first, of the tingling ache in her arm. It stirred her, deep in her slumber, and she moaned softly as she tried to move her arm, to relieve the symptom. But it refused to budge. Penetrating deep into her subconscious, it made her slip from the warm blanket of unconscious and into the cold of the conscious.

And hell, was it cold. As she rose to the surface, she felt the cold that had seeped into her limbs. It was only then that she realized that her arm was beneath her, hand still raised to her face. Not that she could feel it.

She shuffled in the tight constraint of the sheet that covered both herself and J.B. The Armorer was quiet beside her and did not immediately stir as she moved against him. For a moment she wondered if he was alive, but his steady breathing reassured her. For such a small, wiry man he was proving to be one hell of a deadweight.

Heaving, Mildred managed to move him enough to free her arm. She gasped as the tingling fled, a weakness spreading through the limb as she tried to flex it. She paused, counted to twenty, then tried again. This time, it felt more like normal.

She took a chance at sitting up, moving the edges of the sheet from where it was tucked beneath her body. A wan light penetrated the thin material, and there was silence beyond the veil it provided.

One good thing—the storm had ceased. As the sheet slid down her body, she propped herself up on her elbows and looked around.

The sun was on the rise. It had to be morning, she thought. The sky was as it had been the afternoon before, clear, yet tinged with strange coloring. There was no sign that a storm had swept across them.

More importantly, there was no sign of the wag or their fellow travelers.

Mildred got to her feet. Cramp ached and bit into her calves, but she stamped it out. The sound of her feet roused J.B., who mumbled and grumbled his way to the surface of waking while she looked around.

"I'll tell you something, John. We're well and truly screwed."

"I've always liked your positive outlook,' the Armorer husked wryly as he, too, rose to his feet and joined her.

The land that spread in a vista around them was empty and impassive. Flat plainlands spread to all corners of the horizon, broken only by the distant plateaus of hill and mountain ranges, spread unevenly. In between these distant markers and the place where they stood was little except the occasional patch of scrub and rock, and those ridges in the earth that were invisible to the naked eye.

"How the hell did we manage to come so far that we've lost sight of the others?" Mildred whispered.

J.B. didn't answer for a moment. He scanned the horizon, turning a full 360 degrees.

"It shouldn't be possible," he said finally.

"Yeah, well, I don't see anyone else. And what happened to us yesterday shouldn't have happened, either. But it did. The question now is how we're going to find them again. Or anything, come to that."

J.B. was lost in thought, gathering in the sheet that had served them so well. Replacing it in his backpack, he pulled out his minisextant.

"I'll see if I can work out how much we've moved,' he murmured as he took a reading and ran calculations in his head. Then, after a short pause, he added, "It doesn't add up. According to my calculations, we must have walked about four miles. And we should still be able to see the wag."

Mildred stared at him. J.B. was rarely mistaken on such matters.

"How can we have come that far? There wasn't enough time…at least, it didn't seem like it was that long." The more she thought about it, the less sense the previous day was beginning to make. "So where's Doc? Where the hell can that wag have been hidden?"

J.B. just shook his head. He was as baffled as Mildred. The only thing he could think of was to take action. Experience taught him that action usually started a chain of events.

"I dunno about Doc. Mebbe we'll find him, mebbe

the old bastard really has got himself lost this time. But if we start to go that way—" he indicated a south-south-east direction "—and keep on going, we should hit where the wag is supposed to be. Mebbe Ryan got it going again, and they've headed off in the wrong direction trying to find us. If so, then mebbe we'll find some tracks to follow.'

Mildred shrugged. As a plan, it wasn't the best she'd ever heard. But right now, she couldn't come up with anything better.

Stopping only to eat from some self-heats that they carried as emergency rations, and sipping sparingly from their canteens, they began the long trek back in the direction that J.B. had determined had been their point of departure.

With every yard that they covered, Mildred expected to see a dust-covered bump on the ground that would turn out to be Doc, alive or having gone to face the judgment of which he had been ranting when last seen. She scanned the land around with every step, but there was no sign. Perhaps the old buzzard had managed to survive yet again.

They trudged across the hard-packed plain, small zephyrs of dust raised by the steady, rhythmic marching of their feet. The sun rose inexorably, and the temperature rose sharply, unimpeded by the clear skies. J.B. had his fedora to shade him from the worst of the heat, while Mildred improvised a covering for her plaits, using a little of her precious water to dampen the cloth before tying it around her head.

They had been walking for several hours when there was the first intimation of any life on the plain other than their own.

Silence had been the norm, to preserve energy and avoid the need to moisten their tongues as much as the lack of anything to say. But now, J.B. broke that long silence.

"What is that? Two o'clock," he added, indicating an area where there was a cloud of dust raised near the horizon.

"Where's it coming from?" Mildred asked. It was still some way off, but had seemingly sprung from nowhere. Maybe they just hadn't noticed it before, too absorbed by the effort of moving one foot in front of the other. That was a sobering thought: losing their edge, their ability to stay frosty and triple red. It was symptomatic of what had happened the previous day. Something was beginning to make sense at the back of her mind….

"Moving quick," J.B. said sharply, breaking her reverie. She followed his arm, which was still raised. It was true. Whatever was raising the dust cloud was advancing rapidly. Immediately, her coalescing thoughts were driven from her mind by the need for action.

Looking around, she could see that there was little cover afforded to them by the terrain.

"Hostile?" she asked, knowing what J.B.'s answer would be.

"Assume it."

Even as he spoke, the Armorer was unslinging his

mini-Uzi, running checks without even thinking, and scanning the area. The only thing within any kind of distance was a small patch of brown-and-green scrub, with a few patches of purple flowers. How that survived in this climate was a mystery for another time. But not as great a mystery as how they could turn this into some kind of cover.

J.B. gestured that they should make their way toward it. Mildred, checking to make sure her ZKR was ready for combat, nodded. They traveled the five hundred yards to the scant cover. When they had made the best of the brush, JB finally spoke.

"They must have seen us moving. They're heading right toward us."

"Well, let's just hope that we can get a bead on them before they can on us," Mildred countered. "Depends on what sort of weapons they're carrying," she added, knowing that their fate was on the line.

They settled in and waited for the dust cloud to reach them.

As the cloud became more defined, and they could see the center of disturbance that was stirring up the dust, neither of them was sure that they could believe their eyes.

For approaching them, calm in the eye of the cloud, were a dozen men mounted on horses. Piebald and chestnut creatures whose manes swirled with the dust, they seemed almost to glide across the ground. Seated atop them were men whose impassive faces were matched by the stately grandeur with which they rode the rolling plain. Like marble statues, they seemed immobile astride their steeds, man and horse as one living entity on an endless journey.

No less impressive was the manner in which they were attired—furs and skins, woven into breeches and moccasins, with jerkins that left their scarred and pierced chests open to the air. From their bare skin hung bones decorated with different varieties and colors of feather. Their hair was long, worn either loose and flowing in the momentum of their relentless progress, or else plaited and held to the side of their head by a snakeskin headband.

They were armed, but not in the manner that either J.B. or Mildred would have expected. Quivers filled with arrows hung from the saddlebags of their mounts and bows were secured across their backs. J.B. couldn't see a blaster on any of them.

Part of his mind wondered how they managed to survive without the use of blasters, bow and arrow being—like a blade—an instrument with less range and destructive power, effective only if wielded with precision. Another part of his mind figured that Mildred's sure eye and the sweep of his SMG could cut a swathe through these coldhearts...if that was what they proved to be.

For the moment, that was less than certain. As the party of riders advanced, they had a confidence about them. There was no sign that they would raise a hand in anger, yet they seemed to fear no attack.

Mildred and J.B. exchanged glances. This was no

normal situation. The Armorer shrugged and rose to his feet, stepping out from cover. Mildred followed. Both had their blasters at ease, yet their body language spoke of the ability to change to the offensive if necessary.

As the mounted men drew nearer, they began to slow. J.B. studied them. It had been a long time since he'd seen anyone who was dressed and ornamented in a similar manner.

As one, the mounted men came to a halt. They were within ten yards of the companions. As their horses snorted and moved their hooves, the dust settling around them, the warriors—for there was no doubt that this was what they were—sat impassive and silent. It was as though each was taking time to assess the people in front of them.

"You gonna say something, or we just gonna stand here and roast in this heat?" J.B. murmured laconically as the still and silence got to him.

"You and the woman are not attacking us," the Native American at the head of the posse stated.

"We'd defend ourselves, but you show no sign of wanting to attack us," Mildred countered.

The flicker of a smile crossed the man's weather-beaten face. "We have no desire to attack you. Why should we? We have been waiting for you."

J.B.'s brow furrowed. "Waiting?"

He was answered by a brief nod.

"How did you know we would be here? We didn't know it ourselves," Mildred said sharply.

The smile grew broader. "You know, even though

you don't know." The smile turned into a deep-throated chuckle as he caught the bafflement on their faces. "Come with us, and you will soon understand."

"Mebbe we don't want to come with you," J.B. said guardedly.

The Native American looked up at the empty, burning sky. "You'd rather stay out here?"

"It's a good point, John," Mildred said quietly, without taking her eyes from the men in front of them. "It doesn't seem to be much of a choice for us right now."

J.B. sighed. "Guess so. We'll take you up on it," he said to the mounted man, adding, "For now."

Two of the mounted men moved forward from the group, indicating without speech that J.B. and Mildred should mount up behind each of them. Stowing their blasters, both raised themselves into the saddle, settling behind the impassive and silent warriors.

It was only when they began to move off, and Mildred had the chance to survey the territory without the incessant march of her own feet that she realized at least one of the things that had been bugging her since they had first set out that morning.

The dust and dirt floor of the plain was clear.

What had happened to the locusts? Where were the frogs that had bombarded them? The ground should be littered with amphibians. If the live ones had sought shelter, then at the very least the ones who had bought the farm should be starting to stink up in the heat.

But there was nothing.

So where had they gone?

DIM LIGHT SUFFUSED the interior of the wag, heat from the rising sun stifling the atmosphere, making it hard to breathe. The stench of their own bodies filled the wag, the secured tarps keeping in the sweat and heat that had suffused them through the night. The closeness of the air, the lack of anything fresh, gave Krysty a headache that pounded at her skull. She awoke to a feeling like a jackhammer thumping incessantly. Her mouth, too, felt like she'd been gargling from a cesspool.

A blue aura, from the light defracted by the tarps, made it hard to see into the shadows of the wag, and it took her a few seconds of fuzzed confusion to recall where they were.

And how few of them were left.

"Ryan," she whispered, shaking the one-eyed man's arm. He lay across the bench seat in the rear of the wag, one arm raised across his face. She had been in front, slumped at an angle that had left her with a shooting pain in her neck. Yet she knew that she had to cast that aside. Rubbing at the soreness with one hand, she continued to shake Ryan, repeating his name.

Ryan grunted, his good eye opening beneath the cover of his arm. The lid was sticky and the eye sore. For a second he couldn't focus, and all was dark. It was only then that he realized that he was blocking the light with his own arm. He shook his head to clear it as he raised himself, rubbing at the eye to try to remove the grit that clogged and obscured his vision.

As his vision cleared and adjusted to the low-level

light inside the wag, he could see Krysty looking at him. Casting his eye around, he could see that they were alone.

"So it wasn't just the bang on the head," he said, "we really did let them go out there."

Krysty nodded, regretting it as a sharp pain seared her skull. "Some weird shit going on, lover. Now there's just the two of us, and I don't know where the hell the rest of—"

Ryan stayed her with a gesture. "No reason to beat shit out of ourselves for it. Just have to try to find them. Figure it's safe out there?"

Krysty paused, listening to the silence that existed outside the womb of the wag's interior. "Doesn't sound like there's anything—anything at all—going on out there," she said softly.

"Then let's recce and see what we can do about it," Ryan said simply.

They both moved with some hesitation. Their limbs ached and their heads felt fragile. As they took the tarps down from the glassless windows, and from the windshield, they both winced at the light that streamed in. It was airless out there. The stillness of the plains slowed the flow of cooler, fresher air into the wag. Thankfully, the windshield glass had escaped destruction in the storm, so if they could get the engine working again, driving across the plain would not be impeded by a faceful of grit.

The desolation of nothing but flat dirt and scrub, with only distant hills to break the monotony, hit them hard. They exchanged glances that spoke volumes. They could see what appeared to be a mile or so in each direction, and there was nothing to relieve the emptiness. No sign of Doc, Jak, Mildred or J.B. It was as though their companions had been wiped from the surface of the Earth.

"What direction?" Krysty asked, as much to herself as to Ryan. "How do we decide?"

Ryan screwed his face into a mask of indecision, wiped a hand across as if to drywash it from him. "Could be any." He looked up at the sky. The sun was low, not long risen by the looks of it.

Getting out of the wag, feeling the ground beneath his feet and for the first time in what seemed like days, Ryan looked around, circling slowly. There was no way of telling if any of their companions were still living out there. No way of telling in which direction they had wandered.

Lifting the hood of the wag, Ryan asked Krysty to try the ignition. As she pumped the engine, and it tried to pitifully cough to life, Ryan studied it. Although it wasn't firing, and he was no expert, the one-eyed man was sure he could fix it enough to get them going. The question was, what direction should they take? He pondered that while he tinkered with the engine, getting Krysty to turn it over until he had fixed the problem.

If it had been himself stranded out there in the storm, and he'd managed to find shelter, then as soon as he was able he would have tried to either find his way back to the wag, or else to head back toward the nearest ville. Population. Water. Food. He knew that they all carried survival rations, but they would only last so long.

As Krysty got the engine started, Ryan shut the hood and took a look around him. The wag would be visible for a great distance. If they began to head back toward Brisbane, then—

The thought was stopped dead in his mind. Coming toward them was a cloud of dust in the distance. He had no idea where it had sprung from, as it hadn't seemed to be there a moment before. Now it was approaching at a steady rate, and it was impossible to see what lay at the heart of it.

He slid into the seat next to Krysty.

"Meet them head-on?" she queried.

"Yeah. Not too fast. Let them come to us, but be ready to hit them."

Krysty put the wag in gear and steered it toward the direction of the cloud. Ryan checked his SIG-Sauer and Steyr.

It was only as they got within five hundred yards that they could see what lay at the heart of the cloud. "Gaia." Krysty whistled, while Ryan breathed in heavily. Both, without discussion, had expected another wag—like, or perhaps even, the coldhearts who had driven them this far onto the plain—but neither had expected the party of mounted Native Americans.

Krysty brought the wag to a halt. Both she and Ryan got out of the wag, using the open doors as cover, and stood waiting for the approaching party. Neither of them moved. The mounted warriors rode without fear or without threat.

When they were less than a hundred yards away, the

party came to a halt, and the leading rider dismounted. He walked toward the wag, one hand raised in a gesture of peace.

Ryan stepped out from the cover of the door, holding the Steyr to one side as an indication of his own desire to avoid hostility.

"We won't fire on you unless you make the first move," he said slowly, "but we will fire. Make no mistake."

The man standing in front of him, clothed in skins, and with his own skin covered in tattoos and paint, shrugged.

"You fire, then you got the wrong idea. We've got nothing but welcome for you both. We've been waiting long enough for you to turn up."

JAK LOOKED UP at the sky. The first rays of a rising sun had spread warmth on a body that was almost frozen. He felt groggy, his limbs heavy and torpid. He was aware that he had become dangerously cold—that thing that Mildred called hypothermia—and that he had to force himself to move, to eat and drink, to get up from the hard ground.

Every movement had to be wrenched from his body. Muscles groaned and protested, refused to act on command, and teetered on the brink of collapse. It was only by the greatest act of will that, after what seemed like hours of effort, he managed to pull himself up, and to his knees. He had to stop there, blowing hard as though he had been chasing prey for hours, feeling sweat run down his forehead, matting his hair. He could feel a cooling puddle form in the hollow at the base of his spine. Grimly, he consoled himself with the thought that he had at least pushed his body temperature up a little.

Moving into a sitting position, he reached into his patched camou jacket, past some of the many hiding places for his knives, and to the place where he kept his water. He took a long drink, then forced himself to chew on some jerky, even though he felt anything but hungry. He knew he had to build up some reserves of energy, give his body something on which to feed. All the while he kept his senses keen—or at least, as keen as they could be while he recovered. Yet the instinct honed by years of being hunter and hunted, at different times, told him that there was little danger around.

The feeling of dread that had swept over him before he blacked out had now gone. He had no wish to dwell on it, but still it puzzled him as to what had triggered emotions that were usually so alien.

Massaging feeling back into limbs that had started to cramp, Jak rose unsteadily to his feet and took a good look around. He looked up at the sky, studied the position of the rising sun. From this he looked to the plateaus that marked the farthest points of vision.

He realized something that Mildred and J.B. would fail to pick up on—from the position of the distant ranges, misty in the early morning, and the place in the sky of the rising sun, Jak knew that he had traveled a vast distance for the duration of the storm, the kind of distance where he must have been walking for more than twenty-four hours.

It seemed impossible. Thinking back, the span of time did not seem that great. It had seemed only like an hour or two that he had been in the swirling seas of dirt, insects and frogs. Yet there was no sign of the latter around him. Neither would a simple hour or two of walking, even with the protracted period of cold and in-action, account for the weariness he felt in his limbs. Had he been out of it for most of the time that he had walked? Or had something happened to alter his sense of time?

Jak didn't know how the storm could have done this, but he could think of no other reason to account for this. If nothing else, it might explain the strange emotions that had overwhelmed him just before the blackout. In truth, it did not matter now. All he could do was accept it and try to find his way back to where he believed the others would be waiting.

No. Just Ryan and Krysty. It was strange that memory was so hard. Vague impressions came to him: Doc, ranting in the storm, talking crap like usual, with J.B. and Mildred trying to rein him in, bring him to shelter. Then Doc breaking away, losing sight of them all in the solid fog that the plain had thrown up around them.

Why had he done something so stupe as to leave shelter and try to aid them, especially when he knew in his gut that there was little chance, and he would only add to the confusion? And why had Ryan and Krysty let him? The weird shit storm. It had to be that. The frogs and insects were weird on the outside, and the way they had acted was weird on the inside.

Jak just accepted that. There was little point in worrying about it. Now that it had happened, and it could be used to account for why he had ended up where he was, all that mattered was whether it was still affecting him. If it was, then there was no guarantee that he could rely on his instincts and senses to find his friends.

Jak sniffed the air. It was dry and arid, with little scent and only the lingering moisture of the cold night air. He felt it fill his lungs, and listened to the faint sounds of the air currents as they hummed around him, barely there, but discernible if you were attuned.

There was nothing in him that felt wrong, or even unusual. Whatever the storm had brought with it, so it had also taken with its passing.

Jak figured that the best he could do would be to try to head back toward the area where he thought he had left the wag. He couldn't be exact, but reasoned that in this kind of wide-open expanse, a vehicle like the one he was seeking would soon stand out against the vastness of the plain. He thought back, tried to recall the outlines of the land as he had seen it before the storm ascended. It wasn't easy. The wag chase across the plain had made the landscape move with a rapidity that hindered recall. There had been other things to take his attention, after all. But despite this, he was sure of a rough bearing that he could take.

Steeling himself for the long march ahead, he shook himself down, then began to walk, one foot in front of another. Failure was not an option.

After about an hour, he could hear a change in the movement of the air. It was something almost out of the range of hearing, but it was there: a note that changed slightly in pitch—a wag engine, moving away from him. He cursed. No point in hurrying after it. There was too much distance, and already it had moved before the sound reached him.

Shaking his head, he changed course slightly to follow the direction of the distant sound.

This new course took him, within an hour, to the shelter of a rock outcrop that stretched some fifteen feet into the air, with an overhang that offered shade in the increasing heat of the day. He looked up at the clear sky, at the burning orb of the sun, which was still some way from the center of the sky. It was going to get a whole heap warmer. The receding wag noise told him that there was little need to hurry. Perhaps a brief rest would be beneficial.

It was only as he turned to move toward a now welcoming shelter that he became aware of something else.

How could he have missed it? Jak cursed himself. Obviously he was not as triple red as he thought. There were still some aftereffects from his recent ordeal, and his focusing on the wag noise had been at the expense of any other possible dangers.

For now he was aware of other people, about eight or ten, barely moving, not talking. Perhaps resting, or in some way conserving energy? There was the faint scent of a dead fire on the air, embers and remnants of smoke. Not just people, either; horses. Unnaturally quiet, or so it seemed. Jak was shaken by his own inability to pick up on this sooner, but dismissed the feeling. There was no time for this.

He hastened his approach, and also became more stealthy. He scanned the outcropping, wondering how he could make a recce without making his presence known. The rock was about ten yards across, and rose at a steep angle. The portion facing him was smooth, with little in the way of handholds. A few cracks in the rock, with barely existing and ragged foliage drooping miserably, were all that presented themselves.

Looking up, he could see that the ridge at the top of the crop was narrow, only a yard or two that angled upward, and seemed to offer nothing but a sheer drop and no cover.

Taking this as his only option, Jak reached the rock wall and began to climb, keeping as silent as was possible. With each hand- and foothold he paused, holding his breath as though that would prevent any disturbance.

As he reached the apex of the climb, he could feel the effect. Muscles ached and trembled, sweat poured off him. When he was on the ridge that formed a shelter, he paused momentarily, hungrily gulping in air while still being cautious.

Feeling more like his old self, he edged forward and carefully looked over the lip of the rock ledge.

What he saw almost made him exclaim in surprise.

Beneath, sheltered in the shadow of the outcropping, stood a small ville of tepees. The dyed and patterned cloth shelters, supported on constructs of wood, numbered nine. An equal number of horses was tethered a short distance away. The tepees were circled around the remains of a fire: it was this that had scented to Jak, along with the horses. Six men sat around the now dead fire, each with his head bent and perfectly still, as though in meditation. Perhaps they were.

That left three men missing.

Jak slowly rolled over so that he could see behind where he lay. The missing three men were behind him. Two had their long black hair in plaits that they wore loose. The other had his hair, unplaited, held back by a bandanna. All three wore vests of a tanned leather, festooned with feather and clay decorations. Their pants were of the same tanned leather, but were not decorated, except by colored thread in the stitching. Their moccasins were battered and hardy.

They carried no weapons, and they stood in a loose, easy manner that showed no obvious threat. But each man was stocky and heavily muscled. Their faces were impassive, so it was impossible to judge their intent.

Jak knew that he had been unforgivably slack in his approach to the crop, the lack of attention he had paid to his own back trail. Whatever happened now, he had to accept that he was responsible for his own position. Studying them, he could see that the one with the bandanna was closest. He would have to be the first point of attack. He could palm a knife, which would even the odds a little. Nonetheless, at such close quarters, to be outnumbered three-to-one were less than great odds. Especially as he was prone, and they were looming over him.

Jak tensed himself. Would they expect him to attack? Surprise might be all he had…

But it was Jak who was to be taken by surprise.

Chapter Six

"White man…whiter than white man," the Native American with the bandanna chuckled. "Legend never told us it would be like this."

Jak had been poised to spring to his feet and take his chances. But the tone of the man's voice disarmed him. There was no malice in there; no hint of any hostility. If anything, he seemed to take the view that Jak was friend rather than foe.

Instinct would not let Jak completely let down his guard. Nonetheless, he relaxed slightly, the tension slackening in his muscles.

"We don't mean you harm," one of the others said, "but we couldn't risk you attacking."

Jak nodded. If he was in their position, he would act defensively. And he had to give it to them; they were good. It was a more than evenly matched standoff, and they knew it.

"What do with me now?" he asked, aware that while he was still prone he was at their mercy.

"Well, if you're not going to turn around and attack as soon as you get the chance, we were going to offer you food and shelter. You look like you could use it."

Jak looked down at himself as he lay recumbent. He was covered in dust and dirt, with livid bruises and welts raised on his white skin by impact with rocks. Streaks of blood colored his skin. He figured that he had to look a whole lot worse than he felt.

"Why give me that?" he asked.

The three men exchanged looks. The one in the middle sighed, then scratched his chin. He was so casual that it seemed as though they were old compatriots rather than men who had just been facing off.

"Look, Whitey, it's hard to explain. Probably might sound crazy and stupe unless you know already." He studied Jak's blank canvas of a face carefully, then continued. "Maybe you do. Don't give much away if you do. Come with us, and we'll explain."

"Okay. Not trust you, though."

The man with the bandanna laughed. "No more than we can trust you, right now. C'mon."

Beckoning Jak to follow him, he turned and went back down the shallow shelf of rock, starting the climb down. He was followed by one of the others, who looked over his shoulder to ensure that Jak was following. As the albino teen got to his feet, he noted that the third man stepped back, but did not immediately follow his compatriots. He waited for Jak to move. Figuring that he would do exactly the same thing under such circumstances, Jak scrambled to his feet and followed, allowing the man to wait for him before bringing up the rear.

The two leading Native Americans were already waiting for him on the floor of the plain as he started his descent. Knowing this, and knowing that he had another above, Jak would have waited to attack if that had been his aim. But right now, he was more concerned with discovering why these men were acting in a friendly manner toward him. With the wag noise having long since vanished into the distance, it was also a certainty that he would need to make allies to survive. At least, until such time as he was able to begin searching for his companions.

The four men made their way around the outcropping to where camp had been pitched. Those warriors who had been deep in meditation were now on their feet. As Jak was led to them, they already had food and water ready for him. It was as though they had every confidence in his compliance. As though they had been expecting him.

Jak ate and drank in silence. He was determined to give nothing away, and would wait for these men to make the first move. Were these men his captors, or his salvation? He was unsure.

When he had eaten and drunk well, they presented him with a bowl of water in which to wash. While he did, they took down the tepees and stored them on a hide sled, which they then attached to the saddle mount of one of the horses.

Once Jak had completed his ablutions, the warrior with the bandanna spoke to him. "If you ride with me, I'll explain something of what has happened while we journey to our ville."

Jak nodded. Climbing up behind the warrior, he found

himself moving out into the middle of the line of riders. The horse with the sled took up position at the rear.

They set off across the plain, the sun now high overhead, and the heat intensifying with every mile they traveled.

After a while, the warrior with the bandanna spoke over his shoulder.

"We knew you were coming. Some had arrived, and so it was certain that the others would be nearby. It was just a question of tracking you. The one who came upon us of his volition could say little. Too long out on the plain, exposed to the elements. But if we explored in the direction from which he came, then chances were that we would find you. As it happened, we were spared the need to search as you came upon us of your own accord. Truly, we should have known that this would happen. How else could the legends be realized?"

Jak listened, but said nothing. So far, none of it really made much sense to him. This talk of legends was stupe, but if he waited long enough, he was sure that more would become clear.

So they continued. It was near nightfall, the sun descending behind a far range of hills, casting long blue-hued shadows over the sun-scorched plain, before they came upon the area that the Native Americans called their ville. Riding into the shadows, as Jak's eyes adjusted to the gloomier light, he became aware that a small ville of wigwams sat in the shelter of the hillside. The large structures, made of wood and brush woven together to form misshapen mushrooms of shelter, were clustered close to the face of the rock, the beginning of a fire flaring and casting a glow reflected back off the rock. In this improving light, Jak was now able to see that the ville numbered more than twenty wigwams. There was also the suggestion of an opening in the rock, through which he was now able to see another source of light. Dimmer, but steady. Not natural or fire light, but something else. Electricity? Within the confines of rock, this could mean only one thing.

"Mebbe redoubt," he breathed.

The man in front of him glanced over his shoulder. They had ridden in silence for some time, and it was as much surprise at Jak's voice, as it was at what he said, that prompted response.

"So you will say something, then? Even if it makes no sense. 'Re'-what? Never mind, Red-eyes, it'll be talked of soon enough. Maybe the shaman can get some sense out of you."

Jak would be ready for anything. He would bide his time and try to find out as much as he could.

As the new arrivals rode into the ville, they found themselves surrounded by men, women and children. Jak noted that while the men and boys wore their hair long, the women were the opposite. Unlike most communities, where there were no rules or conventions about this, it seemed that it was a tradition strictly observed. Grimly, he wondered how Krysty or Millie would fare in such a place.

The warrior party halted and dismounted. The throng milled around them, and there were questions about where Jak had been found and what he had said. None of these were directed toward him, which he found amusing rather than irritating. It was as though the people were afraid to speak to him directly. He found himself being ushered through the crowd by the man he had ridden with, who brushed aside all of these queries with a few terse words. It was easy to see that Jak was considered of some importance. Mebbe, he thought, someone would soon tell him why.

He found himself being led to the wigwam that was closest to the redoubt entrance. As they approached, he noticed the following things—the wigwam to which he was being taken was larger and more ornate in its weaving than any of the others in the ville. There was little doubt in his mind now that there was a redoubt hidden by the rocks, as the open entrance was unmistakable, down to the support pillars in the interior tunnel, and the entry pad and sec door mechanisms that were visible on their approach. And there was also little doubt that the other members of the Native American tribe were in deference to the inhabitant of the large wigwam, falling back as they did.

The warrior in the bandanna stopped in front of the entrance to the wigwam, indicating that Jak do likewise. He said something in his native language, and after a few moments two men emerged from the interior of the wigwam.

Although he could not see, and did not look back, Jak could feel the people at his rear supplicate as the two men walked into the open. One was tall, barrel-chested, and was dressed similarly to the warriors who had brought Jak into the ville. He had an aquiline nose and hooded eyes, which were as cold as a snake's as they regarded him. He was a man used to being obeyed without question. Where some men had decorative feathers and braiding in their hair, this imposing figure had enough to almost consider it a headdress. He also had scarring on his chest that suggested a number of ritualistic ordeals. Jak was familiar enough with stories of such Native American tribes to guess at such.

By contrast, the figure at his side was, perhaps, more sinister than imposing. Shorter, and much thinner, he was a wiry figure whose frame was similar to Jak's. But his skin was dark and his long hair jet-black. Or at least, it appeared to be so. There was little of it visible beneath the headdress that he wore. It was made from the skull of some animal—Jak couldn't guess which—and was covered with furs, stitched from many creatures, and of differing hues that extended past his neck and shoulders. His clothing, too, was made of animal pelts that had been dried, but not cured in the same way as the leather and hide worn by the rest of the men. It was enough to set him apart and mark him as someone with a unique role in the tribe.

This, Jak figured, had to be the shaman.

The larger of the men held up his hand in greeting. "Welcome, Red-eyes. Can't say you're what we were expecting, but then, the same is true of the other half."

"Seems our friend doesn't know what we speak of," the smaller man interjected wryly, taking note of the expression on Jak's face. Although as impassive as ever in many ways, there was perhaps the slightest flicker of puzzlement at the larger man's words.

"Perhaps not. The prophecies never said that the messengers would know the message that they carried. I wonder if it's possible that they aren't permitted to know."

"That to know would somehow break the spell?" the smaller man asked. He shrugged. "It's a possibility."

Jak was starting to get angry at the way they were talking. It was as though he wasn't there. Worse, it was as though he were some animal being bought and sold at market. Or a slave. And Jak Lauren was no one's slave.

"Hey, talk about me like I'm dumb shit? Fuck you."

Jak turned to leave. Deep down, he knew that there was no chance of his being able to make a break for it. As he made his move, he could see that the whole of the tribe—men, women and even the children—were now facing him. In the manner that they looked at him there was nothing but expectancy. And he had no idea how he could fulfill it.

But that was unimportant for the now. Beyond the faces, he could see only that the densely packed mass of flesh would be a wall of resistance that it may prove impossible to pass, particularly as he could see that male warriors among the crowd had picked up on the change in his posture. His body language now said nothing more than flight. They wouldn't be amenable to that, he was sure.

The bandanna-wearing warrior who had ridden with him stretched out a hand—a large ham of a fist—that encircled Jak's biceps with ease. The grip was loose, but definite. It threatened to close tight at the merest behest.

Jak looked around, his eyes meeting the dark brown orbs of the warrior. In a second, he could see many things in there: the reluctance to violence; the hope that it would not come to conflict; the longing of one who has waited long for a prophecy to be fulfilled. The man did not want to fight, but would if he it was required.

That initial reluctance was all that Jak needed. Slippery like an eel, he jerked his arm from the warrior's grip before it had a chance to tighten. Reflexes just that fraction of a second too slow, the man was left clutching at air as Jak snaked behind him, a leaf-bladed knife palmed to his right hand while the left closed around the warrior's throat. A booted foot to the calf caused the man's leg to crumple, and he dropped to one knee, Jak driving a knee into his back to further bend him to his optimum position.

Red eyes darting around the crowd, seeing the warriors stiffen as they reach for knives of their own, Jak also flicked his gaze toward the chief and the shaman.

"You want him chilled? Be easy," Jak said softly. Then he let the man go so that he slumped forward onto the ground. His constricted throat now freed, he gasped for breath, coughing hard. Jak stepped back, palming the knife once more so that it seemed to simply vanish, its hiding place within the patched camou jacket impossible to ascertain.

A small patch of empty ground had opened up around the albino hunter. The whole tribe had moved back, unwilling to either precipitate the chilling of their warrior or to risk the wrath of the man for whom they had waited so long. Jak stood in the center, aware also that the chief and the shaman had moved back.

"Could easily have chilled him. No need. Tell me what you want, and mebbe we can talk."

The chief, with a sideways glance at the shaman, stepped forward, slowly, hesitantly, unwilling to cause any further problem.

"Ok, Red-eyes, maybe we shouldn't have sounded like we were talking in riddles. Let's start again." When Jak nodded, the chief gestured to the gathered tribe. "We're what used to be called the Pawnee, back before skydark. We moved onto these plains not long after the white-eyes came. They brought us the horse, and we used it to find new pastures on which to graze. We settled where we hadn't been able to before, because of what we'd gained.

"But the white-eye was greedy. Always wanted more. We existed alongside them, but they acted like they wanted us gone. They fought us, drove us into smaller and smaller areas. They called them reservations, which were prisons. All the while, the white-eye ways did nothing but destroy the land and bring the end of all life that much closer.

"Before skydark came, some of us had decided to return to the old ways. We had the jack that the white-eyes had forced us to use, to fit in with their ways. So we used it against them. Took it off them, used it to stockpile things that would help us, determined that we would go back to the ways of our fathers."

"Pretty story," Jak sniffed. "Can't see where I fit."

The chief snorted. "You need to understand why we see you as important, For that you need to know how we got to this point."

"Hurry up, then." Jak shrugged.

Undaunted, the chief continued, although the look given him by the shaman did not escape Jak.

"When the nukecaust came, we had already started to separate from the world of the white-eyes. We had left the lands to which we were sent by the old governments, and we had come to this place. We found shelter, and so we were able to wait out the worst of the nuke winter before the spring of a new life came to us."

Jak was starting to get bored. A lot of stupe talking had never, as far as he was concerned, ever got anyone to anywhere. But he was hanging on, hoping that some sense would soon come out of this, something that would give him some clue as to why he was seemingly indispensable. And who, perhaps, was the "other half" they spoke about.

He knew he'd have to be patient. The chief was speaking as though this was something that had been committed to memory and passed down. It would end only when it had always ended.

One thing that did strike him as amusing, though: it would seem that the shelter from the ways of their enemies had come via the redoubt. Built, of course, by those they professed to be against. He figured that it was not the time to raise this anomaly.

But now he could see that the chief was reaching the

end of his long peroration. It was time to find out what the hell he was here for... or so he hoped.

"As the lands were ravaged by the dreadful terrors of the nuke, and the life that had been given by Mother Earth had been distorted by mutation, it was hard for us to adapt to the new land and the new ways. But we were driven by the knowledge that this was just, in the view of the great spirit that guides us, a way of cleansing. So that the world would be made afresh for us. Then, when this was so, and we were in the right place at the right time, as defined by the stars, then two people would come out of nowhere, delivered unto us so that we could be the people to lead the world."

"An' you figure I'm one of 'em?" Jak questioned.

The shaman nodded. He answered instead of the chief, and when he did, it was clear why.

"Wakan Tanka speaks to those of us who have been blessed with the gift of vision. We are few, and we are just vessels of the spirits, but we are the mouthpiece by which the wise words of Wakan Tanka are delivered to those who would be his chosen people. To my predecessors he spoke of a time when you and the other half would come across our people. You are the ones who will lead us. It is only in my time that he has spoken of the nearness of this event. The stars are in the patterns that he showed me in the dust. The shapes are right."

"And we're supposed show you what?" Jak asked. It sounded like a bunch of crap to him, and his patience was wearing thin. Maybe they could give him shelter on a hostile plain, but was it worth this shit?

The shaman smiled sadly. "That is what you are supposed to know. But perhaps you do without knowing that you do. Such are the ways of Wakan Tanka."

"Sounds like crap," Jak said.

"It would if you had been sent as the unsuspecting messenger." The shaman shrugged. "Perhaps it is part of the great plan that you must discover for yourself before we can discover."

"For now," the chief added, "rest up here and let us show you that we mean you no harm. The answer lies on the plains from which you came. You and the other half, who was also delivered to us by accident. Perhaps if you meet him, then that will mean something to you."

Jak said nothing. It sounded yet another stupe idea to him. It was lucky for whoever the "other half" might be that he had been saved from wandering the plains until he bought the farm, but Jak couldn't see that it would mean squat to him. On the other hand, he had nowhere to go. Play along, and at least he would gain food, shelter and rest for a short while, while he considered what to do next.

"Okay," he said simply.

The chief stepped forward and indicated that Jak follow him. The crowd parted as the barrel-chested warrior strode through, heading for a wigwam that stood on the far reach of the small ville. The shaman brought up the rear. Some of the crowd followed, driven either by the need to witness this momentous event or simply by curiosity.

It didn't escape Jak's notice that in among them were

a few men whose hands hovered close to the sheathed knives that hung from their belts. He had noticed the small hand gestures exchanged between the shaman and the warrior he had earlier bested. They may not be overtly hostile, but they were certainly in no mood to take risks.

Jak would have been the same.

At the entrance to the wigwam, which was the far-thest from the open redoubt entrance, and faced onto the empty plain, a man and woman were waiting for them. Its location suggested that if trouble were to start, then none of the tribe would be at much risk. The man was armed in plain sight, just to reinforce the message. The woman, on the other hand, had her long sleeves rolled up and looked as though she had recently been wash-ing something…or someone.

"Is he awake?" the chief asked.

The woman shook her head.

"We will look upon him anyway," the chief decided.

As the man and woman stood aside, the chief and the shaman ushered Jak into the wigwam. It was dark in-side, the tallow candle casting only the dimmest of light. It took the albino teen a few moments to make out the shape that was huddled on rush bedding.

"By Three Kennedys…" Jak breathed, almost to himself.

Chapter Seven

Three days and nights. That was how long Mildred and J.B. rode with the tribesmen before they reached the cluster of wigwams and tepees that defined the tribal ville. During that time, they had learned very little of who their traveling companions were, and why they had been waiting for them. In truth, the subject had been broached only the once: during a rest period on the second day.

For most of the first day they had traveled in silence, which had suited both Mildred and the Armorer; both were still at the point of exhaustion after struggling against the effects and aftereffects of the storm. Although both had many questions to ask, these could wait. By the same token, they were relieved that the silence of their fellow travelers saved the effort of having to answer potentially awkward questions for themselves.

The first night, as the sun fell and the cold cloak of dark descended upon the plain, they had halted at a signal from the rider at the head of the party. It had seemed arbitrary, but perhaps he had determined visibility too poor to continue. For both Mildred and J.B., riding behind warriors in the middle of the party, it was impossible to know. All either of them could say was that the rest of the party concurred with his opinion. Indeed, by the way in which they had dismounted and struck camp with only the barest of verbal communication suggested that the unit worked like a well-oiled piece of machinery, with every wheel and cog fitting perfectly into a place that they knew only too well.

When a fire had been lit and tepees had been erected for the night, food was cooked, and bowls presented to both Mildred and J.B.

"Eat. It'll help you through the chill of night," intoned the bronzed warrior who handed them the wooden bowls. He waited until they both took a mouthful before nodding, then returning to his compatriots.

The food was good: spiced meat that had been heated in a thin stock, with dried beans added. They were astounded at how hungry they actually were, neither having given the matter much thought since the desultory breakfast of the morning.

Their traveling companions talked among themselves in low, soft tones, yet there seemed to be no secrecy, no desire to keep the newcomers out of the loop. Rather, it seemed as though a quiet, contemplative manner was their natural bearing. In the same way, there was no attempt to mount a guard on the two outlanders. The horses were tethered nearby and left unguarded; neither did any of the warriors seem to even notice when Mildred, and then J.B., rose to move nearer the warmth of the fire. It was only when the warriors made a seemingly mutual—and unspoken—decision to retire for the evening that a guard was mounted.

With the rising of the sun, camp was struck and the party headed off once more with, yet again, little verbal communication.

As they traveled across the plains, Mildred and J.B. were acutely aware that every hour took them, in all likelihood, farther away from their friends. The chances of coming upon them by mere coincidence grew less and less. Yet, at the same time, there was a nagging feeling—unspoken by either—that they had not seen the last of their companions.

The land around them changed as they traveled, so slightly by degrees that it was only noticeable if they stopped to think about it. The flat and arid plains had been replaced by a more verdant landscape. Small groves of stunted trees began to appear at intervals, with spiky, high grass scattered between. This alone spoke of a higher water table, and a more fertile soil, which was confirmed as they rode into a small dip that was too shallow to grace with the term valley, yet provided enough shelter from the elements to harbor some small rodents and mammals along with the lizard forms that had occasionally shown themselves along the way. Trees with overhanging branches, their heavy greenery seeming to drink from the shallow but clear stream that ran between them, provided shelter.

As the warriors halted and dismounted, J.B. could see that the stream emerged from one end of the dip and disappeared into the other. The dip had been not been hollowed out by erosion, but appeared to have been engineered at some point to allow access to the stream. By these tribesmen? The growth of flora suggested that it had been settlers long before the dark of nuclear winter that had originally dug here.

He said as much to the warrior who had brought them food the night before. If nothing else, he wanted to see if the man would open up on this subject: if so, then it was possible that he may be able to find out more about the status Millie and himself shared as people who had been "expected."

The warrior nodded, and said nothing for a moment. He cupped his hands and drank from the stream, as did many of the others. After he had splashed his face with the cool liquid, he drew breath and nodded once more.

"There are many stories and legends about the plains. For many hundreds of years both our people and the white man tried to tame the land. Neither was truly successful. Mother Earth has to be lived alongside, not broken in like a young stallion. There are those who say our people made this. Others say it was the white man. I figure that as wrong. We never try to make changes in the land. That's what the white man did. Where he went wrong."

"You might not be wrong there." J.B. nodded. "Still, we should be grateful for it right now. Although I guess if it wasn't here, you could still find water."

The warrior smiled. "Smart man. Also man with a lot of questions you want one of us to answer."

J.B. chuckled. "That obvious?"

"Only to those who care to see," the warrior replied. "But the answers are not ours to give. That is why we want you to travel with us. When we reach our home, then our medicine man will speak with you. He is privy to the secrets that Wakan Tanka shares only with those who have the ability to speak directly to him. That is how we found you."

J.B. looked at the man, one eyebrow raised. He pushed back his fedora and scratched at his forehead. "You'll excuse me if that makes no sense to me," he murmured.

The warrior shook his head. "Those are the ways of the spirit world. Few of us understand. We are directed by the spirits to do their bidding, and it is only when each has played his part and the patterns are drawn in the dust that the real shape emerges."

"Meantime we have to trust you?"

"Only if you wish to. All I will say is that the spirits told our medicine man that two we have been waiting for would be found in the dry parts of the plain, having been on a vision quest."

J.B. pondered that. He had no idea what a vision quest was as such, but the idea that it suggested to him fitted pretty well with the weird shit and discomfort that he and Mildred had endured only forty-eight hours before. Maybe—just maybe—there was something in what the warrior said.

"I think your medicine man can tell me and my friend much that we would want to know. Mebbe we can tell him something in return. Something we might not know we know."

The warrior returned the Armorer's previous expression of bemusement. "You sound like him, so you might be right," he said with a wry humor.

As the party made ready to leave, J.B. relayed the conversation to Mildred. Remembering she knew of Native American lore from her old, predark life, she still erred on the side of believing it to be a pile of crap. However, there was something in what J.B. was saying; and it was true that they had no better option open to them. With a certain reluctance, she concurred with the Armorer.

And so they set off once more. The rest of the day followed the pattern of the first. They rode until the sun began to fall, finally stopping to pitch camp as the darkness curled around them. The next morning, they rose and began their journey with the rising of the sun.

The land was now much more lush. Scrub grass grew around the trail made by generations of riders, both before and after the nukecaust. The mountains and hills that had once been hazed with blue mist like wreathes of smoke now came into sharp relief, and grew in size with every mile that was traversed by the riders. Now there were herds of cattle upon the plain, fenced in by wire strung along a series of wooden posts. The enclosures were large, but were nonetheless enclosures. Mildred was certain that this hadn't been part of the Native life back in the days of the old west she recalled from movies. Maybe they had learned more from the white man that perhaps they realized.

The cattle looked healthy and well-fed. The land here

had lush grasses. In the distance, she could see grazing animals that had large heads and narrow backs, like the bison that had been all but wiped out before skydark. It was too far to be sure. Could these be the result of some kind of mutation, bred by these people in emulation of their past?

In the distance, and growing nearer by the minute, she could see the clustered wigwams and tepees that defined the ville. They were almost at their destination.

What they would find may just prove to be fascinating. Or it could be merely dangerous.

She knew what her money would be on.

BY THE TIME that Mildred and J.B. reached the tribal settlement that housed their rescuers, Ryan and Krysty had already been settled into the tribal ville inhabited by the men that had found them.

Following their surprisingly peaceful encounter with the tattooed riders, both Ryan and Krysty had agreed to follow in the wake of the party. Exchanging glances as they were faced by the riders' emissary, they both realized that dissent would risk combat that neither was ready to face. Sure, they wouldn't be able to look for their companions; by the same token, it wouldn't be possible for them to find their way back to the wag. But, looking around, there was little sign of any life other than themselves and the men who stood in front of them on foot or horseback.

In truth, they had little real choice.

Gunning the wag's engine back into life, Ryan and

Krysty drove across the arid and uneven area of the plain, surrounded on all sides by the riders. The horses kept their distance, whether from a desire to avoid any collision as Ryan erratically steered the wag over the more erratic excesses of the ground, or from a desire to show that their intent was not to ride sec on the inhabitants of the wag, was unclear. Either way, it allowed Ryan and Krysty to exchange words without fear of being overheard, while also avoiding the worst of the dust clouds thrown up by pounding hooves.

They headed in a direction that took them on a parallel course to the ville of Brisbane. At certain points in the journey, they could see the black ribbon of the road as it moved momentarily closer, then farther from them, barely visible through the dust thrown up by their outrider escort.

"Going back to Brisbane?" Krysty questioned.

"Near. Has to be," Ryan said.

"Then how come we never heard of anyone who looked like this when we were there?" she continued. "It's not as if these guys wouldn't stand out in a crowd. Not if it was the crowd that lived in that pesthole."

"They must keep themselves apart," Ryan reasoned. "The big question is why they would do it."

"Figure we'll get that answered sooner rather than later, lover," Krysty said softly, watching the impassive figures of the Native Americans as they rode at pace with the wag. Their decorated bodies were hardened to the elements, and they did not flinch under the harsh glare of the sun, nor under the scouring of the constant dirt mist that swirled around them. Among the body decoration, she was sure that she could see signs of scarification. From what she had heard, that bespoke of rituals for manhood that would test their endurance for pain. Which, in turn, would explain why it was no problem for them to take the dust and the heat in their stride—or at least, the stride of their mounts.

If they could take that amount of punishment, would they hesitate at handing out similar? And could either Ryan or herself—given the effects of the day before—count on their stamina being enough to handle this right now?

She looked across at Ryan. He didn't notice the look, his attention being focused on keeping the wag on course. But he looked weary. The effects of his concussion had not yet had time to wear off. How would he be if they faced trial and ordeal in any short space of time? Come to that, how would she deal with it?

These thoughts preoccupied her so much that she did not notice that their path had begun to deviate from the road back to Brisbane. It was only when Ryan pointed that out, wondering out loud where they were headed, that she took in the change in direction.

They were now headed away from the ville that stood alone on the dusty plains, their direction taking them toward one of the plateaued ranges that had peppered the horizon.

"Could be a long haul," Ryan commented. "Mebbe not…the way they're taking us across this ground, that might be nearer than we thought…" It crossed his mind that he may have made an error of judgment in heading the way he had when pursued by the coldhearts. If he had taken this route, could they have headed for the mountains and evaded their pursuers? Would they have skirted the storm? Would they still be together as a group, and not scattered to who knew where?

He shook his head, as if to clear it. What had happened couldn't be changed. It had been the best call at the time. He had to stay focused and stay frosty so that he and Krysty could face what lay ahead.

They journeyed on as the sun moved across the empty sky. As it began to sink to the horizon, Ryan could see that the route they had traveled had taken them out of the dust and hard-packed, ridged earth, and into something that had a little more to support life. The wheels beneath him no longer bucked and reared, twisting the steering column so that his arms ached with the effort of keeping them on an even path. The clouds of dust and dirt thrown up by hooves now began to decrease in size and volume. It became easier to breathe as the air became less arid. Their progress hastened as the wag was able to follow the riders with less strain and more speed.

The sun was starting to fall behind the plateau ahead as they picked up speed. Ryan pushed down on the gas, his speed increasing with that of the riders. It was clear that they had every intention of reaching the mountains by the time that the last rays shone over the now blackened outline of the range.

"Any sign of where we're headed?" Ryan asked

Krysty as the near side of the mountain became lost in shadows cast by the descending sun.

She shook her head. "Can't see jackshit, lover. We'll just have to trust in where they're leading us. Can't be far now, though. If they don't live on this side of the range, then they'll have to stop and make camp for the night, surely?'

"I wouldn't like to put jack on anything," Ryan murmured.

The one-eyed man hit the switch for the headlights on the front of the wag, figuring that the battery and the fuel supply could take the extra drain. He cursed as nothing happened. The mechanism had to have been damaged by the way in which the wag had borne the brunt of the previous day's pursuit. He would have preferred a little light, as now he felt he was driving blind literally as well as figuratively.

Gradually, as their eyes adjusted to the lack of light that existed in the shadow of the mountain, they could see that they were being taken onto a trail that led them to the foot of the rock face. Around them, sheltered from the worst excesses of the elements, there were sprouting crops of trees and bush. The trail was worn deep into the soil, telling of regular use. The trees hung over, heavy with leaf and branch, sheltering wildlife that scattered and took cover as the warriors on horseback and the alien roar of the wag approached.

Yet there was no sign of human habitation. Both Ryan and Krysty, without having to speak, were sharing the same thought. If they kept on going, they would run into the rock face. There was no sign of a path around, and there was nothing that suggested a camp or ville of any kind.

Then they saw it—an opening in the rock, hidden by bush and overhanging tree branches, the trail they were following veering away at a right angle. As they drew near, Ryan applied the brakes, following the lead of the horsemen, who slowed as they approached. He drew the wag to a halt, leaving the engine ticking, as some of the riders dismounted and began to move some of the brush that stood in front of the mouth of the opening.

One of the riders came over to them. He indicated an area around the mouth of the opening.

"Take your wag in there, then switch off. We'll move it to a safe location after you have been taken to our elders."

"Your elders?"

The man chuckled. "Nothing for you to get your back up about, One-eye. They're the ones who sent us to look for you. They've been waiting for you for a long time, like you were told."

Before Ryan could ask any further questions, the warrior turned and walked back toward the opening in the rock. Ryan looked at Krysty, shrugged, and put the wag into gear, guiding it toward the gaping black maw of the rock mouth.

Slowly the wag advanced on the black hole. But as they drew near, both began to see more of the place they were about to enter as a procession of dim lights spread a faded yellowing glow over the rock interior.

As the wag nosed into the cave, they could see that the original fissure had been taken and worked into an enlarged space by people working with primitive tools. There were paintings on the cave walls that were as faded as the lighting, though whether they had been daubed thousands, hundreds, or mere years ago was indeterminate.

The cave receded into the distance, curving away from the straight tunnel so that it became impossible to see where it ended. Responding to a gesture from one of the warriors, Ryan brought the wag to a halt and switched off the engine. As they got out of the vehicle, the warrior said, "Leave it here, now. We'll make sure it's secured and hidden from prying eyes. You follow him," he added, indicating a man who had appeared at the farthest bend of the tunnel. "We have to clear any signs of our passage before we can join the tribe."

"Why clear away tracks?" Ryan asked. "Do you fear intruders?"

"Few come this way. Why should they? There's nothing to bring them, and few know that we are here. But if anyone should stray this far from usual white-eye routes, we wouldn't wish for them to disturb us." There was an edge to the way that he said that, leaving Ryan in no doubt as to what disturbance would mean for any unwitting intruder. "And if we make sure we leave no traces, then there is little chance that they may stumble upon us." He dismissed them with a gesture and turned to join his colleagues.

Ryan and Krysty turned to face the man who was still waiting for them. His stance and expression gave noth-

ing away, and he waited in silence as they walked toward
him, speaking only when they were almost upon him.

"Welcome, outlanders. Few white-eyes see our do-
main. Fewer have the opportunity to go in peace and tell.
The prophecy foretells of your coming. I pray for your
sakes that you are not a false dawning."

Without giving either of them the opportunity to
comment, he turned and walked on ahead of them.

As they followed, they could see that the walls of the
tunnel formed in the rock were covered in hieroglyph
paintings that seemed to detail the history of the people
who dwelt within the cave system—for neither of them
had any doubt that this was more than just a simple hole
in the rock—with paintings depicting scenes of skydark
and the long winter that followed in its wake being followed by scenes in which the decorated people of the
tribe emerged from hiding and rebuilt their homes in this
place. There were also images of hunts, and scenes that
appeared to depict rites that the men of the tribe went
through to achieve the status that was the coming of age.
These confirmed Krysty's earlier thoughts about the
tattooing and scarification of the warriors who had
found them.

As they moved along the dimly lit tunnels, they became aware that they were moving on an incline. As
they went deeper into the heart of the mountain, they
were also moving upward.

Along the way, there were other tunnels branching
off this main route. All the passages were lit by tallow
candles that burned slowly, smoke rising from them in

whorls that moved with such a slowness as to seem static. It occurred to both of them that the tunnel system should soon be filled with such smoke, choking anyone within. It was only on closer inspection that they could see that the candles were mounted near small fissures and cracks that attracted the slow-moving plumes. The mountain and cave system seemed to come equipped with its own natural ventilation system that had been put to good use by the tribe that made it their home.

Down the passages they could hear voices, and the sounds of movement and life. Bowls and pans clashed, the smells of freshly cooked food wafted down before joining the smoke plumes in being slowly sucked out to the skies above.

"You cut these out yourselves?" Ryan asked. He didn't expect an answer, as their guide had so far been silent. So he was surprised when his query did elicit a response, although perhaps not so much at the terseness of the reply.

"Most of them were here when our ancestors found this place. Just worked them out a little."

Krysty wondered if honeycombing a mountain with tunnels until it was almost hollow was ultimately a good idea, but held her peace. As long as the bastard didn't collapse on Ryan or herself, it was none of her damn business.

The paintings on the walls, despite their apparent age, were recent. As they continued, she studied them to gain some kind of insight into the people they had landed among. It seemed to her that these were a proud warrior race who worshiped the sun, and believed in living as one with the elements. They took only what they needed, and replaced it with themselves as the time came to buy the farm. In many ways, they had a lot in common with the ways of Harmony, her home ville. Perhaps it wouldn't be too hard for her to find common ground with these people should Ryan find communication a problem.

A colder air now pervaded the tunnel, indicating that they were near the open air. Certainly, the incline of the tunnel, though not steep, had grown greater, and the ache in their calf and thigh muscles spoke of an ascent perhaps greater than they had realized.

The mouth at the apex of the tunnel became visible, if only because it was a hole of dark velvet, sprinkled with the distant lights of the night sky, against the fallow light that illuminated their way. The chill of the cold plains night prickled at their skins.

They emerged onto a mesa ringed with trees and shrubs that provided shelter from the winds that may sweep across the flat plains around, and at the same time provided cover from prying eyes for any who may wish to look from the ground.

This kind of mesa was more common farther south, where thousands of years of erosion had flattened mountain peaks. Here, where many hills and mountains were untouched in such a way, this kind of mesa had to be the result of the same postskydark disturbance that had caused the honeycomb effect in the mountain beneath.

Scattered across the flat rock floor, scattered with a

thin layer of topsoil, were wigwams and tepees, clustered around three fires that burned low and steady, sending dark towers of smoke into the black night. Around one such fire sat a man in a flowing headdress, who was accompanied by a larger man who wore animal furs. Both looked around, their faces shrouded in shadow, as their guide led Ryan and Krysty into the open.

The two men stood and strode over to them. The man in the headdress—obviously the tribal chief to judge by his dress and the amount of decoration and scarification that was visible even in the low level of light—was shorter than the man in the furs. He strode across the mesa with the air of a man who had been waiting for this moment, and could barely contain his excitement. Keeping a pace or two behind, the man in fur—who Krysty could recognize not from his dress but by something indefinable in his bearing as being the shaman of the tribe—was less obviously excited, but could be seen to be using the time to examine the two people who stood with the native guide.

The chief stopped in front of them and held up his hand in gesture of greeting.

"So finally you have come," he said without preamble. "Now the prophecy can begin."

The shaman stood behind him, saying nothing. Ryan could tell that whatever he said next would determine how they were to be treated.

"If it's been foretold, then so it must be," he said carefully, "even though the fates may not tell us of our own role in its unfolding."

"Very nice," the shaman murmured, his voice pitched high for such a large man. "Thing is, it could mean anything. There are two of you, and you have arrived from the desert, maybe having endured a vision quest to determine what you must do with your lives. But maybe you've just got lost, and we found you."

"Mebbe," Ryan agreed. "But if we are the ones that legend foretold, it may be that we have to be ignorant of intent in order to be pure of heart."

The chief held up his hand again; this time, it was more by way of a gesture of irritation. He turned to his shaman.

"Just what the hell are you two talking about?"

The shaman shrugged and smiled. "I think One-eye here was just trying to tell us that he has no idea what prophecy we're talking about, but he doesn't want to buy the farm over it."

The chief sighed. "Well, shit, you can't blame him for that. There's no rule that says messengers have to know what the message is…that's what you're for." He turned back to Ryan and Krysty. "The stars are in the right place, and legends of the Dakota Sioux have foretold of two people since we first came out of the ground after skydark. You're right place, right time. That'll do for me." He beckoned them toward the fire. "Follow us, and we'll tell you all that we know. Maybe that'll help you make sense of things."

Krysty shrugged at Ryan's questioning gaze. These people were being friendly in a way that was alien to expectation at a time like this.

There had to be a catch.

TWO DAYS LATER, and at a distance as far removed from the dark mountains as it was possible to be, Mildred and J.B. finally arrived at their destination. As they rode into the heart of the ville, the tribe turned out to greet the riders who had traveled in search of a legend, and had returned with those who may just have fulfilled the old stories.

Despite the fact that, seemingly, the entire ville had come out of their wigwams and tepees to view the newcomers, it was uncannily quiet. The tribe seemed to be as silent as those who had ridden out to collect the two strangers. Mildred wondered if it was going to be difficult to work out just what it was that was expected of them. Would anyone actually open his or her mouth to tell them just exactly what it was the prophecy foretold?

The riders dismounted, Mildred and J.B. following suit. In among the tribe members who were there to greet them were two men who obviously held special significance. By their bearing, and by the way in which their dress differed, they were plainly the elders of the tribe. The way in which they moved in silence through the throng, cutting a swathe with ease, confirmed that.

"These are the ones you found," one of them said as they reached the riders. It was a statement more than a question.

The warrior who had spoken to J.B. by the river nodded. "It was as foretold. They had been on the plains for some time, and showed signs of a vision quest—"

"Hey, don't you tell me what we showed signs of,"

Mildred said hotly. "We got separated from our party in that damn storm that blew up."

J.B. stared at her. He couldn't believe that she was choosing now to let anger get the better of her. Not when they were surrounded and outnumbered. He wasn't to know that the idea that the storm may not have been as it seemed was one that had been nagging at her subconscious for some time.

"What storm?" asked the elder who had, so far, been silent.

"That damn storm where the winds raised up so much dust that you couldn't breathe without choking, and those damn frogs and locusts rained down like—" She stopped when she realized that the entire tribe seemed to be scrutinizing her, hanging on to her every word.

"Were there such things?" the elder asked of the warrior.

He shook his head. "There was a dust storm. But nothing else." He turned to Mildred and J.B. "If what you say was true, then where were the frogs and locusts that rained from the heavens? Did you see them on the ground? I did not. Neither did my brothers."

J.B. looked at Mildred. "Hadn't thought of it, but—"

"Damn it, he's right, John. It's been bugging me since I first woke up the morning after…"

"Truly, you were on a vision quest."

Mildred had been dreading this moment. All that she had previously dismissed as bull; now it seemed to be coming home to her as truth.

"Could you," she said slowly, "explain exactly what a vision quest is?"

The elder who had questioned her paused to consider his words before speaking. Finally he said, "When a man seeks guidance, or to attain the next stage in becoming a man, then a warrior, he must go out into the wilderness alone, where he will undergo the rituals that enable him to see beyond the veil of this world, and into the world of the Sun and Earth spirits. Then he will be shown things that will reveal to him great truths."

"Frogs?" Mildred asked with a raised eyebrow.

The elder smiled slowly. "Truth is not always boldly stated. Sometimes, the meanings can only be understood by those who take the time to look beyond the obvious."

Mildred said nothing. Maybe those things she had so readily dismissed were not the total crock she had thought. There was little else that could explain such strange and apparently hallucinatory effects. And if that was the case, then just maybe there was something in this prophecy that had been alluded to; if so, then she had the notion that J.B and herself were in for a very weird—and possibly dangerous—time.

Moreso when she realized that the exchange had caused a ripple of murmured conversation around the fringes of the crowd. Looking over them, she could see that the men of the tribe, with their long, decorated hair and bared skins were at the forefront. The women— who had shorter hair, more functional clothes—were at the back.

It was a patriarchal society. The elder had spoken of

men going on vision quests. Not women. Yet here she was, proclaiming an experience that the very same elder was proclaiming as such a quest. Somehow, she had the feeling that this would not go down too well with some sections of the tribe. The looks on the faces of some warriors gathered in the crowd did nothing but reinforce this opinion.

It looked as though her earlier fears could very well be confirmed.

Chapter Eight

Jak rested fitfully and uneasily during his first two or three nights in the ville. Always, of necessity, a light sleeper, he found that his rest was interrupted by the feeling that there was tension and unease throughout the ville, and that it was centered around himself and Doc.

That wasn't exactly a surprise: it was the weight of expectation that worried him. After two days, he had seen very little of the ville, and had been told even less. The woman and man who between them looked after and seemingly guarded himself and Doc had been less than talkative. Given Jak's own natural reticence, it would have been a good time for Doc's loquacity to take center stage.

But Doc was silent. Raving, occasionally, it was true, but mostly silent and either sleeping or unconscious. It was hard to tell which was which. Mostly still, he would sometimes twitch and mutter, shifting position as though in the midst of an uncomfortable nightmare. Then, at other times, he would sit bolt upright, his eyes wide and staring yet seeing nothing, yelling sounds and words that only occasionally cohered into some kind of sense. When it did make such sense as was possible, it seemed to be a continuation of the biblical rant on Revelation and the coming of the end that had spurred him into first disappearing into the storm.

Jak wanted to wake him up and hit him. Stupe old bastard was still going on about the crap that wound them up here. He'd got them into trouble, and still he couldn't change the subject—though it had to be said that Jak was beginning to question his own behavior more and more. To begin pursuit in such conditions had been the opposite to the way in which he would have usually acted. Reflection was something that came rarely and all too uneasily to the albino; now, however, he had the time and space in which to indulge. There was nothing he could do to find an escape route until Doc was ready to move.

He was glad that he had found the old man. Doc was awkward, sometimes stupe…but he was one of them. And in some ways the one whose back needed looking out for the most. One down, four to go. It was better than being alone. But it had its own problems. A fit and focused Doc would back Jak all the way. If—when—Doc woke from this stupor, who knew in what condition Jak would find him.

Meanwhile, Jak wondered about the people who tended him. The woman had said not more than two words since he had arrived. She tended to Doc, using poultices that stank of strange herbs to try to soothe his ravings. His other wounds were minor—scratches and abrasions—and were dressed and already beginning to heal. It was the wounds to his mind that were longer lasting. Nothing was said about them, but twice the shaman had come in and stood over Doc's prone figure, breathing heavily as though hyperventilating himself into a trance state before chanting and singing in a tongue that made no sense to Jak. Then he had promptly left, without sparing the albino youth a glance.

The man—who had obviously been ordered to watch over and guard them—had said little more than the woman. The first night, Jak had snapped awake to find the man sitting in the smoky, darkened wigwam, sitting as still as if he had been carved from rock. Yet he was not asleep. The whites of his eyes shone in the dim tallow light, and Jak could see that they were focused upon him. Unblinking. Giving nothing away. Jak had returned the stare for some time, until weariness had overtaken him once more, and he had been unable to prevent his eyelids from beginning to droop. As sleep claimed him, he knew that the man still stared at him, giving nothing away.

Gradually, though, the warrior had begun to speak a few words. Jak, being a man of few himself, had not known how to initiate a conversation. So many things he needed to know if he was to begin to plan, and yet how to broach the chasm of silence?

He hadn't needed to. It was, surprisingly, the man he could only think of as his guard who started to speak.

Jak was outside the wigwam, breathing in the early morning air, sharp and fresh. Without appearing to take much notice of the activity around him, Jak was mentally pinpointing the routines that he could begin to see taking shape in the community around him: the making of bread by the women; the order in which they gathered their tools and ingredients; the group who went to wash clothing by the small stream that he now knew ran just out of view, around the shelter of the mountain. Always the same time. He knew because he still had his wrist chron. He surreptitiously timed them. They were the same two days running. He knew they would probably be the same the following day. Likewise, the men had their own routines. Those who would hunt were already gone by the time that he had risen. They returned before the heat of the sun became too great. They carried with them strange-looking creatures: animals the like of which Jak had never seen again. Not misshapen, but somehow wrong: like hybrids of creatures he had seen in other places. One that had really shaken him had looked like a dwarf horse crossbred with a puma. Strange and unnerving to see those green eyes and snubbed nose, yet with an extended neck and a tail that was less like a big cat than a horse.

Other men were engaged in the manufacture of weaponry. They whittled and carved bows, strung with fine wire made of gut. Arrows were whittled, sharpened flint heads attached, feathers for flight carefully added. Targets of varying sizes and at differing intervals were used both to test the new weaponry and also the mettle of the men who would use them to hunt or in combat.

Jak tried to be circumspect as he made his study, but he suspected that he would be detected. He was good, but he did not underestimate these people. The manner in which they had been able to sneak up upon him while he had tried to approach them spoke for itself. So he was less than surprised when the warrior suddenly spoke.

"You have nothing to fear. You are not our enemy."

The man was behind Jak. The albino had known he was there, so was not taken by surprise. Slowly, wishing to show no sign of hostility, Jak turned to face him.

"Then why keep me and Doc here?"

"Are we making you captives? You are free to move about, are you not?"

"Long as not go too far," Jak countered.

"Why would you do that while your friend is still in the land of the spirits?"

Jak frowned. He had to have looked puzzled, as the warrior added, "He speaks in tongues that make little sense to anyone except the shaman. Even when he wakes, he sees not us but the spirit realm."

Jak had seen Doc's madness too many times to do anything but wonder at how the Pawnee interpreted it. Nonetheless, it gave him a way to broach the subject that was his concern.

"Suppose want to leave when he right? You saying easy?"

The warrior considered that. "Maybe not. You were sent to us. Destiny must be fulfilled as it was told to us by the Great Spirits. We have a purpose to fulfill. You have, too. You are a part of that purpose. To go against the spirits would be a bad medicine, and I cannot see why anyone would wish to do that."

Jak could see from the man's open expression that he was truly baffled as to why Jak would wish to leave

before this destiny, whatever it may actually entail—
was fulfilled.

"What happens when Doc okay?" Jak asked bluntly.
"Destiny mystery to us. You know?"

The warrior paused. It was a subject to which he was
giving great thought. Whether it was because he was unsure of the answer, or because he was wondering if it
was his place to speak on the subject, Jak could not tell.
Whatever, the albino knew that he could not totally trust
the accuracy of what the man said next, even though it
might give him an indication of what could happen.

"When the old one is well enough, when he has returned totally to this world from his sojourn with the
spirits, then you will go with the chief and with the
shaman to the earth lodge. There you will convene with
the greatest of them all, our father Wakan Tanka, there
to discover the path that we must now take to reclaim
that which is ours."

"AN EARTH LODGE?" Krysty asked. "Up here?"

Martha Is-A-Man laughed heartily, throwing back
her head. "How stupe do you think we are?" she returned. "Since you've been here, you keep looking at us
like we're savage and little better than the meat we hunt.
But you think we got that little going on in our heads?"

Krysty was taken aback. Somehow, because she as-
sociated some of the ideas that she had divined in these
people as being like those of her home ville of Harmony,
she had assumed that she would be in better touch with
their way of life than Ryan. Yet, when she stepped back

and looked at it, she realized that she had come across as superior.

Ryan had adapted better than she had thought. True, he was used to a much more violent and straightforward way of living; societies that were based on the rule of the blaster and of fear. Yet because he had realized that these people based their way of life on other, older ideas, he had stepped back to let them show him. He had questioned that which he did not understand.

Krysty realized, as the women in front of her stared her down, that she had assumed too much. She had acted as though she knew everything about their way of life. And she didn't. Harmony was different. There were some ideas in common, but that was all. It made her realize, perhaps, how much she had missed her home ville.

The women had been skinning, gutting and salting the day's chill. It was messy, necessary, and had exposed Krysty to the strange mutations that seemed to populate the plain. The deerlike creature she had been dissecting with Martha's aid was a perfect example, being unlike anything she had seen before. Its sightless eyes stared up at her, as if questioning what she was about to face.

But it was not the creature that concerned her now. Her eyes flickered to the oiled length of hide that stood between herself and Martha. On it were spread a number of finely honed knives, each with a blade that spoke of a specific purpose: fine, thin blades that were for skinning, thicker, heavier blades for scoring the flesh, carving it. Others were made for the specific purpose of gutting, filleting and preparing the meat and hide for use.

Martha Is-A-Man had a large, thick knife in her fist. It was appropriate, as anything else would have been dwarfed by her large hand. Her name was appropriate. She was a large woman, muscled like a man. Her face was like a slab, and right now it was distorted by a loathing that she had been keeping inside for the past few days. The other women were gathered around the two of them. While the men were going about their business, the women had been set to their task and left isolated on a far reach of the mesa. They would prepare the food, then take it to the lower levels of the tunnel system, where the natural chill of the rock served as an icebox for the already salted meat. So that the blood and waste from the carcasses could be drained and disposed of without contaminating the rest of the area, they had been set apart.

Now this isolation was working against Krysty.

The women gathered, closed the circle around Krysty and Martha. The two women were screened off from prying male eyes, and at the same time were being forced together as the circle closed in.

Krysty could feel the heat from their bodies as they drew nearer. She could see the hatred in Martha's bloodshot brown eyes, the set of her lantern jaw showing her determination. She thought about trying to reason with them: the tribal elders would be less than happy with any damage to her before she and Ryan could fulfil their role in the prophecy; she had no reason to fight, no argument with them; her attitude had been misjudged, but had been bred from enthusiasm for a way of life like that she had once known.

One look at the faces of the women around her, and another glance at the body language of the woman standing in front of her, and she knew this would be pointless.

Martha wanted a chance to prove her superiority. Perhaps she had been the alpha female in the tribe and sensed a threat in Krysty. Perhaps she just plain didn't like her. Looking at several of the women, and thinking back to the way in which they looked at Martha, and the proprietorial way in which she acted toward them, Krysty realized that her Is-A-Man name came not just from the way she looked.

Maybe that was it. Maybe she wanted Krysty, and the fact that the Titian-haired beauty had been oblivious and aloof had irritated her.

No matter. She only knew now that she had to fight.

In her hand she had a small knife that she had been using to pare the skin from the beast's haunches. It had a handle that sat snugly in her palm and a thin, short blade. It was as sharp as one of Jak's leaf-bladed knives, and in truth it felt comfortable, as she had used some of the albino's blades on many occasions. But it would be useless unless she could get in close. And Martha had the length both of blade and reach to make that difficult. The woman was also built in such a manner as to suggest that brute strength could cover any lack of swiftness.

She saw the blade she wanted. A long, thin stiletto-like knife that was used for skinning the main carcass. She dropped the blade she held, dipping down so fast that she had picked up her replacement before the first knife had hit the dirt.

She had to be that fast, as Martha lunged for her as she moved, sensing that those few moments when she had no weapon were the optimum moments in which to strike.

Krysty heard her enemy's breathing quicken, come harder, as she threw her body forward, putting her whole weight behind her thrust.

Bad move: a total commitment to one move left her wide open should it go wrong, should she miss.

Krysty was too quick for her. As she plucked the longer knife from the oiled hide, she twisted her body so that she pivoted away from the lunging Martha. The movement took Krysty into a sideways roll. Exerting all the muscle control that she could muster, she rolled and came up again, feeling the strain in her thighs and knees as she came to her feet, keeping her balance, now almost behind Martha, who had pitched forward and stumbled as the expected resistance of Krysty's pierced flesh was no longer there to halt her motion. Krysty raised one silver-tipped boot and pushed hard, connecting with her opponent's bony rear.

Martha sprawled face first into the dust. Coughing, spitting out the dirt that filled her mouth like the bitterness of her humiliation, Martha scrambled to her feet, scuttling around as she did so that Krysty could not attack her from the rear. She was almost surprised to find that Krysty had not closed on her, and was instead standing some distance from her, balanced on the balls of her feet, her face intent with concentration, waiting for her opponent's next move.

Krysty knew—could almost see it in the woman's eyes—that Martha was beginning to regret the attack. But she could not stop now. The humiliation of backing down in front of the women she had bossed would be too great. She had to follow this through to the bitter end.

She was lucky. Where she would have had no compunction in chilling Krysty given half the chance, or at least inflicting some serious damage upon her, the redhead had no such intent. Chilling or maiming a member of the tribe—even in self-defense—would put both her and Ryan in an untenable position.

For a few moments the two women circled each other, each mirroring the movements of the other. The crowd around them pulled back slightly, partly to give them more space in which to engage, and partly to avoid being pulled into the combat by default.

Krysty liked that: it said to her that the malice and intent was draining from the crowd. It was just down to whether Martha wished to continue. Krysty knew that the woman's pride would dictate that she couldn't back down, but how much effort would go into the next attack? It all depended on whether her heart would be in it or not.

For Krysty had little doubt now that she could take the woman out. In this tribe, the woman's place was to stay in the ville, to prepare for the comforts of the men. They were trained in the domestic ways of tribal life, but the skills of combat were foreign to them.

Martha showed that by making another sudden but

clumsy lunge. She had been relying on her anger and hostility to give her impetus. With that replaced by doubt, she was slow and obvious.

Krysty could not resist a small smile flickering across her mouth like a twitch as Martha came toward her, arm outstretched. Stepping to one side, Krysty was able to parry the arm, put out a foot to trip her opponent, and follow her down to the ground, knee in the small of her back to stay her, knife arm trapped in an armlock. Blood stopped, nerves trapped, the knife fell from her lifeless fingers.

"Now you listen, because I'll say this only once," Krysty hissed, "I won't think I know everything about your ways if you'll stop wanting to stick a blade through me. I didn't ask to be here any more than you asked for me. Let's leave it at that, or else next time you get to ask the spirits about me in person. Okay?"

She let the woman's arm go, and Martha let her shoulder and face fall into the dirt, sobbing at the pain. Krysty stood, stepped back and turned to the others.

"That goes for all of you. Do we have an understanding?"

Faces refused to look at either her or the woman on the ground; eyes would not meet hers. These told her all she needed to know.

"Good. Let's get back to work before someone notices and asks stupe questions. That'll do none of us any good."

The women returned to the hunt chill. Martha picked

herself up and looked at Krysty. It was partly hurt and
fear, but there was something else there: not respect, but
an understanding that Krysty had spared her.

Chapter Nine

As he sat studying a distant thunderstorm, J.B. thought that settling into the ways of the tribe had been odd, yet much easier than he would have thought possible. They had a rigid structure to their way of life. It seemed to him that this was partly because it had always been this way, and partly because they had opted to keep it this way rather than change and evolve. It was as though the tribe had been frozen—just as Mildred once had—waiting for the moment when they would be thawed out to fulfill its destiny. Then things would change. But not until then. It was as though staying the same reminded them of this.

But things weren't that simple. When Mildred had emerged into a world of which she had no knowledge, she had changed her way of reacting to the world to survive. J.B. wasn't sure that these people could do that.

In the past few days he had been shown the way they hunted for food, how they farmed the land to feed themselves by augmenting their own diet, and also growing feed for the livestock they kept. He had seen them as they made the weapons that aided their hunt, aided their defense, and would presumably fuel any kind of attack that they may be compelled to make.

It was, in some ways, an idyll; a model of how to live. Nothing was wasted. Everything was put to some use. Waste products from ammo and wags were unknown to them. The kind of crap that accumulated in any ville from trade goods was unknown to them, as they did not enter into any kind of barter or trade with outlanders.

It was a good way to live; J.B. could see that. The trouble was, he could also see that it was only a good way if everyone else lived that way. He supposed that was their aim, and what the prophecy was about. But J.B. had traveled too far, seen too much to trust to any kind of fate that would look kindly upon him. Fate was neutral at best, hostile at worst. To assume anything else was to beg for trouble.

There were a lot of coldhearts out there. They had blasters, ammo, grens, explosives of all varieties. There was little an arrow, a knife or an ax could do against that. While the Otoe stayed aloof, that was fine. But if they thought their destiny would lead them to engage against outlanders who were armed in this way…

J.B. let the thought drift away, not wanting to consider his position. He wanted to talk to Mildred about this, but even that was proving difficult because of the ways of the tribe. As a woman, Mildred was a new tribe member whose way of life was radically different from J.B.'s. She was set to the more domestic tasks of life. Her place was to serve and support the men as they engaged in their endeavors. It was not a question of inferiority; rather, J.B. thought, it was about everyone having his or her place, and that being defined by sex. And there was no stepping outside that.

He grinned to himself. That was probably driving Mildred nuts.

He didn't hear Little Tree come up behind him. The man who had spoken to him during their journey to the ville had become his contact. While the others seemed to be wary of the newcomers, perhaps in awe of their status as carriers of the prophecy, Little Tree had not. J.B. had picked up from some of his comments that the warrior was a man who felt apart from his fellows. Although very much a part of the tribe, there was a restless intelligence and curiosity to him that made the others wary of him, as he was apt to question. This same facility made him feel separate, as he experienced the isolation of those who do not idly follow.

So it was no surprise that it formed a bridge between the Armorer and the rest of the tribe.

"Pretty impressive sight. But not funny, as far as I can see. Unless it's the laughter of relief that we are not on the end of nature's little joke," he said softly.

J.B. turned toward Little Tree. The two men were standing on a raised hillock that stood at the end of an enclosure. Cattle with enormously misshapen heads grazed behind them, uncaring of their presence.

"Wasn't that making me smile." The Armorer shrugged. Not wishing to reveal his train of thought, he indicated the distant storm. "Looks hard. Real hard."

Little Tree nodded. "Most of the time, we get sun, maybe some rain, and the rivers that run beneath give us water through the wells. Wakan Tanka provides. But sometimes it's like Ictinike takes over, and it's time to put up with his idea of a joke. Then the clouds gather and bang heads before crying with pain. When they do this, the rains come so hard that the ground cannot open fast enough to drink it in. So the rivers become seas, and everything in its path becomes as fodder for the floods."

"How long since that happened here?"

Little Tree shrugged. "Ten, twelve moons back. Before that, maybe twice as long. When it did, many cattle lost. Most of the crop went west. All the wigwams. Most of the earth lodges."

"How many buy the farm?"

Little Tree shrugged again. "Three…no, four."

J.B.'s face must have showed his astonishment. "With flooding as bad as you've just said?"

It was Little Tree's turn to smile. "Ah, there are things about which you are yet ignorant. It's no accident that we have made our home in this area. Come, leave the wonder of Ictinike and come with me. I get the feeling someone like you is going to like this. A lot."

With which air of mystery, he turned and walked away. J.B. gave the distant storm one last glance, and then he, too, turned away.

MILDRED WAS FINDING adjustment hard. There had been times in the recent past when she and Krysty had been forced to adopt subservient roles when they landed in villes whose views on a woman's place were decided and inflexible. She could remember a time when they had been forced to bide their time working for a mad bitch who traded in textiles. She had felt then—and saw little reason to revise that opinion now—that she would rather face down a mob of stickies or crazies single-handed than pick up needle and thread. She wasn't exactly doing that now, but she wasn't far off. And back then, she'd had Krysty with her. Now she was alone, and it made more of a difference than she would have thought.

She was looking for anything to distract her. So when one of the women with whom she was making clothing from hide said something that offered her a way out, it was more than welcomed. It was simple enough: a comment that Mildred shared her name with a tribal elder.

"What, there's a guy called Mildred?" she said, trying to keep the sardonic edge from her voice. She needn't have worried: the humor was lost.

"No," her companion said, straight-faced. "Milled Red lives in an earth lodge near the great shelter."

Mildred did not answer immediately. There was a lot to consider. She realized the earth lodges were used as sacred places by the Otoe. Perhaps it had not always been thus, but over time they had become thus. She knew it was unusual for anyone to be living in one. And the fact that it was a woman. Tribal elders were rarely, she gathered, female. To be as such, this woman had to have earned in some way immense respect.

Last, and something that had set her wondering in a different direction, there was the "great shelter." What, why and where? These were key questions that could be of great significance.

For more than one reason, then, Mildred wanted to meet this person.

"I'd like to meet her," she said simply. "Would now be possible?"

The women engaged in sewing looked at one another. Mildred could see that usually their task would be stuck to until the bitter end. There would be no stopping for reasons that could not be explained as for the common good. Yet, at the same time, it was true to say that Mildred—along with J.B.—was way outside the norm. How could they deny the messengers of the spirits?

The woman who had raised the subject looked nervous, but still said, "Yes, let us go now."

She rose to her feet and held out her hand to Mildred. She was a little over five foot, and slender. Mildred was not a large woman, but she was taller by a few inches, and had the muscle tone of a warrior. She dwarfed the woman as she stood over her, which was somewhat ironic, as the woman had been introduced to her as Running Steer. She didn't look like she had the power in her for such a name.

Pushing that thought to one side, Mildred allowed the woman to lead her from the wigwam and out into the sunlight.

Once again, Mildred surveyed the land on which the tribe had made their ville. She had time to ponder on this as they made their way slowly to the fringe of the enclosures. The tribe had chosen to build and make their homes some distance from the nearest range of mountain and hills. Down here, the land was undulating in a series of waves, with the odd hillock to give vantage onto the flatlands of the plain that lay beyond. It was fertile, and obviously farmed well. Yet she could see the storm clouds in the distance. If those clouds ever came this way, then she could see why they would need what the woman had called "the great shelter."

They moved toward the center lodge. The roof was so low that it would be impossible for anyone—even someone as small as Running Steer—to stand upright, unless the floor of the lodge was sunk into the earth. The woman turned to her as they reached the entrance to the earth lodge. "Very few people get to meet Milled Red now. She is old, infinitely so, and sleeps much of the time. But she has much knowledge to impart, for those who understand."

Mildred's heart sank. The woman sounded like she was a dementia sufferer who roused from her slumbers only to pontificate like Doc on a bad day. She could see how such obtuseness could be taken for mysterious wisdom, but had no wish to buy into it.

So it was with some surprise that she followed Running Steer into the earth lodge, which she had expected to be dark and depressing, only to find that it was strongly lit by several tallow lamps, the walls covered with colorful tapestries that depicted scenes of Otoe life, and strange mythical creatures falling beneath the arrows of two figures.

In the center of the lodge, on a bed of skins and furs,

reclined a woman whose age Mildred would not have liked to guess, even with her medical knowledge. She was small, wizened and crippled with arthritis. There was no flesh on her bones, and her skin was stretched like a mask against her skull. Her eyes were closed as they entered, a younger woman beside her quietly sewing.

As they reached her, and before Running Steer could speak, the old woman's eyes snapped open. Mildred almost gasped out loud. Contrary to the clouded and unfocused gaze she had been expecting, these eyes were hazel, piercing and bright. They held within them the intimations of a great intelligence and humor that had not been decayed with the aging and betrayal of her body.

"So you've brought her to see me, young Steer," she croaked. It was a deep, cracked voice, age making her vocal cords rasp. Mildred could only guess at what the woman had sounded like when younger, though the humor was still in her intonation.

Running Steer nodded. "She is the one with the name like yourself, O wise one."

The old woman gestured impatiently. "Yes, yes, I've gathered that. I might be old, but I'm not as a child in my mind, even though I need looking after like one." She turned her attention to Mildred, and the younger woman could feel her older woman appraise her carefully. She nodded slowly. "A woman. A black woman. Not a white-eye, but not what the slow-witted medicine man would have expected."

"Is that a problem?" Mildred asked.

"Not for me. Messengers come in all forms. Maybe for him. I hear your fellow traveler is a white-eye. Male, but not of us. Nor of you. That may be giving him more problems."

"How so?"

The crone chuckled. It was so low and harsh in her throat that it sounded like someone gargling gravel. "The ones to lead us to the lands and prizes promised by the Great Spirit are supposed to be of us. If we have followed the ways of the father, then why does he not conform to that and send us two warriors? Why does he send us a white-eye, and a woman who is black? I say why not? It tests our belief and faith in the father. But there are those who cannot see that. They believe that the letter of the law is all that counts."

Mildred was taken aback. The last sentence the old woman uttered was a phrase that she had not heard for so long. Since before she had been frozen. Since before skydark.

The sense of what the old woman had spoken before this had entered her consciousness but had not been assimilated. She was too shocked by the implications that sprung to mind from Milled Red's utterance.

The old woman could see this, and smiled gently.

"The spirits work in mysterious ways. So did the white-eye before skydark came down. You are perfect for the role of messenger, as you are not from this world. I can see that. You are from the time when people lived in great cities of chrome and glass. Of stone. Of the fossil fuels that were pulled from the earth with nothing put back. Our ways are alien to you, but so are the ways of the white-eye in this new world."

Mildred looked at the woman with a sense of awe. "Just how old are you?" she breathed.

The old woman wagged a bony finger. "Not as old as you think, my fellow name holder. Unlike you, I do not come from the time before the nukecaust. I have lived more moons than I can count, but the skies were still black and winds still howled when I was born into this world. No, my dear girl—I have the right to call you that—when I was born the white-eye had already triggered the end of one cycle and the beginning of another. But there were those still living who had witnessed the world before, and had tried to withdraw from it, not wishing to be part of the destruction. Sad that the white-eye tech would not pay heed to such wishes.

"I have lived through the coming into the open once more of the Otoe. Seen the feeble grasp we had on the hostile world become stronger. The Earth Mother has allowed us to rebuild as we respect her. And now there are those who say that the time has come for us to show the world that ours is the right way. Those who would say that your deliverance to us is a signal for this to begin."

The old woman paused, as though waiting for Mildred to ask the question that she knew had come into her mind.

Mildred felt as though the key to survival for herself and J.B. hinged on what she now felt compelled to ask.

IT WAS A REDOUBT. There was no doubt about that, and
J.B. was puzzled. Here, the Otoe had everything they
could need to forge a new world, yet they chose to ignore it.

Little Tree had taken him to it with little compunction. A sunken entrance was hidden on the far side of
the enclosures in which the cattle quietly grazed. The
Otoe had not bothered to disguise it as perhaps it once
had been; rather, they left the entrance openly uncov-
ered, for easy access.

As the two men had lowered themselves into the access shaft, J.B. knew that it was something similar to
that which he and his companions had seen before—not
a large military redoubt, but rather a kind of way sta-
tion. Subdued lighting flickered on as they entered the
shaft, and by the time they were at the bottom, the whole
of the corridor was bathed in light.

Without a word, Little Tree led J.B. through the cor-
ridors, detailing all that lay within as though this was
the first time the Armorer had seen such a place. J.B.
did nothing to disabuse him of this notion. Instead he
noted that the dormitory areas showed signs of use—
presumably as sleeping areas when the storms came—
but that the kitchens, stores, and particularly the armory
were untouched.

"There's a lot of ordnance and tech down here that
could help you," he murmured.

Little Tree shook his head. "You have to understand
one thing, particularly if you are the unknowing vessel
of the Great Spirit. This is white-eye shit. This is what

made the world go wrong. We are grateful we were shown this place for shelter, but to touch anything else would be to ask for bad medicine. To deny our heritage and pervert our destiny."

J.B. felt that it was a waste of good firepower, but opted to keep his own counsel. Instead his attention was caught by a wall map in one of the untouched rooms. It was clearly of the plains area, and showed a network of underground redoubts and bases in the region. He had never seen so many clustered together, and it told him that the plains had been an area that whitecoats and military considered of great importance.

But why?

"WHY?"

It was a simple question, but it held within it many strands of meaning. Mildred studied the crone's face and noted the knowing smile that spread across it.

"Because," she began carefully, "there are many things that become lost with the passage of time. Stories passed down can become distorted and changed. Not with the intent of deception, but because of a lack of understanding. Words get lost. Words like metaphor."

The old woman's eyes flickered from her nurse and Running Steer to Mildred, asking if she grasped the real meaning. Mildred nodded. Grunting in satisfaction, the old woman continued. "We have legends among our people that go back beyond the time of the nukecaust. Legends that go back beyond the time when the white-eyes first came to this land. To before they brought us the horse, and we traveled across these plains. Such are the ways of the spirits, that the coming of those who would seek to oppress us also made us free to roam. The ax had two heads. It always has two heads.

"Now, in our legends we have the twins Dore and Wahre'dua. They were fighters and defenders. Their mother was slain by a monster, and so they swore to avenge her by becoming slayers of monsters in their turn. This was how they spent their lives, for it was their mission. The notion of twins who fight in tandem to right the wrongs caused by monsters is something that runs through the way in which stories are told. You follow me?"

Mildred nodded. The old woman's eyes darted across the others in the room, and she gave a brief cough of a laugh as she could see her meaning sail across their heads.

"Good. Understand that Dore and Wahre'dua would slay on sight. They would not always know who they were defending until the monster had been laid to rest. This could cause them to make mistakes. That they did not was because of the spirits, who guided them. That is how people see it always to be. But I wonder if the stories we hear are only the ones in which they were proved to be right. Others would reject such notions. They are the ones who are always right, and believe only in right. But Dore and Wahre'dua were only men, after all. And men do not always know the full stories of why they must act."

"I understand. Dore and Wahre'dua were figures of legend, but before the legend was the flesh," Mildred said. "And flesh is fallible, and must take care not to put itself in the line of monsters with no defense."

Milled Red nodded with some satisfaction. "I see that you understand the truth behind legend very well. I have one more thing to say to you. We have another figure in our legends. A terrible monster called Itopa'hi. Sharp-elbows. He is an ogre whose greatest joy is in eating men. He has spikes on his elbows, on his face, and on both sides of his head. But that is not the most terrible thing about him. The worst of his ways is that he has two faces, one looking one way, one the other. Each can be different to the other. This makes him hard to fight, for you can never tell which way he is truly looking, or can you guess his true intent."

Mildred bent and took the old woman's hand. "Him, I recognize. A monster like that exists in every people's myth and legend. Because he exists in truth. I know, I've met him often enough. Your words have not been wasted on me."

And as the old woman smiled once more, Mildred Wyeth felt the years and the distance between her past and present melt away. For once, she had come close to someone other than Doc who could in any way understand what it felt like.

And make no mistake, she would heed the words of the wise woman. For the wise woman could have been herself.

Chapter Ten

"Vision quest? What fuck—"

"Hush, now, my young Jak, for I suspect we are about to be enlightened."

Jak glared at Doc. Glad as he had been to see the older man, and also that he had regained both his good health and a measure of his sanity, still, he was annoying. If Jak had been forced to choose any of the others with whom he would like to be stranded in a ville peopled by a tribe whose ways were in some respects alien to his own, Doc would not have been the first name to spring to mind. Right now, he just wanted to hit him.

The shaman nodded appreciatively. "Thank you, Theophilus. You are right. I will explain to you the manner in which this ritual takes place, and why."

Jak shook his head. The Native American had spent so much time with Doc that he was even starting to talk like him. One Doc was bad enough, but two...

"Every young man, when he reaches the age where he must attain his manhood, has to go through this ritual. Alone, he will go into the wilds for a period of some days. There is no water or food for him, and he must not partake, as this will block the channels through which he can communicate with the Grandfather."

"He talk to his grandfather?" Jak snorted.

Doc glared at him. "Not the father of his father, but the Great Spirit. That is what they call him when not referring to him by name," he intoned solemnly.

Jak was glad that his face could not be read easily by anyone. Any half-wit stupe knew that going into the wilds without food or drink for days would make you see things. It wasn't talking to gods; it was called buying the farm. But he allowed them to continue.

"When a young man talks to the Grandfather, then it will be revealed to him what his purpose in life may be. When he returns home, then he sits with me in a sweat lodge and we discuss what he has seen. If he is unclear, then I can help him to understand what his path must be."

Make it up for him, depending what you want him to do, Jak thought. However, he opted to hold his peace.

"So you see," Doc said in an excited tone, taking up where the shaman had finished, "we did not go through this when we were the right age, but as we have been sent as the unknowing messengers of the Grandfather, we now have to travel forth and discover what our mission must be."

"Thought knew that," Jak mumbled. "They tell." He indicated the shaman and the chief, who had sat silently beside his medicine man throughout. They were in an earth lodge, away from the rest of the tribe, symbolically separated while their mission was discussed.

"Exactly," Doc replied. Then, when Jak's blank look

exasperated him, he sighed and continued. "We have not discovered it for ourselves, and if we are to fulfill the prophecy, then we must know this, and we must take the lead. We have been brought here, and now the way in which we must proceed will be shown to us."

Jak could feel the anger boiling inside him. For days he had wanted to try to get away from the ville, perhaps steal into the redoubt to see if there was anything that he and Doc might be able to use—a wag, maybe, or some more ordnance—to make a break and look for the others. If Doc had survived, sure as hell that Ryan and the others were out there somewhere. Yet Doc foiled him at every turn. It was as though the old man had finally seen a reason for why he had been flung into this world.

The tribe had not been hostile. On the face of it, they had been friendly. But they didn't talk much. That would normally have suited Jak. But when they spoke, it was in their old tribal tongue, and much of what they said in common language was odd. It was as though they had learned it to talk to outlanders, but had little opportunity. Probably why the shaman was starting to talk like another Doc.

More importantly, everywhere that Jak went, everything that he did, he was aware of being watched. Not with any hostile intent, but he could feel eyes boring into him. The tribe wondered when he would make his purpose clear. But it was more, even, than that. Jak had finely attuned senses, and whenever he strayed more than the tribe would feel comfortable with, he could sense a tension run through them. Like one of their own bows, so tight that it sang in the wind, forever on the brink of snapping.

They may have felt that he and Doc were sent by Wakan Tanka, but they were also sure that they weren't going to give him the chance to run before the prophecy had been fulfilled.

While this ran through his mind, Jak had been silent. He knew that Doc was watching him with eager anticipation; the shaman and the chief with something that was closer to apprehension.

Jak knew himself, and his abilities. He could also spot an opportunity in the tightest of corners.

Finally he shrugged. "Okay. Not young anymore, though—'specially not you, Doc."

A huge grin broke on the old man's face. "Not in years, perhaps, but in the ways and spirit of the Pawnee we are but infants. This is why we must go through the rituals of the young. I knew you would understand, Jak."

Jak said nothing. What he understood, and what Doc figured he did, were far apart. But there was no reason for Doc to know that.

Not yet.

"THAT'S STUPE. You people want something, but you won't play by the rules to get it."

Ryan raised an eyebrow. In all the years that he'd known Krysty, she had never played by any rules, or even acknowledged that such things existed. But now, when it came to playing every card...

The Titian-haired beauty turned away from the elder

caucus of tribesmen—including the medicine man and the chief—who sat in front of her and Ryan. She had risen to her feet in anger as she spoke, and now she walked to the edge of the natural room formed in the rock, and looked down a corridor where cool air drifted against the warmth generated by the small fire and the close gathering of men.

"But I don't understand," one of the warriors said tentatively. By his tone she could tell that he was speaking the truth.

"Neither do I," the chief added in clearer tones. "Why would you wish to put yourself through such an ordeal?"

"Why not?" she asked wearily. "Why do you think I shouldn't?"

"Because you are a woman," the medicine man said calmly. "In our way of doing things, this is not a woman's task. It is something that they are least able to cope with. That is why men do it. It is just not part of their lives."

Krysty turned back to the gathering. Ryan did not turn to look at her. She knew why; he was letting her lead to make a point.

She sighed. "That's true of the women of your tribe. But I'm not. I'm from outside. If your spirits have sent Ryan and me to lead you, and you say that he must go on this dream quest to discover exactly what the spirits want him to do, then how am I supposed to know what they want me to do unless I go, as well?"

There was silence in the room. Through the echoing caves and passages, Krysty and Ryan could hear distant sounds of life that seemed to contrast with the confused and uncertain quiet of the elders.

"She speaks the truth," Ryan said gently, choosing his words with care. "You say to me that the spirits reveal to the man on the dream quest a truth that is personal, and varies from man to man. That is why it is necessary for the medicine man to sit with him in a sweat lodge and divine meaning from the visions. So if that is so, then Krysty can only know her own truth if she experiences the dream quest. Is that not so? Would mine not be the same as hers?"

The chief looked at the medicine man, who brooded in silence.

"One-eye speaks true," he said heavily.

"But—"

The chief's protest was stayed by the medicine man's raised hand. "Women of the tribe do not go on dream quests. But this woman is not of the tribe. Indeed, if she and One-eye are messengers from the Grandfather, then can they truly be mortal? Are they not some strange demon state between the living and the dead?"

There was a murmur of agreement.

"Very well," the chief said finally. "You will both leave tomorrow at sunrise. Two men will lead you to the place where warriors must begin the quest. From there, you will have three days to commune with the spirits."

UNKNOWN TO EITHER PARTY, J.B. and Mildred had been having a very similar argument with the Otoe chief and shaman. J.B. could not help but think that although the tribe's way of life was in many ways a peaceful and idyllic existence, the rigid code by which they lived could be constricting. The look on Mildred's face when she was told that she would not be accompanying the Armorer on the vision quest was one that, if directed at J.B., would have caused him to rapidly rethink his decision.

After much argument, it was only when Mildred insisted that they consult the elder Milled Red that the shaman began to unbend. Shrewdly, Mildred argued that there may be a precedent; one so distant that only the elder might remember it.

So they found themselves in the earth lodge that Mildred called home, the shaman and chief treating her with deference as they put the question.

The old woman paused as though in thought.

"Did you understand our request, old one?" the shaman asked with deference.

Milled Red snorted. "I'm not deaf or stupe, I'm thinking," she snapped. Her eyes glittered with anger, and also with amusement as she fixed her gaze on Mildred. "Those who come from the outside are expected to abide by our ways when they are with us. Yet they are not raised with those ways. The differences between us are for a purpose. I would suggest that although we have no precedent for this—never, in the time that I have known—then perhaps it is the time to set such a precedent."

"But it is such a step—" the shaman began.

Milled Red cut him short. "An exceptional circumstance demands an exceptional decision. If you cannot see that, then you are not worthy of your position. And I think that you are," she added smoothly. "Mildred should join her fellow messenger. They are joined by fate, and who are such vessels as we to set them asunder?"

Her eyes met Mildred's, and the latter could have almost sworn that the old woman winked at her.

The tentative glance between the chief and the shaman showed that the old woman's words had been effective.

The course was set.

Chapter Eleven

"I wonder if those on our tail will stay there the whole while, or if we shall be able to shake them."

"Not if you talk so loud…"

Doc contained a wry smile. Jak was in a bad mood. It was not really surprising. Doc could see that the warriors who followed their every move would cramp his style.

They had been given horses by the men who were to act as their guides—though it was obvious they were also guards—and had ridden for several hours before the warriors had given them the command to halt. This, like most communication, had been done with a gesture. Doc had attempted to engage them in conversation, but had been unsuccessful. Why he had even bothered was something of a mystery, even unto himself. He suspected it was something to do with the fact that he was to spend days in the wilderness with a lad who brought new meaning to the expression taciturn.

Further, although he had enjoyed his long conversations with the shaman—learning along the way a number of things about the Pawnee that he was sure would be useful before too long—he had noticed that the tribe as a whole were a silent people. They preferred their own language to that which Doc spoke; and even in this they were inclined to reticence. Doc liked to talk. Sometimes, perhaps, to his own detriment. But he liked it, nonetheless, and he missed the chance to cross swords for the occasional verbal thrust and parry with the good Dr. Wyeth.

Doc's mind stopped wandering aimlessly and snapped sharply into focus. The others: that was why he wanted their tail to be lost. And he was sure that Jak echoed this.

When he spoke again, it was in a much softer, quieter tone. Barely more than a mumble. But with Jak's sharp ears, it did not have to be more than this.

"If we evade them, then which direction?"

Jak's incline of the head enabled him to murmur directly toward Doc. "They bring us due east. Ville southwest of where found me. Good place to start as any."

Doc considered that. "That's a lot of ground. Particularly for two men without food, water or transport of any kind."

"Saying we should give up?"

Doc pondered. "No. Merely that we should try to get some."

Jak's impassive white visage flowered momentarily into a vulpine grin before returning to its neutral state. "You think right" was all he said.

As Doc looked around, he could only conclude that the idea was all very well; the reality may prove to be a little different.

Now, having left the safety of the shelter and the

scrub that surrounded the old redoubt and hills where the Pawnee had pitched their ville, Doc and Jak were exposed to the harsh climate of the post-nukecaust plains—hard-packed earth with a light film of dust as a topsoil. The occasional burst of violently colored foliage held little hope of anything that could be eaten. Consequently, there was little sign of whatever could survive here, and could in itself be hunted, chilled and eaten.

And dry: the land was parched, and about to lose more moisture under the clear skies and the unrelenting glare of the sun. When they set off, it had still been the cool, damp dew of sunrise. There was moisture in the air, but it had burned off as they had progressed, and now that it was nearing the middle of the day, Doc could feel the sweat gather and evaporate before it had a chance to run, leaving white salt marks on his skin and clothes. He had already shed as much as he dare, trying to balance his increasing body temperature against the burning rays. Glancing across at Jak, he was momentarily astounded that the albino still wore his patched and heavy camou jacket, and seemed to be barely breaking a sweat.

Sweat…water… Doc's mind wandered back to the matter at hand. He was aware that he was beginning to wander, and that he had to keep it together if he was to be anything other than a liability to his companion.

It was a condition of the quest that they have dreams and visions while they were out in the wilderness. Given that they were forbidden to eat or drink during this time, it was not hard to see why these visions would come to them; with a wry smile to himself, Doc figured that he didn't need lack of water and food to have hallucinations of this sort.

Therefore, it made sense that they would be placed in a region where such temptations were beyond them. Which was all very well; however, it did them little good if they were to search for sustenance to fortify them for the breakaway that they hoped to make.

Doc hoped that Jak's finely attuned senses—those that had made him a hunter of both man and animal—would come to their assistance. For he feared that he would be of little use.

RYAN AND KRYSTY reached the top of the plateau and lay panting on the hard rock that fringed the wind-blasted surface. Unlike the plateau that served as a camp for the Dakota Sioux, atop the honeycomb of caves and tunnels they called home, this had no raised rock wall to shelter the flat surface from the elements. As a result, the earth was dry and dusty, a few straggling plants and sickly trees clinging on for dear life. Even the hardiest of birds would not nest here. The only water came from the skies, and was sucked hungrily by those few flora that dotted the surface.

"Gotta admit, lover, they're not giving us any chance to cheat or run," Krysty said ruefully, still breathing heavily from the climb.

Ryan rose to his knees, gulping in the dry, warm air and instantly regretting it. Though his body craved the oxygen, he could already feel that his throat was parched, drying with each hungry intake.

"Bastards got every option covered," he husked.

It was true. At the back of both Ryan's and Krysty's minds had been the idea that they might use this opportunity to make a break for it, to head off and try to locate their lost companions. More than that, perhaps: the chances of easily tracing J.B., Mildred, Doc or Jak were nonexistent. But the chances of riding into disaster at the head of a Dakota Sioux party to fulfill a prophecy about which they knew nothing were greater. Maybe the so-called quest would reveal something to them. Krysty had a greater belief and knowledge of these things than Ryan; for his part, the one-eyed warrior believed mostly in what he could touch, feel and see. And as a battle-hardened veteran he could see nothing but disaster ahead. The Sioux had no real idea of what the prophecy meant in practical terms. So the chances of anything that resulted from Krysty and himself leading them into the future being what they wanted were slim.

The quest should have given them the chance to flee from this powderkeg.

Escorted by a phalanx of Sioux warriors, they had ridden out from the caves as the sun rose. From one outcrop of mountain to another was a good two hours' ride, and the sun was starting to beat down by the time that they arrived at their destination.

Looking up, Ryan was at first disbelieving. They were expected to climb to the top of the rocks and stay on the plateau for three days and nights without food and water. It gave them no option to escape. From the looks on the faces of the Sioux warriors as they watched

Ryan and Krysty begin their ascent, it was obvious that this was a prime concern.

The climb was hard. The rock was smooth, with little in the way of hand- or footholds. For the first few yards it was relatively easy, but the higher they climbed, the steeper the ascent, to the point where—near the lip of the plateau—the rock swung out, necessitating a swing that took the body almost horizontal.

The rock was scarred by great slashes that looked like the marks of giant claws. Too deep, wide and long to be as such, they were also impossible to use as holds. But they did give Ryan an idea. Unsheathing the panga, he started to hack at the clay. It was tough, and it bit back at the blade, but it would yield. The blade would be blunted and would need to be sharpened, but that was for another time. Right now, all that mattered was that the rock gave enough for him to make the hand- and footholds that would take them to the top.

It was slow progress. The rising sun began to pound him with waves of intense heat. He could feel the muscles in his calves cramp as he dug his combat boots into the small holes he had hacked into the face of the mountain, taking the weight as he clung with one hand and cut with the other. He could feel, rather than see, Krysty clinging to the rock beneath him. The occasional upward glance showed him that there was still a long way to go. And that lip…

His back ached, strained and protested as he twisted his muscles, reaching with one hand to grope for the edge of the rock while feeling the skin tear from his other hand as it gripped the hold he had cut, indented to make the rock take some of the weight.

The worst of it was when he felt his feet swing free into the air, his torso partly over the edge and onto the plateau, his center of gravity almost dragging him back. Muscles burned as he hauled himself over, pausing only for the chance to breathe deeply before looking back over the lip and extending a hand to help Krysty up and over.

And now they half crouched, half lay on the plateau. Not bothering to look over the edge, knowing the warriors would still be there, pitching camp and waiting, they breathed deep and hard, resigned to their fate.

It was going to be a long three days.

FOR MILDRED AND J.B. the journey to a place where they could undergo the vision quest and so see their part in destiny took far longer. The Otoe had chosen their home on the plains with care, and so they were surrounded by territory that was lush by comparison with other areas. To go beyond this, and so to attain an area that would have the deprivations necessary to reach the trancelike state of the dream, entailed a ride of more than a day.

Little Tree was one of the guides who led them to this place. While the other tribesmen who rode with them maintained the kind of silence that seemed to come naturally to the tribe, and was only increased by the language gap, Little Tree had formed a bond with J.B. over the weeks that caused him to feel the need to talk.

So it was that, when they stopped at a creek to water the horses and themselves, Little Tree beckoned to the

Armorer to follow him. Under the guise of leading their horses just a little farther downstream, the two men found the necessary space to exchange words in a barely audible undertone.

"You know why we are with you," Little Tree began.

J.B. nodded. "To guide us…"

He left the words hanging, guessing what his friend had to say. Little Tree grimaced and spit into the creek.

"Guide, yes. And more. But you know this, I think. You did not know of the prophecy, nor did you come to us willingly. As such, there are those who think you would run if you had the chance."

"You think we would?" J.B. asked.

Little Tree let the ghost of a smile flicker across his face. "I think that if I was in your position, I would be thinking of such a thing. You do not know what you face. You do not know where your traveling companions are, though you may have a mind of where to begin searching. I would be thinking, wondering if it would be possible."

"And your telling me it isn't?"

Little Tree smoothed the snout of his horse, gently tickled it under the lower jaw, and looked back at Mildred and the other men, some distance away.

"All I can tell you is that we have our commands. We must see that you fulfill the quest, and that you do not run. We are not to move unless it becomes necessary. But if you make it so, then we must stop you, come what may. I do not want to have to do this."

J.B. followed the man's line of sight. There were five

warriors surrounding Mildred. That made three-to-one. Not good odds. J.B. and Mildred still had their blasters. It was a sign of the ambivalence that the Otoe felt: they had allowed them to keep their weapons as a sign of faith, yet would still mount a guard over them to prevent their flight. Three men with bows and axes to one blaster-wielding combatant made for reasonable odds in J.B.'s reckoning, but he and Mildred would be in flight, and so the Otoe would have had first shot. There was no way that the shaman or the chief could have figured on Little Tree's sense of loyalty to his new friend clashing with that to his tribe.

Not that it did. J.B. could see from Little Tree's expression that he did not feel he was betraying anyone: rather, he was trying to keep a balance and play his small part in fulfilling the prophecy.

For this, if nothing else, J.B. opted to say, "Okay. We'll go with it. Might as well see what this prophecy means before we think about trying to find our friends."

Little Tree's expression was one of great relief. "I am glad you say that, my friend. The future is already there for us, we just have to trust in the Grandfather." With which he grasped J.B.'s forearm in his fist.

The Armorer understood what this meant to the warrior, and how much it had taken him to speak. Question was, how was he going to put this across to Mildred on the rest of their journey without giving the warrior away? Certainly, the look she shot him as both he and Little Tree rejoined the rest of the party demanded a response of some kind.

But it was only a few hours later, as they left the water and scrub behind to enter an area of arid dust and rock, that she was able to steer her mount close enough to the Armorer that she could ask him without fear of being overheard. With one eye on the guide party that rode with them, he dismissed her question with an imprecation to wait. She was less than pleased, but how else could he avoid implicating Little Tree, who had risked the greatest thing a warrior had: honor.

Eventually they came to the place where the desert area of the plain truly began. At a signal from their guides, they drew their horses to a halt and dismounted.

"Now you go," one of the men said. His words were halting, as though he had trouble with a tongue other than his own. But he was obviously the senior of the party—or else why should he be the one to speak, and not Little Tree? Automatically, Mildred marked him down as the one who she would have to take out first…if it came to it.

While this went through her mind, the man continued. "You keep walking, and let the sun decide your path. You do not come back this way until three days have passed. We will be waiting."

J.B. and Mildred turned and began their march into the desert. They could feel the eyes of the warriors upon them, but did not look back.

"Hope you got a good reason why we we're not making a break for it," she whispered to the Armorer when she figured they were out of earshot, which was some distance, as the empty land and sky were silent almost

Get FREE BOOKS and a FREE GIFT when you play the...

LAS VEGAS

GAME

Just scratch off the gold box with a coin. Then check below to see the gifts you get!

YES! I have scratched off the gold box. Please send me my **2 FREE BOOKS** and **gift for which I qualify.** I understand that I am under no obligation to purchase any books as explained on the back of this card.

366 ADL E4CE   166 ADL E4CE

FIRST NAME   LAST NAME

ADDRESS

APT.#   CITY

STATE/PROV.   ZIP/POSTAL CODE

7	7	7	Worth TWO FREE BOOKS plus a BONUS Mystery Gift!
🍒	🍒	🍒	Worth TWO FREE BOOKS!
🔔	🔔	♣	TRY AGAIN!

Offer limited to one per household and not valid to current subscribers of Gold Eagle® books. All orders subject to approval. Please allow 4 to 6 weeks for delivery.

The Reader Service — Here's how it works:

Accepting your 2 free books and free gift (gift valued at approximately $5.00) places you under no obligation to buy anything. You may keep the books and gift and return the shipping statement marked "cancel." If you do not cancel, about a month later we'll send you 6 additional books and bill you just $31.94* — that's a savings of 24% off the cover price of all 6 books! And there's no extra charge for shipping! You may cancel at any time, but if you choose to continue, every other month we'll send you 6 more books, which you may either purchase at the discount price or return to us and cancel your subscription.

*Terms and prices subject to change without notice. Price does not include applicable taxes. Sales tax applicable in N.Y. Canadian residents will be charged applicable provincial taxes and GST. Offer not valid in Quebec. Credit or debit balances in a customer's account(s) may be offset by any other outstanding balance owed by or to the customer. Offer available while quantities last.

If offer card is missing write to: The Reader Service, P.O. Box 1867, Buffalo NY 14240-1867 to the point of being deafening. J.B. relayed the conversation that had taken place between Little Tree and himself. Mildred listened attentively, then looked at the vast expanse of emptiness that surrounded them for a full three-sixty.

"Yeah, well, I guess he has a point," said quietly. "They couldn't have chosen better if they want us to have no cover. The thing is, I don't think that was really why they brought us here."

J.B. risked a look back at the place where they had left their guards. The warriors had pitched camp, and were seemingly oblivious to their charges. "No, they don't seem that concerned. Can't work them out, somehow. They trust us and don't."

Mildred thought back to what the old woman had told her. "They want this prophecy to be real, and they'll do anything to make it that way. But if they have to force it to happen, then it won't be so…real, I guess. It won't be the spirits, it'll be man, and it won't have so much power."

J.B. snorted. "If it happens, then it happens. No matter how. Still the same result."

Mildred smiled. "That's because you're a pragmatist, John. These people just think differently."

"Guess so. But I don't care how they think," he spit, "as long as we can get our asses out of this in one piece. That's what's real enough."

Mildred shrugged. He was right. All the spirituality in the world wouldn't save them if, when they took their place in bringing the prophecy to life, it came to combat. The only thing that mattered then was skill and cunning.

Meantime, they had three days and nights to survive in this wasteland, maybe just so their ravings could be interpreted by a man who already knew what he wanted them to see.

Looked at like that, she could see exactly what the old woman had meant.

She only hoped they could live through it.

SO IT BEGINS. Three pairs of people, thrown by fate into a situation that bore no relation to anything they had ever known; each pair wondering if the others were chilled or alive, and if they would ever be able to find their friends again; none knowing that their friends were experiencing the same situation through which they persevered, and for the same reasons.

From the moment that they first encountered the storm that seemed to bring locusts and frogs, and yet left no trace of either, they had been in a world that seemed almost like a dream in itself. Three communities had eschewed the old ways of the predark world, communities that believed in ways and values that predated the kind of rationale that even the oldest of the friends had known from birth.

In what way did those values tie the people to the land on which they now lived? That land that was once so fertile, and was now arid and presenting nothing but struggle to people who face the hardships with stoicism.

The worlds of the dream and the mystic were things

that were alien to the friends, but were worlds that would soon become familiar to them. Whether they wished it or not, they would experience the vision quest.

Chapter Twelve

Jak looked down at himself. The camou jacket glass and metal bits glittering among the patches in the glare of the sun, was now gone. The heavy boots on his feet were no longer there. He felt different, but in a way that remained just beyond explanation.

He moved his hands to check for the .357 Colt Python that had served him so well. To check for the leaf-bladed throwing knives that felt as comfortable in his palm as though they were part of his skin.

Gone.

There was no indication that he had ever had these items about his person. Indeed, his person seemed to have changed.

Jak had fallen to his knees under the weight of the sun, and now, as he raised one hand, he saw only a paw covered in a light, mottled fur, claws where once there were fingers. He tried to stand, but found that as he reared up he was unable to keep balance, and toppled backward so that he landed on his spine, twisting it instinctively as he fell so that he was almost on all fours again from the moment that he hit the dirt.

He shook himself. Why should he do that? All he

knew was that it felt good. He raised his hand once
more—or should he think of it as his paw?—and felt his
face. Tentative because of what he may find, and because he was unused as yet to the way that this foreleg
moved in place of his arm, he patted delicately at his
face. No scarred skin. Just fur. And a long snout where
his nose used to be.

Twisting his head, Jak could see that he was now a
coyote. A hunter still, but of a different kind. He sniffed
the air and could tell the difference between his old and
new self. The old Jak had been attuned in a way that
most humans were not; but this was on another level.
There was a tang to the air, of conflicting scents that lay
beyond the boundaries of the human olfactory system.
Similarly, his hearing was sharper still, and his sight was
clearer.

But where was Doc? Looking around, he could see
that there was no sign of the old man. He should be
here, but…if Jak was now coyote, then did anything
make any sense?

Suddenly a sense of freedom swept over him that was
almost overwhelming. If he had changed in this way,
then there was no need to go on with the stupe dream
quest. He could do as he wished.

Aware, now, of the gnawing in his guts, he knew that
his first priority had to be food and water. He had to find
sustenance.

Jak began to trot ahead, sniffing at the air to determine where he may find something to hunt and chill.
But there was nothing. He continued to walk, wonder-

ing if he would starve in this new form as he had been starving in the old.

"What do you want, young coyote. What is your wish?"

Jak stopped. Ahead of him was a large rock with several small ones laid around it, as though in obeisance. The rock had spoken to him. It had to have. There was nothing else around. ·

"Do you speak me, rock?" he asked. Even though his words emerged as guttural yowls, he knew that they were understood.

"Yes, it is I, the Great Spirit. I will aid you in your quest."

"Grandfather, seek food, for am hungry. Must eat, or buy farm."

"Young coyote, you are of good soul, so I will aid you. Head due east for one hour, and you will find a small hill. On the far side, there is a village where they revere your kind, and they will feed you."

"Grandfather, thank you. But what can give as offering to spirit?"

"You still carry a knife. It is a good weapon and a fine piece of work. As something with meaning to you, it will be a gesture that would please me."

Jak was puzzled. Without his jacket, where could he keep a knife? Twisting his head back, he nuzzled in his fur. There, halfway down his back, was a knife. He was sure he would have felt it when he fell, but… Pulling it out with his teeth, he found that it was not one of the leaf-bladed knives, but a more ornate blade, with a carved bone handle. He laid it down in front of the stone.

"Now go, young coyote, and feast."

Jak left the stone and set off in the direction he had been instructed. Was it his imagination, or had the stone sounded like Doc? But how could that be? Doc was not here. Like walking on two legs, he was something that seemed to be a dream.

After some time, Jak came to the hill. Breasting it, he saw the village on the other side. The earth lodges and wigwams were richly decorated. Cured meat was hung out to dry in the sun. As he approached, he was greeted by tribesmen who recognized in him a hunter of great repute. The stone had not lied. He was revered and welcomed here.

Sitting to feast with the tribe, he tore with his teeth at the meat that was offered to him. It tasted good and filled his belly. Yet he was aware that he could not eat with the speed of the men around him. They were paring at the meat with knives. Ornate, beautifully carved knives like the one that he had given to the stone.

"Wait. Thankful for meat. Must do something important, but back soon."

Jak left the puzzled men and ran back, away from the village, and toward the stone. Why had he given the knife to a stone that could have no use for it? It would, at least, be performing its intended function if he took it back.

Reaching the stone, he took the knife in his teeth, from the place where he had left it, and placed it back in his fur, from whence it had come.

"Forgive, Grandfather, but have need."

The stone was furious. "Do not take back that which is given freely and as a gift. Disrespect to the spirits. If you have no respect for them, then they cannot be of aid to you."

"Spirits cannot fill belly," Jak said as he began to run back toward the village.

He thought it was over. He had taken back the knife. He did not expect to hear the stone rise up from the earth and begin to follow him, yelling curses as it came after him.

Jak knew that he could not lead the stone back to the village. Not because he wanted to spare the villagers, but because he did not wish to be dishonored in their eyes. Even as he turned and ran in the opposite direction, away from the hill, he knew that there was something wrong in this notion.

But right now he did not have time to consider this. The stone moved fast, though how it traveled he could not tell. He knew only that it seemed to be gaining on him. So he pushed himself harder, running until he felt that his lungs would burst and his legs would go skittering from beneath him.

He came upon some caves, where bears were sitting in the shadows. Breathlessly he yelled at them as he approached, pleading for their help as he knew he could not best the stone on his own.

"Keep on running, coyote," one of the bears yelled back. "We do not want anything to do with the stone. We will not offend the Grandfather."

Cursing them, Jak kept running. He passed a group

of trees where mountain lions idled in the branches, awaiting the arrival of prey. Normally, he would have considered himself to be fair game for them; but they did not move from their perches. He called up to them, pleading for assistance.

"Keep on running, coyote," yelled one of them in return. "We will not interfere with the wishes of the Grandfather. The stone will do what it must with you, and that is the way it should be."

Yelling curses back at them, Jak kept on running, aware all the time that the stone was gaining on him. It called out to him in a voice that seemed to grow louder and more resonant with each call.

Ahead of him, on the plains, buffalo grazed peacefully. Jak ran for them, screaming for their help. Normally they would scatter from him; this time he hoped they would rally to him. But they did neither. Instead they stood calmly and peacefully, allowing him to run through them, and allowing the stone to follow.

"Keep running. Away from us, for we have no wish to argue with stone," one of the buffalo cried.

Jak would have cursed, but he was short of breath. It seemed as though his time was now up.

But yet there was the promise of salvation. A flock of Bull-Bats, not normally seen at this time, flew overhead.

"Hide, coyote, and we will help you," one of them cried down to him. Jak did not look up, nor look back. He was just grateful for their aid. His eyes searched rapidly for a place to hide, and seeing a small crevice in a group of stones, he dived into it, squeezing himself into the dark place.

Outside, the Bull-Bats swooped, with each pass unleashing wave upon wave of guano on the stone. The acid guano hit with force, chipping at the stone, breaking off more with each revolution, until the stone rolled to a halt, nothing more than a trail of pebbles.

"Come out, coyote, all is safe," the Bull-Bats called.

Jak emerged from his hiding place. "Grateful. Why do this?" he asked.

"Because it is funny," one of the Bull-Bats replied. And as Jak watched in horror they swooped, gathering the pieces of the stone. Each pebble and shard was clutched in their claws and placed in a pile. The guano that had previously acted to break up the stone now became like a glue, and welded the pieces together so that the stone was once more complete.

"Did you think that anyone could help you when you have gone against the spirits?" roared the stone. "There is no escape from the path you have chosen, coyote. You made the decisions, and you must stand or fall by them."

And the stone began to roll, coming after Jak once more. In a blind panic, fear overcoming every instinct that he usually relied upon to guide him, Jak found himself turning and running. Somewhere, deep in the recesses of his mind, he knew that this was not what he would usually do, that he would use instinct with rational thought to work out a plan that would at least give him a fighting chance. But he was not Jak the man, he was Jak the coyote, and animal fear now consumed him.

Running blindly, he did not see the steep bank ahead of him. He did not think about what lay over the lipped edge. He just ran and jumped, hoping that he would be able to reach the other side.

But the bank gave way to a ravine, with a wide gap between this side and that. Jak found himself floundering in space, his momentum not enough to carry him to the far bank. Instead he began to fall, yowling in fear as he fell faster, knowing what was about to happen and yet being able to do nothing about it.

The pain as he hit the bottom was immense. Every bone broke. Nerves screamed. Organs felt bloodied and pulped as the weight and momentum of his body crushed him against the floor of the ravine.

Yet he was still alive. He could still see, hear and feel through the fog of pain. And he was aware of the rock, rolling to the edge of the ravine, far above, and hurling itself off. The Bull-Bats hovering overhead, laughing.

"This is what happens to those who try to deceive the spirits and the fates," the rock intoned as it fell.

They were the last words Jak heard before the rock landed on him, and all went blissfully empty and black.

FOR A MOMENT, Doc felt that he was back home again. The skies were blue with a smattering of white cotton that carried none of the taint that he was now so used to; rather, it had a purity and beauty the like of which he had not seen for many a year.

The land around him, as he stopped and looked, casting a gaze all around as though seeing for the first time, was lush and verdant—pasture with grazing horse and buffalo, trees waving in a distant breeze, the speckle of faraway birds in flight. It was as though the recent times were nothing but an insane nightmare from which he just awoken, fully refreshed.

He heard a cry from behind him and turned. It was a woman's voice, and he expected to see his beloved Emily coming toward him, perhaps with the children playing happily around.

What he saw told him that this was not real. It may seem that way, but it was far from being concrete and actual. Doc was familiar with hallucination and madness: so much so that he was able to almost detach a part of his fractured mind and view from two angles. So, although everything seemed to be as real and as beautiful as the world he had so long ago left behind, he knew it was artifice because of the glaring anomaly that now confronted him. It was not his Emily who came toward him, but the vacuous blond Lori Quint, whose childlike demeanor had so enchanted him until she had bought the farm, and left him alone. Like all the others.

She was not dressed as he remembered her. Gone was the miniskirt, the high boots…gone, too, was the mane of blond hair. Still the color of ripe corn, it was now hacked short. She was dressed like the Pawnee woman that he had been around until…recently? How recently? That part of Doc's brain that could detach started to wonder what was happening to him. A curiosity that was crushed rather than piqued when he looked down at himself for the first time and realized that he was dressed not in his usual frock coat and vest, but in skins and furs. He felt the side of his head; his hair was in long braids.

Still feeling outside the situation, he yet knew that he had spent all day farming, tending to the crop that was growing around him. And that his wife—he knew some-how that Lori was his wife—had come to fetch him.

"Good day, husband?" she asked. Her voice was the same as he remembered it, but her words sounded strange and out of character.

"Tolerable," he answered. Ah, at least he was still himself. "What have you been doing, my dear, while I have been out here?"

"I have made your meal. Also fed and tended the horse you gave to me."

Doc was aware of an irritation as she said that. For a moment he did not know where this feeling came from; then it seemed as though he could remember. A hunt with others of the tribe, where they had tracked and killed buffalo before stopping at a waterhole on the way back to their village. At the waterhole, he had seen a horse that he desired: wild, beautiful, with a spotted pelt that was unusual. To have such a creature would mark him apart in the tribe. He had left the others to water-ing their horses and had approached the horse. He had expected it to bolt, but it had been calm, almost as though waiting for him.

Securing the horse had been no problem, and when he had brought it back to the wigwam in which he lived with Lori, he had given it to her as a sign of love.

They had no children, and he had given the horse almost as a way of compensating. And she, in her turn, had loved it as such.

Except that now, as he walked with her from the crop fields back to their home, he knew that he was starting to resent the time she spent tending the creature. They ate their meal in near silence, swapping few words. It was the easy silence of those who have spent long in each other's company, and feel no need of words to communicate. Doc felt more secure.

But this changed as darkness fell and Lori said, "I must go and feed him before we settle for the night."

He was not sure who "we" might be: Lori and himself; or Lori and the spotted horse. He said nothing, just nodded at her words. But, waiting until she had left the wigwam, he rose and followed her at a distance, making sure that she could not see or hear him.

The spotted horse was roaming free in a small enclosure at the edge of the village. He had to pass other wigwams and earth lodges in her wake, and he knew that the way she was with the horse was not just his own knowledge. The whole village would grow quiet at his approach.

Yet there was nothing that seemed amiss as he watched her from a safe distance. She called the horse to her, and it nuzzled her as she fed it from her hand. There was a strange intimacy there, but nothing that he could call amiss. When she turned back toward him, it was all he could do to stay in the shadows and reach home before her.

In what seemed like an agony of real time, Doc went

through three days and nights where he toiled by day, then followed her by night. Each night was the same. He was aware that the three days was significant some-how, but it was something that seemed to be just forever out of reach.

That was driven from his mind by the events of the fourth night.

Doc followed Lori, expecting things to be as they had been on previous nights. When she reached the enclo-sure, however, it seemed empty. With a fear gnawing at his stomach, Doc waited while she called and whistled for the spotted horse. Then, to her obvious surprise as much as his, a man stepped from the shadows. Tall, lean and muscular, he was dressed in buffalo robes painted with pictures of a spotted horse.

For a moment Lori shied away, and Doc tensed, ready to go to her aid. But he was stayed as she leaned forward, as though in recognition.

"Do you not recognize me?" the man said in soft, honeyed tones.

"Yes," she replied nervously, "but it cannot be."

"It is. I have been sent to give you that for which you have craved. The barren years are over for you. You have shown me love, and I will show you in return."

Doc watched, both horrified and fascinated. The man who was about to seduce his wife was the spotted horse he had brought back for her. How this could be, he did not know: yet he was certain.

The man dropped his robes. Naked under the light of the moon, he was finely honed and muscled. Holding out a hand, he helped Lori climb into the enclosure. He took her in his arms and kissed her. She melted into him in a manner that Doc could not recall her doing to him for many a long year.

The man undressed her until she was naked in the moonlight. He kissed her down the length of her body while she trembled in the cool night air. Then she did the same to him.

The transmuted horse-to-man laid her down in the grass, and Doc crept closer, despite himself. He watched, appalled, while the man copulated with her.

Doc did not wait to watch her rise and dress. He said nothing when she returned. He said nothing as she returned to the horse every night. It was now a horse again, and didn't change. She tended to the horse as the seasons changed and her belly grew heavy with child. The village rejoiced that they should be blessed after so long. Doc said nothing.

Not even when she gave birth, and there, emerging from her, was not a child but a spotted foal.

She was shunned by the village, and when she had recovered from the birth, Lori fled one night, taking her foal-child with her. Doc did not see her go. He no longer lived under the same roof, and although he felt shame for what had happened, he still lived under a dark cloud. He was not shunned by his fellows, but treated rather as an unfortunate who had been tricked by evil spirits. He found this pity almost more shameful, and harder to bear than the shunning that had driven his wife from him. For, despite what had happened, he did not blame

Lori. He had failed her as a husband, and blamed himself for bringing the horse back to the village.

Years passed. Doc felt as though he lived them in real time, even though a part of him couldn't believe this was so. It was a lonely time. He didn't feel that he could truly trust anyone after what Lori had done to him; neither did he feel comfortable with his fellow tribesmen, as they all knew his shame. His wife taken from him by spirits.

His life continued. He farmed, hunted, and somehow managed to get along with a tribe of which he no longer felt a part. But there were days when he wished that his life would just come to a close. It wasn't that he was miserable. It was worse. It was that everything felt empty.

Then, many years after Lori had run away with her foal-child, Doc joined the warriors on a hunt. It was spring, and the buffalo and deer were moving across the plains. Those who had been following the herds had returned with tales of a strange creature they had seen, but only at a distance. It was like a horse, yet no horse they had ever seen before. With it were a small group of other horses, that seemed to be more like the norm. The herd was unusual, as they were all spotted.

Much time had passed, and the fact that these horses, and the strange creature that led them, were spotted, didn't register as significant with many. But for Doc, it had a resonance. It was as though this was what the Grandfather had kept him alive for: when the next hunt party sallied forth, Doc made sure that he was a part of it.

It was three days before they came upon the herd. Another two as they followed at a distance. Doc knew, as soon as he set eyes upon them: the strange creature, mostly horse but still bearing some resemblance to her former self, was Lori. Almost entirely transformed, but still with a human face, and with the breasts that he remembered so well.

He didn't know what he would do when the time came to confront her, but as he saw her with the horses, he realized that one of them was the foal-child with whom she had fled the village. The others, he knew, were also her children by the horse-man-spirit that had caused her to flee.

The men hunted the horses, determined to take them back to the village and tame them for mounts. On the fourth day, they approached them. The horses did not bolt. To the surprise of the tribesmen, the horse-woman approached them. Doc knew her, of course, but the shock of the others as she came close enough to be recognized was unmistakable.

"You have come for me, husband?"

"No. I have come with the others to round up your children, so that they may serve us."

"I cannot allow that. They must stay free. They are not welcome anywhere because of my shame, and the manner in which I was tricked. Even you, my husband, deserted me. And now I am this."

Doc realized that he had felt the wronged one for years, where in truth Lori had been equally, if not more, wronged.

"Wife, I have been wrong. I should not have let you go. You should not have been left to come to this state."

"Then do what you must," she said simply.

Doc understood. He raised his bow, and with a clean shot pierced her breast. As she slumped, and life flowed from her, Lori returned once more to her human state, a smile upon her face.

The rest of the warriors stood back. Doc dismounted and walked toward Lori's children. They waited until he was among them, then nestled close. In a way he could not explain, he knew that they had been waiting for him. He would atone for his desertion of their mother by caring for them. They were outcasts through no fault of their own, but he could give them a home where they would be safe and secure.

And he knew, too, that he would no longer be alone.

This knowledge was the last thing he could recall, although he could never explain how things, once more, changed at this point and he became, once more, the man that he had been before.

Chapter Thirteen

Ryan had changed. He didn't know quite how, but he knew that he was somehow different. He had been on the plateau, on his hands and knees, crawling to find some kind of shelter from the relentless rays of the sun. Krysty had been there, close by; she, too, had been on all fours. He could hear her breath, shallow and harsh, at his rear. His own breath had come with razor-sharp edges that sawed painfully at his throat. To make even the gasping rattle that begged expression would have been a pain that was unnecessary right now: he focused on keeping that pain down, using it as the wedge to drive between himself and the pain that racked his whole body.

He had felt as if all the moisture had been sucked from his body by the sun; as if they had been laid out on the dust- and dirt-covered rock surface to fry like pieces of meat. This was supposed to show them the way of the spirits? It would be funny if the test that was supposed to set them up for the fulfillment of the prophecy did nothing more than chill them. The Grandfather spirit Wakan Tanka wouldn't find that so amusing. Nor would the tribal elders. Ryan would, though. Fireblast, it would slay him…

He knew he was thinking stupe thoughts, and not concentrating on finding a way in which they could shelter, maybe find some water. The scrub plants up here were weak and pathetic, but they still managed to cling on somehow, which meant there had to be some moisture to be found up here. That could make the difference between buying the farm and surviving a little longer.

How long had they been here? How many days, months, years…hours? He had no idea. Time seemed to stretch out and curl in on itself so that he was not sure how long it was since yesterday or the day before that.

That was when he realized that he was different. How and when it had happened he could not tell. One moment he was Ryan Cawdor, and the next he was and yet was not.

It was still hot, but a different kind of heat. Not the relentless pounding of the sun, but a kind of diffused, all-encompassing heat that came only from a fire within an enclosed space.

He was no longer outside. He was inside. He had no idea how that had happened, only that he felt like he had been here for a thousand years. Perhaps longer.

His eyes focused. What had seemed at first like blackness had been the dim light of a cave lit only by a fire. Now that his vision was adjusting to the gloom, he could see that in front of him stretched fur-covered legs, ending in huge black paws. He started to lick them, knowing that he had always done this, and would continue to do so for as long as time existed.

The mouth of the cave was in the distance. They

were far back within, hidden from the world outside and sheltered from the elements. It was a long way to see, yet his new eyes were good enough to view the world beyond the cave. He could see a vista of lush, verdant plain in the distance. But near to where the mouth of the cave entered the outside world, the land was more desolate. Stony, with little scrub, and no sign of growth or life. He knew—again, he was not sure how—that the cave was situated where the Macha Sicha and the prairie met. The badlands where nothing could live, and the lands where all could prosper.

The cave stood at the point where life and death were poised, facing each other.

And he had a task to perform.

Inside the cave, by the light of the fire, he could see a woman. She was immeasurably old—as old as himself, and he could not measure the time that he had been here—and sat hunched and bent about her task. In the reflection of the flickering flame, he could see that her face was lined and weathered, her skin the color and texture of a shriveled walnut. Indeed, her whole body resembled nothing so much as this, as she seemed to disappear into herself.

She was dressed in rawhide, and it gathered in folds around her, emphasizing how old and small she had become. For a thousand years she had sat in this same cave, and she would sit a thousand years more if that was what it took.

On her lap she had a buffalo robe. She was measuring against it a blanket strip that was decorated with dyed porcupine quills. It was two-thirds complete, but there was still much work to be done. Her eyes glittered in the firelight as she counted, her lips moving soundlessly as she calculated what remained to be done.

Ryan watched her intently. No, not Ryan: he knew that his name now was Shunka Sapa, and that he had sat here since she had begun the blanket strip. Sat here because he had an important task to perform, but one that he could only do at certain times. So he had to wait, bide his time, and then be ready to act swiftly when he was called upon.

The old woman put down the blanket strip and the buffalo robe, and took up the skin of a porcupine. There were many skins by the side of where she sat, and the floor of the cave was littered with the bones from which these had come, as well as the bones of all those who had been used before. The air was sweet with the decay of their flesh. Some scents were fresh and pungent, others older and just a faint suggestion that lingered in the close, still air of the cave.

While Ryan watched, the old woman took the quills from the skin and placed them in her mouth, gradually flattening them so that they would be easy to work into the blanket strip. It was a slow, laborious process, and it took her forever to flatten just a few. That she had been doing it so long showed when she took them from her mouth and, satisfied, smiled to herself. Her teeth were nothing more than stumps in her mouth, flattened like the quills by years, decades, centuries of chewing. Flat almost to her gums, they were discolored and slablike.

This first task having been completed, she took the bowls of juices and dyes that she kept by the side of her seat, and worked the quills into them, dividing the numbers so that she had the right amount of each color to add to the pattern she was forming. The dyes took some time to take hold, but she appeared to be in no hurry.

Ryan was content to wait. He watched her, still licking at his immense black paws.

When the dyes had taken hold, the old woman grunted and nodded to herself. Taking up the blanket strip once more, she began to work the dyed and flattened quills into the design, filling up more of the space that had been left blank and open. It was a beautiful design, possibly the single most beautiful thing that Ryan had ever seen. Yet it was also awful in its beauty, as it was a design of the universe, and to see it complete would mean that everything was finished, and so would all come to an end.

The finished blanket strip would mean the end of the world.

She worked slowly and assiduously, investing in her work a care and attention that meant time was immaterial. She would take as long as it took, and nothing would deter her. She would work until there was nothing left of her, until she had shriveled into nothing. She would give her all to this blanket strip.

Still Ryan watched, his eyes never wandering from her hands as they moved across the blanket strip. Every quill that went in, Ryan knew its exact position. He understood that it was important he know this.

When she had finished with the dyed quills, she sat back for a moment, nodded and sighed to herself. She mumbled a few words, chuckling softly. Ryan did not understand them; they were in a language that made no sense to him, though whether that was because it was a native tongue, or because he was now a dog, he did not know. Perhaps it did not matter. He would have liked to have known what she said, nonetheless.

She took up another skin and began to slowly strip it of quills. In the oppressive heat of the cave, it seemed as though she did that with an infinite care; almost as if she slowed down the longer she carried on. Ryan felt the air grow heavy around him. He kept licking his large black paws, his eyes unmoving from her. The heavier the air grew around him, the more he was aware that he needed to stay focused. That the time to act would soon be upon him. He did not wish to be found wanting.

The old woman began to flatten the quills with her stumps once more. It was something that he knew he had seen thousands of times before, and that he would see yet many more thousands of times before the end of all time.

Yet this time it was a little different. Halfway through her task, the old woman paused. She took the half-chewed, half-flattened quills from her mouth and laid them upon the blanket strip. She rose from her chair. This alone seemed to take an infinity, as her extreme age and the amount of time that she had spent seated caused her to seize up, and her aged body took a long time to unbend.

When she was finally on her feet, watched all the

while by the black hound that Ryan had become, she shuffled her way across the cave floor to where the fire burned. A large earthenware pot rested on the flames, supported by a structure of crossed sticks, rooted in the stone circle that contained the fire.

The pot was full of a bubbling liquid. Wojapi. The sweet red berry soup sustained the old woman, and was the stuff from which life itself was sustained.

The old woman grasped a stick that protruded from the pot and began to stir. She intoned and chanted to herself as she did this. It was almost singing, except that her voice was flat and toneless, so no notes could be discerned.

She kept stirring. Her back was turned. If she took as long over this as she had over any aspect of the blanket strip, then Ryan knew that he had the time in which to act. And he knew what he had to do.

Rising to all four feet, he stealthily padded the few yards between where he had lain watching, and where the old woman had worked. The blanket strip lay upon the buffalo robe. With his forepaw he scattered the quills that she had been flattening, and then set about worrying and working loose some of the colored quills that she had spent so long inserting into the blanket strip.

Her work was good. It was almost a pity to discard so much of it. Yet he knew that he had to. The longer the blanket strip took to finish, the longer the world could live. He was all that stood between life and the end of all things. The thought of that did not help him, nor make his work any easier. If anything, it made the clumsy paws fumble all the more; the unfamiliar teeth

bite and catch on the quills, each miss-hit making his
mouth raw, salt blood mingling with the taste of the dyes
and the old woman's spit.

He heard her move behind him. He scattered those
quills he had unpicked until they were lost in dust and
shadow, then returned to his position in time to see her
turn around. When she saw what he had done, she
screamed and cursed at him in that tongue that he could
not understand. Her manner, though, was unmistakable.

Almost crying, she returned to her seat. Seating herself, she surveyed the damage to her blanket strip. He
had removed all that she had done while he had been
watching her, and this time a little more besides. He
knew, though did not exactly remember, that it had not
always been this way.

With a resigned sigh, the old woman picked up a porcupine skin and began to pull out the quills. When she
had enough, she placed some in her mouth and began
once more to chew.

As it had always been.

As it would always be.

KRYSTY HAD NOT SEEN them before, so she could have
no idea why they would wish to do this. Why the spirits would be so mischievous, and wish to scare her so.
She did not realize that her reputation as one who was
scared of nothing had spread from this world into that
of ghosts and spirits, and had angered those who lived
in this realm.

She had not seen the four of them, gathered high in

the rocks by the light of the moon, sitting in a circle and swapping ghost smoke while they talked.

Their chief drew long on his smoke, then blew it out into a pattern that lingered on the night air. "This woman, she is brave. She fears nothing. That is what they say about her. But there is always something that causes fear. It is our job to do that, and as long as she walks, seemingly afraid of nothing, then there will be no fear of us among the others of the tribe. That is not how it should be. We must change that."

"How can we do that?" asked one of the other three.

"We must find a way. Let us now make a wager. The one of us who succeeds in scaring her will have the advantage of being chief."

The other three ghosts looked at the one who had spoken.

"You must feel sure that you can succeed. No one would willing give up their position, or wager idly upon it," he said to the chief.

The chief said nothing. He smiled and blew more smoke at the moon.

"Very well then," said the others, "we will take you up on this wager. And whichever of us wins," they continued, each thinking that he alone had the best chance, "will take your place."

The chief ghost smiled at them in a way that made them eager to beat him. "Then let us see," he said simply.

So it was that, later that night, Krysty was returning home when she saw a most unusual sight.

She had been walking alone, as was her custom. Others in the village were scared of the ghosts that stalked in the night, but Krysty did not fear them. That which was not alive could not touch you, let alone chill you. So she was surprised, rather than scared, by the skeleton that jumped out at her as she walked down a narrow passage between some rocks. Under the light of the shining moon, chosen by the ghosts as it would reflect most upon their ghost skin, or in whatever form they chose to appear, she could see that skeleton shimmered in the dark.

"Let me pass. I mean you no harm, and you cannot harm me," she said.

The skeleton laughed. "Oh, stupe woman, do you think that I cannot harm you? I can steal your breath and take your life if I so wish."

"Only if I give it willingly, which I will never do, stupe ghost," she countered.

"Very well, then. Let us make a wager. I will play you at hoop and stick. If you win, then you continue on your way. If I win, then you will join me in becoming a skeleton. Will you agree to this?"

"I will," Krysty said. But she did not trust the skeleton. Everyone knew that ghosts were wily in the ways of trickery and mischief. She knew that he would seek in some way to deceive her, and so steal her breath.

"Good." The skeleton laughed and looked around for a stock with which to play the game.

He had not expected Krysty to be so suspicious of him, nor to have no fear at coming close to him. Those were not the normal ways of humankind. So it was that while he was turned away to look for a stick, Krysty dived toward him and took hold of his bones. He yelped in shock and surprise as she bent him in a circle so that he now formed a hoop of bones. As she did this, she pulled one of his bones from his lower leg, laughing all the while.

"See, how do you like this for hoop and stick?" she asked, using the leg bone to spin the gasping, yelling ghost. "How about we change this game to one of shinny ball?"

"No, no," the ghost yelled, knowing only too well what was about to happen to him.

With a swing, Krysty hit the hoop of ghost bones and sent him skittering away from her along the pass. As he rolled out of control, she threw the leg bone after him, calling, "You lose, ghost. You are nothing to be frightened of, and you are easily bested. You will have to do better than that."

She turned and continued on her way home, not knowing that other three ghosts had been watching and listening. So it was a surprise, but not a shock, when another ghost appeared in the pass in front of her, also choosing to appear in the form of a skeleton.

"Ha! Two ghosts in one night. What a lucky woman I am," Krysty said with some sarcasm. "What games do you wish to play with me, ghost, so that you may steal my breath?"

But this ghost was more cunning than his brother, and so decided to try another way.

"I do not wish to steal your breath, or play games

with you," he said. "I have no wish to wager with one so brave, wise and clever as yourself."

"You say flattering things, ghost, but you must have a purpose," she said, "or else you would not appear before me at this time, and under such a flattering moon."

"Yes, it does make me look good," the ghost agreed, "but it is also flattering to you. A brave and beautiful woman like you makes me wish for nothing more than to dance with you."

The ghost held out his arms, inviting her to join him in an embrace that was to be nothing more or less than a dance. Yet Krysty was not as stupe as the ghost seemed to think. A ghost dance would do nothing more than steal her breath and lead her into the realm of the chilled. She had no intention of falling for such a simple trick.

She moved toward the ghost, saying, "Yes, I will dance with you ghost…"

Then, when she was within touching distance of the bones, the arms of the skeleton outstretched and waiting for her, she suddenly darted beneath his embrace and stole two of his ribs. The ghost looked down in surprise, and while his glance was not upon her, she snatched his skull from his neck bones.

"What are you doing with me, woman?" the ghost asked, confused.

"You want to dance with me, yet we cannot dance without music," Krysty said. And she began to beat out a rhythm upon the ghost's skull, using his ribs as sticks.

"Stop, stop, you are giving me a headache," the ghost cried.

"It is much less than you wanted to give to me, so be thankful, ghost," Krysty replied as she continued to beat a tattoo upon his skull.

"Enough, enough," he cried, until she wearied of the joke and threw his ribs down the pass, tossing the skull after them.

"Now begone, ghost, and do not bother me again," she said as she walked on toward the village.

When the third ghost jumped down in front of her, she was not in the least surprised.

"This is beginning to get boring," she addressed the skeleton. "Can you ghosts think of nothing else to do to pass your time, other than appear before me as I try to walk home? Your attempts to trick me are pitiful."

"Ah, I have too much respect for you to try to trick you, or to make stupe wagers with you," the ghost replied. "I offer you nothing more or less than a simple challenge."

"You intrigue me, ghost. A spirit that does not wish to trick me? That is unusual."

"I have seen you with the other ghosts, and know that there is no point. I offer this challenge. Wrestle me. If I win, you come with me. If I lose, I leave you alone."

"That is simple enough," Krysty said, mulling it over. "Very well, I accept your challenge, ghost."

"Good. Then let us engage…"

The skeleton moved toward Krysty. Rather than back away, she mirrored the move and took a step toward the ghost. It ducked in toward her, and she feinted back before sidestepping so that she could move around and behind the skeleton. The ghost turned so that its skull grinned at her, glinting in the light of the shining moon.

"So, you do not wish to touch me. Could it be that you who are supposedly afraid of nothing are scared of one little ghost?" he crowed.

"Perhaps I just wanted you to think that, ghost," she countered, moving with a speed that took the skeleton by surprise. Before he had a chance to move, she had plucked his rib cage from him, his arms falling to the floor. His skull wavered precariously atop his spine.

"What are you doing?" he asked, bewilderment large in his voice.

"Showing you what I think of you as a wrestler. One move and I was able to better you," she said. "Now it is time for me to play."

With which she took the rib cage and climbed the rocks so that she was looking down on the pass on the far side of which was a river.

"See what a good sled you make, ghost," she said, turning the rib cage so that she could ride upon it, and throwing herself down the scree, the bones chipping on the loose stones beneath. She yelled with excitement and joy as the bone sled sped over the rocks, coming to rest in the shallows of the river.

She picked herself up and shook herself dry, climbing back over the rocks until she was in the pass once more, facing the wobbling ghost head.

"Now go and find your bones and leave me be," she said, leaving the ghost in her wake.

The chief of the ghosts had been watching this with

interest, and knew that to defeat Krysty would require something special.

So it was that she turned a bend in the pass to find the chief ghost as a skeleton, seated atop a spectral steed that was also nothing but bone.

"I have come for you," he boomed, hoping that the stomping of skeleton hooves would unsettle her.

Krysty laughed. "Is that the best that you can do? I am a scarier ghost myself," she said. She began to make faces and yell at the horse, distorting her features so that they looked inhuman. The horse reared up on its hind legs, and the chief ghost yelled with shock and surprise as he was unseated, landing on the floor of the pass with a bump that scattered his bones across the dirt.

Krysty took the reins of the skeleton horse and calmed it. She looked at the skull of the chief ghost, then laughed again as she left the horse, moving among the debris of skeleton bones and throwing them as far and wide apart as she could manage.

"See, you are not scary, ghost. None of you could steal my breath, no matter what tricks you may try. For you have no power over the living, and you cannot harm us. Lucky the man who soon realizes this."

With which she mounted the skeleton horse and set off toward her village.

A short time later, she rode into the village to find that all had come out to greet her. Her skeleton mount had been seen from some distance, and there had been alarm that ghosts were riding on the village to attack. Then, when it could be seen that she was riding the steed, the concern turned to amazement and speculation about what could have occurred to make such an unusual event.

As soon as she had pulled the mount to a halt and climbed down, it vanished into a puff of ghost smoke, its task done, and the villagers gasped. Many voices, talking at once, asked her what had happened. Breathlessly she explained how the four ghosts had revealed themselves to her, and how she had bested them.

"Truly, you are the most courageous among us," the chief told her, "and you have much to teach our people about showing bravery and lack of fear in the face of the enemy."

Krysty was pleased about that, and was about to answer the chief, when suddenly she froze. All that was in her mind about bravery and courage fled, to be replaced by fear and dread. She could not move, and she felt the cold sweat of terror prick at her scalp.

To the amazement of the gathered village, she started to scream, long and loud, and with barely room for breath.

"What is it?" the puzzled villagers asked themselves, turning to one another. "What is it that has caused such terror in one who has shown no fear in anything that she has faced?"

"Look," said a small girl, stepping forward from the crowd, "I can see what it is."

And, as she pointed to an area on Krysty's breast where she herself was staring as she screamed, the villagers saw that a small bug had landed upon her jerkin.

It was this that had put so much fear into the heart of one who had been so fearless about ghosts.

"It is nothing—see?" the little girl said as she plucked the bug from Krysty's breast and held it in the palm of her tiny hand. The bug fluttered its wings and flew away as the little girl laughed. "How can you be so scared of that?" she asked, giggling.

And as she watched the bug fly away, Krysty wondered at herself, and realized that there was a great lesson for her to learn in this.

Chapter Fourteen

J.B. was a mouse boy. He lived in a log. At first he had no recollection of how this had happened to him, but as he sheltered from the elements, taking sustenance from the food brought to him by other mice, slowly it came back to him, and he began to remember.

His name was Wahre'dua, and he was one of two children. The other was called Dore. This was his brother, yet as he envisaged his brother it was not a boy who came to mind, but a woman with dark skin and braids. The name Millie was in his mind. Millie was Dore. She had another life before they were reborn as the brothers, and although others might see her as a small boy, he would always see her as he had first known her, just as he knew she would see him not as the mouse boy but as a grown man.

This was confusing. There was something else that he needed to recall, something that was important. Yet, try as he might, he couldn't bring this to the front of his mind, as the memory of his brother and what had happened to leave him here was too strong, and would not be denied.

Wahre'dua and Dore had been with their mother and

father. They had traveled far while their father hunted. One morning, while father had been away hunting buffalo and mother had been cooking, he and his brother had been playing. They had seen the stranger, but paid him no heed. People came and went as they traveled.

This man didn't pass. He stayed. He wasn't a remarkable man, yet there was something odd about the way that he looked. It was as though smoke rose above him, obscuring him so that although he looked as other men, so it was that you couldn't fully bring his face to mind when you wished.

The man talked to their mother. She wished to carry on with her task and did not seem to return his conversation. This did not deter him. He kept talking, then went on his way.

In the afternoon he returned. The boys played, but could hear him. Their mother still didn't wish to talk. The stranger tried to tempt her with magic tricks, but she didn't pay him heed. Finally, in a rage, he killed her. When their father returned, he was saddened, but was a practical man. He decided that he couldn't return with both the boys, and so he took Dore, leaving Wahre'dua to live with the mice and become an animal.

But the mouse boy didn't wish to be separated from his brother. So he resolved to find his father and his brother. Despite the fact that he was only a boy, he knew the way in which they traveled, and returned to their home village.

He waited for his brother to be alone, and then the two boys played. But he knew that his father would want to trap him if he realized that Wahre'dua had re-turned, and Wahre'dua was still angry with his father for leaving him, so he whispered into his brother's ear that he should forget every time they parted company.

Remembering this, he went to play with his brother. The two of them hunted and trapped until the sun began to drop in the sky and Dore had to return home to their father. But, having done so much, Wahre'dua forgot to tell his brother to forget.

So Dore, excited, told their father of what he had been doing. And so it was that the next day, when the mouse boy came out of hiding to play once more with his brother, he was surprised when their games were interrupted by their father. He tried to escape, but de-spite all he had learned, their father was still the better hunter, and he captured the mouse boy, who came to live with his brother and his father at last.

Yet his father still wasn't happy with Wahre'dua. Now that he was home, the mouse boy forgot his anger in the joy of being with his family once more. He missed his mother in a way that he hadn't while he lived wild, but he was determined to make up for this by winning the love of his father, and so making his own feelings for his father grow to what they should be.

To do this, he determined to show his father what he had learned, and that he should be a good hunter like him. He also resolved to teach these things to his brother. Dore was brave like Wahre'dua, but hadn't lived the same life, and so was cautious where his brother was fearless.

The two boys trapped slugs and rattlesnakes. The slugs were to show that they had no fear of the things that others quailed from because of how they looked and felt. The rattlesnakes were to prove to their father that they had no fear of that which could chill them with a swiftness that would brook no mishap. One wrong move, one second of time lacking in judgment, and they would be no more.

They were successful because the mouse boy was an excellent hunter, and his brother was a quick and skillful student. They soon had many trophies that they could bring before their father. Yet this didn't please him. He was disgusted with Wahre'dua, and it seemed that the mouse boy could do nothing to please his father.

And this was how the mouse boy and his brother became great hunters—because their father would not show pleasure in the exploits of his mouse boy, Wahre'dua.

For the mouse boy was the stronger of the brothers because of his experiences, and so he could always bend Dore to his will. And Wahre'dua had a plan that would make their names as great hunters.

They would travel to the forbidden place where U'ye, the great female maw of the world, lived. There, they would chill her as proof of their skills.

"But she will eat us whole," Dore said.

"Not if we are clever," mouse boy replied.

In front of the place where U'ye lived there was land covered in flints. "Follow me," Wahre'dua told his brother as he threw off all his clothes. Dore did so, and then watched as his brother rolled in the flints until they covered his body.

"I see. These will protect us as she cannot eat us until they are gone," Dore said, throwing himself into the flints and covering his body from head to foot.

The two young hunters then went to U'ye and challenged her. The female maw took them up, and started to slowly chew the flints from their bodies. Yet they couldn't find the place where they could strike the chilling blow. They were still struggling to find this when she had stripped them both of flints, and was about to consume them.

"Oh, brother, we are about to die," Dore cried.

But Wahre'dua smiled, for he could feel one flint that the female maw had failed to find. It had lodged under his foreskin, which he pulled back so that he could retrieve the flint.

When this was in his hand, he wished that it would be a flint knife, and magic made it so. It was then that he realized that he had the power of magic.

Wahre'dua took advantage of U'ye's surprise to strike a chilling blow in her diaphragm. This was the only place in which she was vulnerable. With a cry, she expired, and the force of her chilling caused an earthquake that rippled across the land, telling all of the boys' triumph.

Soon, word of their victory spread, and the boys became well-known for their feats of monster slaying. Dore learned magic well from his brother, but always it was Wahre'dua who had the greater powers.

So it was that they began the times that made their legend stand tall. Horned water panthers were keeping their tribe away from the waters that they needed to survive, so Wahre'dua and Dore decided to chill the panthers. But how to gain access to the panthers?

"Listen to me, brother," Wahre'dua said, "for I have the stronger magic and I know this will work. Chop me up into pieces and cook me so that I am an offering for the horned water panthers."

"But brother, I cannot chill you," Dore cried.

"Do not worry, it will be all right. You take your part, and I will take mine."

So Dore took a knife to his brother and chopped him into pieces that he then cooked in spices. He carried this to the place where the panthers lived.

"Who are you that dares approach us?" they called.

"I am Dore, and I have an offering for you."

"For that alone we will let you live. Now begone," the panthers cried.

Yet no sooner had the panthers gathered around the platter of cooked meat, to gorge themselves, than Wahre'dua reconstituted himself from the pieces. The panthers were surprised, and before they had a chance to act, Wahre'dua had moved among them all, chilling them with his flint knife. He called upon Dore, who had been in hiding nearby, and who rushed to join his brother. Between them it took the brothers little time to lay waste to the panthers, and once more the tribe was able to use the river and have water.

When the chief of raccoons used his people to stop the tribe from hunting, once again the brothers used their trick to get among the raccoons and chill them.

It wasn't long before their growing reputation as monster hunters spread farther across the land, and attracted the attention of spirits who didn't wish them well. The Honpathotei, a tribe of flat-head spirits, challenged the brothers to a race. If the spirits won, then they would be able to stop the brothers from chilling any more monsters.

The spirits were convinced that they would win, as they hadn't the encumbrance of the flesh. But they didn't reckon on the magic that the brothers held, and to their surprise they were defeated.

"You would have us do as you wished if you won, so now you must do as we wish," the brothers told them.

The spirits weren't pleased, but an oath was something that couldn't be easily broken. Their displeasure grew even more when the brothers told them what they had to do.

The flat-head spirits were divided into two armies, each commanded by one of the brothers. And while the brothers watched from a hill, the two spirit armies fought at their commanders' behest until such time as they had wiped each other from the face of the Earth.

"See, brother, none will doubt our power to do good now, should we be called upon," Wahre'dua told Dore.

But despite their power, and their willingness to use it only for good, their father was frightened of the magic that they held. For that reason, he hadn't wished them to take part in any of their monster hunts. But now that they had bested the flat-head spirits, he knew that the time had come to speak of what had happened to their mother. In this way, he knew that they would set out to avenge her chilling. And while they were gone, it would give him a chance to leave: for he knew that they no longer needed him, and he was scared to be in their presence now that they had this power.

"The man that chilled your mother wasn't a man. He was disguising himself with magic. In his real form he is hideous to behold, as he has two faces, each with spikes, and his body is covered in these spikes. He comes from a tribe called the Sharp Elbows, who are all like him. They are monsters who bring fear to all whose path they cross. I will tell you where they live, and I want you to go and find them."

So their father told them of the land in which the Sharp Elbows lived, and sent them on their way, hoping that by the time they returned, he would be gone.

But this wasn't to be, for the brothers were driven onward by the desire to avenge their mother, and so they made their way to the village of the Sharp Elbows far quicker than anyone could have imagined.

"We will use our old trick," Wahre'dua told his brother.

"But what if they know of it?" Dore asked.

"Even if they have, our magic and our will to chill them is stronger than their will to survive. I know it," his brother replied.

And so it was to be proved. Dore chopped up his brother, cooked him in spices and took him as an offering to the Sharp Elbows. But they seized Dore and would not let him go.

"So, this meat is the mouse boy whose mother I ripped to pieces." One of the Sharp Elbows laughed.

That was his big mistake. The knowledge that their mother's murderer was among the Sharp Elbows before them spurred the brothers to greater feats of hunting and magic than even they could have believed. Dore broke away from the Sharp Elbows who held him with fury, and his brother came back into being with an anger that drove him on. In no time, the Sharp Elbows were no more. Those creatures whose savagery and incredible spikes had made almost invincible were now no more.

The whole of the world knew of the brothers' triumph as they returned to their father. He had known that they had the power to beat the Sharp Elbows, but even he could not have reckoned on their achieving this so swiftly.

Now, more than ever, he feared their power, even though he was their father. So he sent them off on a quest to discover the corners of the world, so that they may rid it of monsters. And while they were gone, he ran away to hide.

During their journey, the brothers made friends with the powers above, the Great Spirits that govern the world. These spirits recognized the power of the brothers, and the things they wished to achieve. So the powers above taught them how to make bundles of peace and bundles of war, and how the magic of these bundles could help them in their task.

So it was that the brothers set about their task of ridding the world of monsters, using wisely the bundles that had been bequeathed to them by the powers above. And soon came the day when there were no more monsters to slay. When this day came, the brothers turned their bundles of war and bundles of peace over to the world, telling them to use them with care, and wisely.

Now it was the time to go in search of their father. For they missed him, and they realized something important: that although the slaying of monsters was a great and good thing, they could not have done it without the values that their father had imparted to them, and without the same blood that flowed through the veins of all of them.

But their father was very afraid of their power, and had hidden himself well away from them. They searched for many years, before they came upon the sweat lodge of the Wanapri. This tribe of ghosts had been asked by the brothers' father to protect him, and so the ghosts tried to keep the brothers from seeing their father.

Although it was impossible to chill a ghost, it was possible to get past them by magic. Yet the brothers did to wish to do this: it was their magic that their father feared, so to use it would only prove to scare him more. Besides, they had no quarrel with the ghosts.

So the brothers built a sweat lodge of their own, in which they lived, hoping that this would tempt their father. Eventually, their father came to them.

"Why did you hide from us?" Wahre'dua asked.

"Because I left you when you were young, and you gained magic that you gave to your brother. I have always wondered if you count me with the monsters because of making you the mouse boy."

"Father, you did what you had to. And the spirits brought Wahre'dua back to us. Without his knowledge, I could not have done what I have. These things happened at the command of the Grandfather, whose manner is not always plain to see. But you are our father, and we are of you," Dore said.

With these words, the brothers were reconciled with their father, who was no longer afraid of them. And with this reconciliation came the time for them to ascend from the mortal world, where their task had been completed according to the plan of the Grandfather. So their father ascended into the heavens and went into a star.

The brothers followed him. Dore went into the moon, as his magic—although strong—wasn't the same as that of his brother. And Wahre'dua, who had the greater power, ascended into the sun. From these places, the brothers could look down upon the world and see the good that their work had caused. They could keep watch that monsters did not again stalk the world, and that the people used the bundles of war and bundles of peace with care. They could also each look upon their father, the star.

In the time of their ascension, Mildred and J.B. became themselves once more, and not Dore and Wahre'dua. And as they did so, they recognized that there were lessons that they had been taught during their time as the brothers that would be important to them in the time ahead.

Chapter Fifteen

And so it was that the two people spoken of in legend as the ones who would lead the tribe to their destiny came back from the wilderness. Three days and nights on the plains with no food or water, and only the tangled imaginings of their own dehydrated bodies and the visions of the spirits to sustain them.

When their time was up, the warriors who had stood guard over the companions, to prevent their attempting escape and also to ensure that no real harm came to them, went to the places where they were and brought them back to the villes. They were placed in earth lodges, cool, calm and quiet places of contemplation, where each, in turn, was given water and food, and allowed to rest and recover from their ordeal.

In each ville, as the pairing who would lead the tribe to destiny recovered in peace and tranquility, the tribes waited for word. They were eager to move now that the stars were in alignment, and the words of those who would lead them were as pearls of dew in the early morning air.

KRYSTY AND RYAN told their stories. The shaman listened carefully before returning to the section of caves where the elders of the tribe sat waiting for word. Briefly he told them of the dog that Ryan had become, and of the manner in which Krysty had put paid to the four ghosts who sought to disprove her bravery.

"There is a lesson in here for us," he concluded. "Eternal vigilance and determination will see us to our goal. One thing we must not do is to take our magpie eyes from the prize. Distraction will be our undoing. In the same way, we must not forget that the bravery is about more than facing the enemy. It is about facing the small things in ourselves that can do more to distract us from the course on which we are set."

There was a muttering of agreement among the tribal elders as they sat in the dimly lit, smoky cave room. The tribal chief spoke for them all when he asked, "And what do the dream quest visions tell us about those that the spirits have sent to lead us?"

The shaman shrugged. "One-eye is stubborn, and focused. He will be a great leader. He knows when to fight, and when to not. He is, perhaps, the better judge of a situation. The woman is a warrior with courage that goes beyond what anyone would expect of a woman who is slighter in stature than most male warriors. But she is perhaps inclined to be carried away, and forget those things in herself that may yet hold her back at a crucial moment. Follow her in battle, but let One-eye make the decisions about how we move."

The chief nodded. "So shall it be," he said simply.

DOC AND JAK spoke of their visions. For Doc, to discuss that which he had seen in a moment of what appeared to be madness was no great trial. For Jak, who did not often choose to talk at all, let alone of things that were from within, the process was considerably more difficult. Doc spoke at length: so much so, in truth, that the shaman was glad when the old man with the white mane finally shut up. He learned much of what Doc had seen, but it was sometimes hard to disentangle the actual vision from the discursive manner in which the old man appeared to veer off at tangents to discuss things that he had seen in the past—bizarre tales of a land in the past from which he claimed to come—and analysis of that which he had experienced as metaphor and symbol. None of this concerned the shaman. Such analysis was his task, and all he sought were the details of the vision.

As such, it was a relief for him when he turned to Jak, and briefly—not without a little embarrassment in his manner as he relayed something that seemed to him to be so fantastic—the albino youth told him of his experiences as a coyote.

The shaman thanked them both for what they had told him, and left to consult with his chief.

"What has Wakan Tanka told us through these men?" the chief asked.

"The Grandfather works in a manner that is bizarre in many ways," the shaman replied with a wry grin. "Certainly, the manner in which he has manifested to them has done little to make their waking minds comprehend what he wishes them to do. And yet, to me it tells us so much about how we must use them, and what their strengths may be."

"Then the Grandfather has done his job well," the chief said after some thought. "For if we are to use these men to lead us, then it is right that the spirits that have guided them to us should also tell us of their strengths and weaknesses, so that we may not be deflected from our course."

The shaman agreed. "The old man is a strange one. He has much intelligence and cunning, yet his mind is inclined to be easily clouded and befuddled. Only such a lack of judgment could lead to a man into taking a horse spirit into his home and losing a wife. He acts upon an impulse to be both altruistic and also to do that which he feels is right. Yet he may not have a grasp on what the long-term consequences of his actions may be and so may lead our people into a situation that will be our downfall. We must follow, but also watch carefully."

The chief pursed his lips and nodded slowly. "I understand. But what of the small white one? What can he offer us?"

"Ah, now he is a completely different matter. He is a hunter of immense skill, strength and cunning. He is cool, almost to the point of not caring whether he does himself harm. He has a fine judgment, and when he does make mistakes he has the ability to think as he runs, and to extract himself from such a situation. Yet he also expects and demands this same level of skill and of truth from everyone else, and this is his weakness. If he is deceived, or his call on the skills of others is wrong in some manner, then it is possible that he may place himself—and by extension our people—in jeopardy. It is essential that we watch him, and learn of his limits, so that we may be able to use our own judgment on those times when he may inadvertently place our people in danger."

"And you think that we can do this? That the spirits have chosen well for us?"

"I have confidence that any who may oppose us will have a mountain as tall as any on this plain to climb if they wish to go up against us."

The chief grunted softly. "This is as it should be."

MILDRED AND J.B. sat together and told their story to the shaman. As soon as they had both recovered from their exposure, and their minds were able to function as their brains rehydrated, they had realized that the dream quest vision in which they had each seen the other had not been mere coincidence. It had been something beyond their understanding that they had shared in a manner that went beyond the world as they knew it.

"These things aren't possible," J.B. had said at first.

"John, we've seen weird shit for as long as I've known you. Hell, it was certainly weird shit to me, where I came from. And isn't that proof enough that things that are beyond normal experience can happen?"

"But—dark night—spirits and gods? That shit is only legend," he countered softly.

"Maybe, but who's to say what are spirits and ghosts, and what are things that happen in the natural universe that we just don't have a way of controlling? What if we share some kind of link not because of some prophecy, but because of something else out there that makes us share?"

"Something?" J.B.'s voice was puzzled, even suspicious.

Mildred thought about what the old woman Milled Red had said to her before they had been sent out on the dream quest. Should she share this with J.B.? She didn't like the idea of keeping anything from him, and yet she was not totally clear on what the old woman meant. She had only the vaguest notion of how science, nature and myth could be tied together.

If only J.B. had shared the secret of the redoubt with her. Their combined knowledge could provide the great leap forward that they needed.

Instead, before she had the chance to form words that would answer his questioning frown, the shaman entered and the moment was lost.

As he listened, the shaman was excited. He tried to keep his feelings from display, but as soon as they had finished he rushed to tell the chief. As he stood in front of his tribal leader, the words pouring from him, he could not believe that he was telling once more the greatest legend in the history of the Otoe.

When he had finished, he looked expectantly at the chief. The elder was surprisingly impassive.

"You are not pleased?" the shaman asked.

"I am more than pleased," the chief replied. "For these two to share the vision of Dore and Wahre'dua suggests that they are, indeed, the reincarnation of our legendary heroes on the flesh. With them at our head, we will surely be the ones who fulfill the prophecy. There can be no doubt about this. We will be the chosen ones."

"So you feel that the others will not have a chance?"

The chief shook his head. "Even if they have been fortunate enough to have strangers enter their midst at the right time, then it is little more than a jest from the Grandfather. The stars are right, so they must find someone to lead them at this time. But they do not have the monster slayers of legend. Anyone who leads them does not have the weight of tradition behind them. No, I am sure that we will be the people who will emerge triumphant."

"Then surely it is time that we should tell them that we are not alone," the shaman mused. "If they have to lead us into the promised lands, then they must be aware that there may be those who would seek to obstruct them."

"In time," the chief said slowly. "We do not want them to be distracted from their task until the last. They must only understand this when they are ready to fight."

Chapter Sixteen

Krysty drew back the bow. She could feel the tension in the taut string, the pressure pulling at her biceps, making it ache as she held the arrow steady, her eye focused on the target that stood at the far end of the plateau. It was a great distance. The tension needed to propel the arrow that far demanded a strength that she knew many of the watching warriors doubted in her.

Very well. Time to prove them wrong.

She held the bow until her muscles felt like they were singing with the same tension as the string. When it felt like she could hold it no longer, and she was as sure as could be that the target was centered in her vision, she let fly the arrow.

The sound of the thin wooden shaft cutting through the air hummed in the ears of the gathered men as they watched its progress. Before they even had the chance to register fully that she had let it fly, the arrow had thudded home to its target.

"Looks good from here," Ryan murmured, moving up beside her.

"You got one eye," one of the men countered. "You wait till we have a proper look before saying anything."

There was a wariness in his tone that added extra weight to the words. The warriors waited in silence while one of them walked slowly across the plateau to examine the target.

In the tension-filled silence, Ryan reflected that the men of the tribe were ambivalent about outlanders leading the trek toward the promised land. Although the prophecy had always foretold that this would happen, and they had always accepted it as the word of the Grandfather, they seemed to have a deeply born reluctance to accept outside help. Part of it, he was sure, was down to Krysty being a woman. The concept of a strong woman who could be the equal of, and fight alongside, the male warriors of the tribe was one that was alien to them. But it was more than that. To go back to the ways of their forefathers and live as their tribe had lived before the white man had taken their land, it had been necessary for the Sioux to isolate themselves. Perhaps there were other tribes like them scattered across the lands; the ones that Ryan and his people had encountered in the past had been more inclined to integrate with other survivors. Regardless, it left the Sioux with a long-ingrained distrust of outlanders.

Which put himself and Krysty in an awkward position. They were told—even though they had no knowledge themselves—that they had been chosen to lead. And the men they would have to lead did not have the faith in them that may become necessary.

All this ran through his head as the Native American

walked to the target, pulled the arrow out and walked slowly back.

"Well?" Krysty asked.

The man shook his head and avoided eye contact with her, looking instead at those gathered near.

"Center of target. Could split an ant's head," he said, but with little satisfaction in his voice.

Right, Ryan figured, they wouldn't accept her no matter what. This wouldn't be easy.

JAK AND DOC WERE having no such problems. In the shadow of the mountain, the Pawnee had adapted well to these two strange outlanders. As the Native Americans who would accompany them on the trip into the unknown lands went through a process of selection, so the two men who had been sent by the spirits to lead them were proving themselves.

For Jak, there was little question about his skills. Already, before his trip onto the prairie wastes, he had proved himself as a hunter when joining the parties that wandered the plains. Now, in combat practice, he was proving himself as a man who could not be bested in hand-to-hand combat. His skill with the leaf-bladed knives made him unstoppable. To prove to the tribe that he did not need these as an advantage, the albino hunter even made a point of removing his camou jacket and the weaponry stowed within. Unarmed, he put himself up against the best fighters that the tribe possessed. Each man he faced found himself deprived of his weapon, and on the receiving end of ax or knife taken from—and used against—him.

Doc had more to prove. For much of the time that Jak had been able to establish his credentials, Doc had been semiconscious and recovering from the exposure that he had faced in the storms that had led them to this place. His bearing on recovery had impressed the Pawnee. To a tribe that had little or no experience of outlanders, the way that Doc carried himself was impressive. What Jak was used to as Doc's wandering mind was, to the Pawnee, a sign that he was a man used to communing with the spirits.

For this alone, he was to be respected. But if he was to lead them, alongside Jak, on their trek to the promised lands, then he would have to prove himself as a warrior as well as a shaman.

So it was that one fine morning, as the cloud scudded across an otherwise clear sky and the chill of a northeasterly breeze was dimmed only in the shadow of the mountain, Doc faced four warriors across a circle of dirt that had been marked out. While many of the women went about their daily tasks and paid him no heed, he was aware that many of the men of the Pawnee had taken leave of their normal activities so as to be able to watch. Among them were the chief and the shaman.

As he looked carefully around, Doc noticed that Jak was conspicuous by his absence. He nodded to himself in satisfaction. It was good that the albino had made himself scarce. That way he wouldn't be obliged to step in if Doc could not handle the challenge he had set himself. That way the chief, the shaman and the men of the tribe would not be looking to see if he would step in. They would evaluate Doc solely on what he did for himself, which was exactly the way that Tanner wanted it to be.

"Gentlemen," he said to the four warriors who stood across the circle from him, "let us begin."

He eyed them warily. The circle of dirt that had been cleared had a circumference of five yards. Small, but not so small as to be confining. Those who were watching hung back a few yards behind the line of the circle.

The four warriors carried small axes, each with a knife sheathed at their waists. They were dressed in loincloths, painted in war markings. There was no way that they were taking this with anything other than the utmost seriousness. They fanned out around the edge of the circle, so that they covered almost 180 degrees. Each warrior held himself so that he was evenly balanced. There was little chance that Doc would be able to tell from their body language alone which one of them—if just one—would be the first to move on him.

Doc moved languidly up and down, looking sideways on at the four warriors. He was stooped forward slightly, head down, looking up at them from beneath his mane of silver hair. His feet dragged slightly in the dust, kicking up small whirls around his heels.

The old man looked incongruous when compared to the men who faced him. He was fully dressed, his frock coat hanging off his shoulders. It seemed as though it would constrict him if or when they should pounce. He also carried his silver lion's-head sword stick, holding it so that the silver head was clutched lightly in his loosely bunched fist.

Too many clothes. Too casual. It seemed as though he was setting himself up to fail.

The shaman and the chief exchanged glances. One was thinking that the man seemed too casual, and that it was a ploy that may just cause his men to drop their guard. The other was wondering what reserves of strength and magic this man who seemed to speak with the spirits may hold within himself. To go up against four warriors with nothing but a flimsy piece of wood...

With a yell that was intended to unnerve his opponent and disarm him as an attack was launched, one of the warriors hurled himself toward Doc. His ax was raised and his free hand reached out to grab at the old man's coat.

Seemingly frozen in shock, Doc deceived his attacker. At the last, when the man's hand touched the fabric of the frock coat, Doc sidestepped and shrugged. The coat fell easily off his arm, pulled down by the weight of the warrior as his momentum and balance carried him forward. With a few deft movements, he made space for himself away from his floundering attacker.

It was space that he needed. Before he had a chance to draw breath, another man was coming for him, ax and knife offering a twin threat. He was almost on Doc before the older man had a chance to move.

This, perversely, worked to Doc's advantage. He pitched the sword stick into the soil, the tipped end digging into the dirt and twisting so that it came around and across, into the shins of the onrushing warrior. Balance disrupted, the man stumbled. Doc drew the sword stick from the soil. With a deft flick of the wrist, he dealt his adversary a sharp blow to the back of the man's exposed neck, his parted and plaited hair forming a line that was an inviting target for Doc.

Stunned, the warrior sprawled in the dust as Doc moved farther away from his two attackers, moving around the line of the circle so that he was now approaching the two remaining warriors before they even had the chance to move on him.

"Gentlemen," he whispered, the tone of his voice now giving a different feel to the word than in his previous utterance. He could see indecision in the eyes of the two men who faced him. They had not expected him to dispose of their comrades with such ease. It wasn't fear that he saw; rather, it was the sudden knowledge that they had underestimated their opponent, and were unsure of their best course of action.

Indecision led to hesitancy, a fraction of a second's delay in reacting. That was all Doc needed. The briefest of vulpine smiles flashed across his face. It couldn't have escaped the two men who faced him.

If they were already in doubt, then Doc's next move was enough to show them that they were novices when it came to close combat.

With a speed that defied the eye, Doc revealed to them the sword hidden within the stick. The rapier-thin blade, honed from the finest Toledo steel, glinted in the light.

It had momentum enough to blur in an arc and catch even the weakest of sunlight in this shadowed glade.

Reacting quickest, the man to the left of the old man feinted and tried to duck inside of the blade's whirling arc, his ax discarded and his knife now unsheathed. Doc dropped to one knee and flicked his wrist deftly, reversing the angle of the blade so that it almost sang in the air as it seemingly defied the laws of nature to come back and lick at the man's exposed wrist, slicing the skin and drawing beads of blood, causing the knife to drop from his nerveless fingers.

It hadn't been for sheer dramatic effect that Doc had dropped to one knee. As the man had approached him, from the corner of his eye Doc had seen his comrade draw back his arm and unleash his ax. The change in height effected by his dip had enabled Doc to evade the spinning ax as it sailed harmlessly over his head.

A neat move, but he had no time to stand on ceremony and reflect on how smart he may have been. While one warrior stumbled, pain momentarily fogging his reflexes, the other pulled his knife and rushed at Doc.

The old man rose to his full height and parried the thrust of the knife, made by his adversary as he closed. The steel of the sword and the coarser metal of the knife blade squealed and scraped against each other, sliding down until the hilt of both met, drawing the two men close so that Doc could see into the warrior's dark eyes, and smell his herb-scented breath as he came almost nose-to-nose. For the briefest of seconds, they were locked into stillness.

Doc grunted loudly. He was slightly more on the front foot than his opponent, all he needed to aid the effort that saw him push the man away.

While the warrior stumbled backward, Doc stepped farther back, the better to deal with the man he had cut, who was now recovering his wits and reaching for the knife with his uninjured hand.

A sweep of the blade kicked up dust, catching the knife blade and pitching it beyond reach. The back stroke of the arc saw the blade hack at the warrior's shins, causing him to stumble. As he floundered, Doc stepped forward and reversed his arm, so that he was able to club his opponent with one sharp, brief blow that caught him behind the ear, rendering him unconscious.

One man remained standing. There was still no time for Doc to pause or rest, for that man had recovered balance and was now heading for him, anger causing him to forego any attempt at retrieving a weapon, relying instead upon his bare hands.

It would be simple to disarm him, if only Doc had fast enough reflexes. But the efforts of putting down the three men had taken the edge from his speed, and he was in the act of raising the sword blade when the warrior hurled himself at Doc, coming in at waist level and under the arc of the Toledo steel.

Doc groaned and gasped for air as the man caught him in the midriff, driving him backward so that he crashed on the bone-jarringly hard earth with the weight of the warrior driving all the air from his abdomen. Lights danced before his eyes and blackness started to encroach on the edges of his vision. His lungs felt as though they were ripping as he struggled for air. Yet he knew that he had to catch his breath before the similarly disabled man on top of him had such a chance.

From somewhere deep within him—possibly the wells of sheer stubbornness that had seen him through so much in his strange life—Doc found the strength to heave the man from him, rolling with him so that he was now on top. He felt his adversary's hands start to close around his throat. But the grip was weak, as though the man beneath him struggled for breath and strength.

It was all the impetus Doc needed. With one mighty effort, he raised his arm and crashed the silver lion's-head on the temple of the man beneath him. It was not the sharp, decisive blow he had shown to his previous opponent. It was hesitant, stumbling… Twice, three times he raised his arm and, almost painfully slow, crashed it down again. Each time he felt the fingers of his opponent weaken just that little more.

The fourth blow, as weak as it seemed to him, had just enough force for the cumulative effect to render the man unconscious.

Gasping, his head both pounding and reeling as the sudden influx of oxygen from his now regulated breathing began to flow around his system, Doc hauled himself to his feet. Swaying slightly, he looked around, surveying the carnage that surrounded him. Four warriors, all rendered incapable.

Vision slightly blurring, he looked across at where the chief, the shaman and other men of the Pawnee stood watching him. There was a low murmur in the crowd, and it sounded approving rather than hostile. Despite his "chosen" status, it had briefly crossed Doc's mind that rendering four of your hosts' best fighters incapable was not, perhaps, the best way of making friends and influencing people.

"You have done well," the chief said. "You have proved yourself the equal of Whitey in besting any who would oppose you."

"I do not know about that," Doc demurred, aware of the rasping breathlessness in his voice. It was a judgment that Jak probably wouldn't be too happy about, and that thought alone made Doc smile to himself. Still, it was nice to hear.

"Does that mean I get the job?" he asked in as bright a voice as he could manage, light-headedness lending him a flippancy that would otherwise have been out of place.

"Eh?" The chief looked at the shaman, puzzled.

The stoic medicine man shrugged. "Spirits can make you crazy," he muttered.

"Oh, good. I am so glad," Doc said, confusing them further.

With which, consciousness escaped him and he fell forward slowly, face-first into the dust.

FOR MILDRED AND J.B. the path toward fulfilling their destiny had little in the way of such high points. The interpretation of their shared vision quest, and the manner in which it tied in to the great legends that powered the progress of the Otoe, meant that they were seen by many as above reproach.

J.B. had already had many a chance to prove himself when out hunting, and in the patrolling guard that kept the children and the women of the tribe feeling safe, riding out at night to keep clear the boundaries of the ville. Mildred had not had this chance, but despite her sex, the wise words of the old seer Milled Red had proved to be correct in some manner. Her color set her apart from the white-eyes, of which J.B. was a part, and this enabled the tribe to see her in a different light. She was an outsider in the land of the white-eyes, just as they were. So she did not face quite the hostility that Krysty had faced with the Sioux in being able to take part in activities that were the preserve of the male.

And now that she and J.B. were linked with Dore and Wahre'dua in the minds of the tribe, they were now both seen as being not a white-eye and a woman; rather, they had become symbols of the way in which the monster-slaying brothers had given themselves to the world. The whole world, regardless of race or creed.

When Mildred went once more to visit the old woman, she remarked upon this. At first, it seemed as though Milled Red had paid no heed. In an irritable tone, she sent the woman who tended her to fetch fresh water, complaining that the herb tea she had been given by her nurse was brackish. It was only when the nurse left the earth lodge that Mildred saw the light sparkle in the old woman's eyes.

"It is a shame to treat her like that, for she is a good

girl in many ways. But not of the brightest, and perhaps inclined to open her mouth before her mind has formed any thoughts."

"So there's nothing wrong with the tea?" Mildred asked with a smile.

The old woman shook her head with an air of impatience. "Of course not. It seems wrong to scold the child in such a way, as she makes such good tea. But I wished to speak with you with some degree of privacy. First, I must ask you—does it not strike you as strange that you and your friend should have the same vision?"

Mildred thought about her answer. What was the old woman expecting her to say? She chose her words with care.

"We're close. We've shared many things. We've also heard much about your tribe and its legends during—"

The old woman waved a hand dismissively. "No, no, that's not what I mean. In the time since our people have returned to the old ways, I have never heard of any two people—even the closest of brothers—having such a shared experience. I am also suspicious of anything that fits too nicely. And this does."

"In what way?" Mildred asked, a glimmering of the old woman's meaning sparking at the edge of her consciousness.

"Simply this. At a time when all thoughts are focused on the prophecy, two people arrive from nowhere. Then they are sent on a dream quest and have an identical vision. It is as though the legend were being written around them by an unseen hand."

"The spirits?"

The old woman shrugged. "Oh, well, you might call it that. But I am old enough to remember a time when such things were not blindly believed. And there is nothing wrong with a little healthy skepticism. You should cease trying to humor me, and be yourself."

Mildred could not resist a chuckle. "Okay, you got me there. I suppose I do find it hard to believe in spirits without anything else to go on. But what's the alternative? That something else is guiding us? Some unseen hand?"

Milled Red sniffed. "That is no less possible. The old bases from white-eye military days, when our people were workers in thrall to them. They are scattered around here like gopher holes. I have never seen inside the one that we are near, but I suspect that your friend may have done."

Mildred nodded. "I wouldn't doubt that John was itching to have a look around. Even though your people don't use the tech, it would still seem like a good idea to him to check it out."

"You haven't spoken of this, then?"

"No, there hasn't been enough time for us to be alone—" she paused, hearing the nurse return.

Milled Red waved her hand in agitation. "There isn't much time, then. Listen well. You must talk to him about what he has seen in there. The white-eye bases hold the key to the prophecy as much as the spirits. The two may even have become the same over the years, one as a way of explaining the other. I have thought this for many years, but those living now could not understand how things used to be, and would not want to question. I like you. It has been refreshing to speak with one who is not small in horizon, just the once more. I would not wish harm to come to you because you are unprepared."

Her voice had dropped to a harsh whisper as the nurse entered, so that she would not grasp the gist of the conversation.

"You are having trouble speaking. I must make you more tea with honey," the nurse said in a worried tone.

"Don't fuss, girl, it was nothing more than a clogged throat," Milled Red replied. "Make your tea, but don't worry."

Mildred left the old woman, with the nurse fussing over her, and went in search of J.B. The words of the old seer were racing through her head. If this area was riddled with old tech and military bases; if there were anyone still alive in any of them, mad, inbred and mutated but still with a rudimentary grasp of how the tech worked; if there were something that worked still on an automatic program…

She did not have to search long before she found him. The Armorer was with a group of men, making bows from finely carved wood, bending the soft, yielding flesh so it was shaped by the tension of the string that ran between the ends.

"John, there's something I'd like to talk to you about."

"Sure," he replied, infuriating her as he showed little sign of moving from where he sat, among those she didn't want to hear their conversation—accidentally or otherwise.

"I've got to be getting on, so could you…" She indicated that they move away.

J.B. frowned. "Okay, but it'd better be quick."

As they moved away, and she tried to ignore his puzzled expression, she was acutely aware of the eyes of the others following them. She made small talk that baffled him even more, until he finally snapped.

"Millie, what the hell is going on? What did—"

She silenced him with a gesture and, looking around to check that they could not be easily overheard, told him of her conversation with the old seer. When she had finished, he nodded shortly.

"Yeah, I can see why you wouldn't want that overheard." He paused, then added, "She might have something. There was certainly a shitload of activity going on around here before skydark."

"Why didn't you say anything about this before?" she asked, exasperated.

"Because I never had a chance for more than a brief recce," he replied, pondering the matter, "and it didn't occur to me that there could be anything going on. Just figured that they'd all be as useless as this one seems to be."

"Except it's only useless because the Otoe don't want to use it." Mildred sighed. "I think we should check this out."

It was easy to approach the redoubt. The tribe thought nothing of the old base, and it was open at all times. Yet they could rarely be bothered to enter without some purpose, so it was essential that Mildred and the Armorer have a reason to enter, in case they aroused suspicion.

J.B. went to Little Tree, explaining that he was more familiar with the old habit of map reading than the Otoe-preferred methods of scouting land, and so he wished to consult the old maps that he had seen when the man had shown him the redoubt.

Little Tree shrugged, figuring it would be no problem, and he accompanied them to the redoubt, where J.B. showed Mildred the wall chart that mapped the maze of redoubts that littered the plains area, completely oblivious to the significance it now held for them.

Mildred whistled low, then spoke as quietly. "With all that shit under the ground, it's a wonder that we just don't fall through and have done with it."

"It is kind of impressive, in a way," he agreed.

She looked over her shoulder at Little Tree before saying softly, "It means that there's a whole lot of computer tech that could still be running, or a whole lot of inbreds who could be doing it. Maybe that's why we had the same vision. Some kind of tech that can bend our minds."

"Mebbe there is," J.B. said sourly, "but that kind of figures that something out there knows what these people believe and is moving us all about like pieces in that old game you and Doc like. And that's just as hard for me to believe in as spirits and ghosts."

"So maybe it taps into what we're thinking, what they're thinking. That's a whole lot of maybes."

J.B. collected a number of maps from the wall and from old storage units. Map reading would enable him to orienteer that much better.

As they left the redoubt, then parted company with Little Tree, both J.B. and Mildred were wrapped in their own thoughts. Only when they felt it was safe, and they could not be overheard, did they give them voice.

"You saying to me that something is guiding us, like spirits or some rogue comp, even coldhearts who might still be hiding out underground?"

"I don't know, John. I really don't. But it's a possibility we need to think about."

"Mebbe you're right," J.B. stated. "Tell you one thing—there's some weird shit happening out there. We've seen that. And the farther out there you get, the weirder it is. Something's causing that to happen. Mebbe the same thing made us see what we did. Whatever it is, we need to be triple red if it can fuck with our heads. 'Cause even if it isn't actively hostile, it sure as shit isn't friendly."

Chapter Seventeen

The stars were in alignment, and the time had come for preparations to cease, and for the fulfillment of the prophecy to begin. The warriors who would accompany the pairs on their quest into the plain, in search of the answer, the secret that would enable their tribe to become the one that would lead the world to a better way, were finally selected.

Now, on the night before they began their journey, the revered explorers were the subject of a celebratory feast. In each tribal gathering, all were gathered in their finest garb. Sweetly spiced meats and potent brews were consumed, and the explorers were given the finest of send-offs. The shaman of each tribe conducted ceremonies that would cleanse and protect those who were to venture forth, ensuring that the spirits were on their side, and they were safe from vengeful or playful ghosts.

And then, when the shaman of each tribe had concluded his ritual, the chief of each tribe stood in front of the assembled throng and delivered an address that was intended to stir those who were to stay behind and wait, as much as it was intended to spur on those who were about to depart.

And it was then—only then—that, in each tribe, each pair of chosen ones realized that they were not alone.

THE SHOCK OF HEARING the chief elder's words as they rang out across the plateau made Ryan pause. A sliver of spiced jackrabbit halfway to his mouth. Slowly, he turned to Krysty.

Looking at him from across three rapt warriors, lost in their leader's words, the Titian-haired woman raised an eyebrow. As soon as they could find a moment when they could not be overheard, it was vital they talk.

TALK WAS SOMETHING that Doc could never help. Even before the Pawnee chief had finished his speech, the old man leaned across to Jak and whispered urgently in his ear.

The albino teen was less voluble than Doc, and a sharp elbow to the older man's ribs soon silenced him, if only for a moment.

When the chief had finished, and music had started to play while a ritual dance began, Jak took advantage of the silence and leaned into Doc. "Sorry for hurt. Should keep mouth shut till safe."

"I know, I know," Doc said, "and you were perfectly correct, dear boy... But you realize what this may mean?"

"Hell of a big chance." Jak shrugged.

"Not really. We started from the same place, and couldn't really wander that far in the time we were apart. If there are two other tribes on this plain who have the same aims, then..."

"Yeah, mebbe. What that shit Mildred say about not chilling chickens?"

"Counting, dear boy, and you're right. Nonetheless, it is now our imperative to—"

"Get away from rest as soon as possible," Jak finished with a decisive nod.

Doc grinned. "Exactly."

FOR MILDRED AND J.B. the revelation was not exactly the shock it may have been for the others. The Otoe had gathered in one of the fields that had been left fallow for the season. A ceremonial fire had been lit, and the tribe had gathered around it. Despite the surprise they both felt at the words of the chief, they remained stoic, betraying no emotion even to each other, let alone to the warriors around them.

But Milled Red had been carried from her earth lodge to witness and partake in this feast. As the oldest member of the tribe—even if a woman—it had been almost a necessity that she see the beginnings of the goal for which she had been waiting all her life.

Mildred and J.B. used the cover of the celebrations to approach her.

"Oh, well, I think I know what you want to ask me," the old woman said before either of them had a chance to speak. "If I knew of the other tribes, why didn't I mention them?"

"Something like that," J.B. murmured.

The old woman shifted painfully, grimacing, then said, "Think of it this way. If I had mentioned it, you would have been itching to escape and search for your companions. For which I would not blame you. But— and this is important—by staying here and learning much of the prophecy, and looking back at the old times, as I'm sure you have," she added with a wry smile, "then are you not better equipped to try to find your companions once you have left the village, and are no longer under close observation?"

"So how do you know that we won't just make a run for it and leave all thoughts of the prophecy behind?" Mildred asked. "After all, you might be skeptical, but you're still Otoe."

The old woman laughed. It was a harsh, grating sound, but not without warmth. "True enough. I have always lived with the idea of the prophecy. Yet I have never been convinced by stories that have no real basis. It may prove to be true. Yet even then, that is no guarantee that it will give the people exactly what they wish for. There is some old saw about being careful when it comes to such matters.

"No. The reason that I am convinced that you will see this matter through has little to do with the Grandfather, and everything to do with fate. It is a much harsher taskmaster, and shows neither favoritism nor interest. You have been set on this course by blind chance. Blind chance has thrown your companions an equal lifeline. Of course, we don't know that for sure. Coincidence is a friend of this land, however…

"You will follow the path that fate and chance has set you. In many ways, there is little else you can do."

The old woman gave a little chuckle as she finished. Despite the tenor of her words, her voice betrayed no malice. She was simply stating the facts as she saw them.

J.B. looked at Mildred. There was resignation both in his tone and written on his face. "She's right. It's like we're caught in a current, and we've just got to see where the tide takes us."

MILDRED AND J.B. WERE riding at the head of their party when the first storm hit without warning. The skies were clear, the ochre-tinged blue forming a haze over the sun as it beat down on them. There was no sign of any cloud cover, and yet it seemed to J.B. that in the blink of an eye, a vast bank of dark, thick, broiling cloud had grown almost directly above them. The air grew thick, charged with static, and although the temperature did not change, the kind of heat had a textural change that was palpable. From a dry scorching on any exposed flesh, the air now became clammy and sticky, sweat forming on their skin and weighing heavy as the moisture seemed to increase in mass, almost too weighty to move and roll down their necks and backs.

"Where the hell did that come from?" Mildred murmured, casting a wary eye at the cloud, which was black and gray shot through with yellow.

J.B. shrugged. "Seemed to appear when I blinked."

"I wonder what it's going to do."

As if the elements had chosen to answer her directly, the first drops of rain began to fall. As heavy and round as the globs of sweat that would not dislodge from her brow, they hit the ground around the gently pacing horses with a force that kicked up globs of muddy dust, pitting the surface of the prairie with tiny pockmarked craters. They hit the flanks of the horses, stinging like stones tossed from a distance, causing the animals to snort and toss as the strange intrusions disturbed them.

They were no less disturbing for those who rode on their backs. The heavy, mordant parcels of water seemed to sting the skin as they landed.

Chem rain. That was no ordinary cloud that rumbled and danced above them, unleashing its deadly load.

Yelling to one another to find cover, the exploratory party turned its horses, scanning the land around for something that would provide cover. Anything, given the urgency of the circumstances, would be a relief.

Was it fate or the hand of the Grandfather that saw them close to a small rock hill, with a cave in the face? Or was it that the storm was only happening because they were near to the cave?

If the latter, then there was a chance that something omnipotent was manipulating them. But they could not waste time to wonder about that. They had to take their chances as they arose, and so they rode for the cover that the cave provided. Their faces, forearms, any exposed skin, itched as the rain hit it with an increasing force. Skin became waxy, then soapy, as the acids locked into the parcels of water were freed by contact and ate away at the top layer of epidermis on every rider.

As if this were not enough, the rain was now falling harder. The drops fell so closely together that they became almost like a constant stream. Sheets of rain fell in front of them, making progress akin to riding through a waterfall. The streams of liquid made their skin blister and ulcerate at a rapid rate; the going underfoot became treacherous and thick, a quagmire that caught at the hooves of the horses, making them slip and stumble.

Yelling instructions or encouragement to one another became impossible as the coruscating rains fell harder, driving into their mouths, nostrils and eyes, making it all too easy to lose their bearings.

More by luck than judgment, testament only to their ability to set a course against all obstacles, the exploratory party made it to the cave. They had scattered, but somehow all managed to find their way to shelter. Using water from their canteens to wash the chem rain from their eyes, they looked out on the land. It was lost now beneath a bubbling, churning river of mud and water that was swept along by what kind of a current they could only guess.

"Better not rise too much," Little Tree murmured to J.B. "You notice something? This is no big cave, and it gets narrow down the back, there."

J.B. squinted into the darkness that lurked behind them. It was a dim light, but even so he could see that Little Tree was right: the cave quickly narrowed as the walls and ceiling closed in a funnel. He turned and looked at the river of mud that was flowing past the opening. The rain still fell, and the mud lapped closer and closer to the mouth of the cave, seemingly inexorable in its search for them.

And then, as suddenly as it had started to fall, the rain ceased. The sheets dried to a few desultory drops that glittered with chemical colors in the sun that now poked yellow fingers through the dark of the fast-scattering chem cloud. In less than a minute, the storm cloud that had lain so heavily was gone, the rain now nothing more than a memory as the skies returned to their ochre-streaked blue. As the exploratory party watched from the cave mouth, the rivers of mud hardened and baked with a ferocity and speed that was almost shocking. Where only seconds before there had been a churning quicksand of viscous fluid earth, there were now hard-baked ridges of dirt that rose and fell, tracing the contours of the flow in a way that would make progress on horseback slower. Columns of steam rose from the ruts as the air reclaimed the water, the rains now rising back to…what? Nothing but blue, now that the cloud that had birthed them was gone.

"The spirits are playing with us, testing us," Little Tree said softly.

Mildred looked at J.B. "Yeah, or someone or something.…"

Wary now of the elements that lay beyond the cave, the exploratory party mounted their steeds and ventured out into the now clear day.

Was this an error of judgment? It seemed that way, as in only a few short minutes they found that the same baking heat that had dried the mud rivers and scattered the dark clouds had now left them with no shelter from its piteous glare. Not wishing to drive their mounts too hard, the party had started at a sedate pace. Yet even now, after such a scant passing of time, it seemed to be too fast. Under the relentless rays of the malicious sun, they slowed almost to a crawl. The heat was dry and oppressive, weighing down on them like molten lead. Their skins itched from the chem burns, and began to fry under the sun. It was hard to concentrate, to form any kind of coherent thought, but it did occur to Mildred that the weight was a constant theme: first the rain, now the heat. As though something was attempting to sap their strength as they ventured toward the area that was their goal.

Any further such train of thought was arrested by what she could see and hear ahead of them, through the haze formed by the heat and rising water vapor.

RYAN, KRYSTY AND THE Sioux party had also experienced an anomaly in the weather, but theirs was more familiar to them. They had seen clouds form and gather in the distance, each swirl of darkness on the horizon to east and west. Yet their part of the skies remained clear.

Krysty's hair gathered at her nape, giving her forewarning of what was to come only a few moments before the first wisps of moving air signaled the beginnings of a windstorm.

"The Grandfather sends this to test us," one of the warriors yelled.

"More likely because we're stuck between the two cloud pressures," Ryan murmured to Krysty, "but whatever's causing it, we need to find shelter."

The woman nodded. It was unnecessary to add the need for speed that she felt, as Ryan was already ahead of her. A dust storm caused by raging winds was what had got them into this situation, and he was damned if he was going to let the intemperate climate catch him out a second time.

Ryan turned his horse, scanning the land for some kind of shelter. There was little. They had traveled from the safety of the hills that had housed them to a region that was little more than arid scrub. They would have to use the hide sleds that some of the party carried behind their mounts to construct a makeshift shelter.

"Tether the horses, use the banking to make shelter," the one-eyed man yelled above the already rising and screeching gales. Dust and dirt from the earth around rose in swirls and eddies, already rising high enough to start gritting their eyes, catching in the nose and mouth.

Nearby a small rise in the land formed a shallow bank. It was little, but all they had. As quickly as they could move in winds that started to grow in ferocity and buffet them as they moved, the exploratory party dismounted and tethered their mounts to whatever they could find—scrub, stunted tree root and branch—and struggled against the elements to form the sleds into a primitive shelter against the angle of the bank.

The earth was loose, and it was hard to drive in pegs that could secure the hide. Even then, it was almost flat to the ground, and was cramped when the warriors secured themselves against the dust and dirt that whipped like stones against the hide.

There was barely enough air to breathe, and that which could be gasped was rich with the sweat and fear of the people whose sweat-spangled skins rubbed against one another. But still the dust and dirt rained and blew, and everyone in the party tried to draw shallow breaths to make the oxygen stretch in the confined space.

Perhaps they didn't notice it at first because of the noise made by the storm, but as the wind abated the clash and clamor of combat became apparent to them.

"Fireblast! What the fuck is that?" Ryan breathed.

When he had struggled out of the shelter and into the now still day, he couldn't believe his eye....

JAK HAD SNIFFED THE AIR not once but several times as the war party made its way across the sparse grasslands of the plain. Stunted trees dotted the expanse of flat lands that gave lie to the hills that lay in the distance. The airless skies above them beat down a hazy heat that made every step taken by their mounts seem to pound into them.

"Dear boy, if you cannot blow it out, then at least swallow it down. Your infernal sniffing is driving me to distraction," Doc said testily.

Jak gave him a blankly impassive look.

Doc shook his head. "Quite right. Remiss of me, lad. Any problems you may have with mucus are the least of our worries right now."

Jak's expression didn't change, though his tone revealed a certain exasperation. "Not got anything to gob out," he said. "Change in the air, but not make sense."

"In what way?" Doc questioned, raising his aching and weary head for the first time in what seemed like an age and looking around him. The dull landscape and monotonous skies seemed to him no different from anything they had been since they had begun this forsaken journey. His gaze also took in the warriors who rode with them. They seemed as exhausted by the weather as he did, their mounts as slow and plodding. If any of them were listening to the exchange between Jak and himself, they seemed not to show it—unsurprising, as he had long since decided that the grasp of English held by many of them couldn't get a grip on Jak's unique use of the language. Come to that, it was something that he, too, found occasion to question. But no matter. It was apparent that the albino youth was unsettled by something, although in his usual way he did not let in show in any obvious manner.

Jak hadn't answered Doc immediately. He looked around him, red eyes squinting in the bright sun, the slightest furrow on his brow betraying his bemusement. Finally he said, "Weird. Air not smell like change coming. Not look like, either. But something not right."

"What?"

Jak shrugged. "Just feel it. Bristle, like when know being watched. But nothing else. Not right."

"My dear Jak," Doc murmured, "there are many things that are not right about this area. I feel sure that nothing would surprise me."

Yet even so, it was still a shock when, within a few minutes of this pronouncement, Doc bore witness to the sudden appearance of dark clouds that crowded in over them. At first, they weren't noticeable. With no prior warning, and no real need or desire to stare up into the sun, none of them saw the wisps of darkness that seemed to appear from nowhere, growing incrementally over the space of a few minutes until they began to cast a shadow over the sun. Only then did the war party look up to see the heavy, broiling clouds that were forming and obscuring that part of the sky that lay directly above them, forming a low ceiling of dark that brooded and threatened to let loose the load that made its belly sag ominously overhead.

Jak shook his head, turning to Doc. "Not right. Skies like this smell, make air change. Air not changed."

"Are you sure about that?" Doc replied, suppressing a shiver. Yet he didn't know whether this shiver was from a kind of fear, or because the temperature seemed to fall with a bizarre rapidity. "Seemed," he felt, because in the distance he could see the land lit up by the sun.

Before he was able to articulate the bewilderment he was feeling, the first flakes of snow began to descend. Ice-cold to the touch, the snow made the war party and its mounts shiver as it landed upon naked skin.

The warriors stopped their mounts to gather blankets from the hide sleds that trailed behind some of the horses. They didn't notice at first that the snow didn't melt away as it touched the plains, and that the sparse grassland soon became a lush blanket of white.

Doc looked around for cover. It was impossible. The land had been monotonously flat for as far as he had been able to see when they were mounted; and now it was hard to see more than a few yards in front, as the snow was now falling in a thick curtain that made visibility poor.

As well, the layers of snow that gathered on the ground dissolved to icy water when coming into contact with the body heat of the war party and their horses. Doc could feel his teeth chatter despite attempts to still them, and a numbness that spelled danger began to creep up into his limbs from his extremities. Unless they were able to find or construct some kind of shelter, he knew what would happen next: a torpor that would sweep over them, lulling them into an unconscious sleep of what would, in every sense of the word, be a chilling.

Willing himself to move, Doc tried to find Jak in the all-consuming white that obscured his view.

"Jak, we must do something," he heard himself say in a faraway voice that told him the cold was already beginning to take its toll.

"Work—keep warm and make shelter," Jak barked. Of course, the boy was right. If they warmed themselves by exertion, they could stay conscious long enough to take advantage of whatever shelter they could create… But it just seemed so hard….

Doc felt the snow form a blanket around him that now felt warm, the numbness seeming to be comforting. He did not know that he had fallen back and was looking at the sky until he felt hands plucking at his sodden coat, hauling him to his feet. He opened his eyes, almost unsure of the orientation of the earth. He seemed to be at an angle that made little sense to him. It was only as he pitched forward again that he realized that his inner ear had gone haywire.

"Doc, take this," Jak yelled, thrusting an ax into his hand. "Help us."

Doc teetered on his toes, unsure as to whether he could stay on his feet. As his vision cleared from a snowblind bleariness, he realized that while some of the warriors were clearing snow from the ground, others were constructing a makeshift shelter from the skins and hides of the sleds, into which they could crawl and take the horses. It would have been some kind of undertaking under any circumstances, let alone with a blinding and freezing hail of snow. Yet Jak and the shivering warriors were making the best of things. The heat from their bodies rose in steam like the jets that issued from their noses and mouths. Hypothermia was kept at bay by sheer exertion, driven by the knowledge that only this shelter could offer them any kind of hope.

For a moment Doc stood as frozen as he felt, observing them as though looking into a glass snow globe from the outside. Dimly, he could recall buying such a token for Emily when he had traveled into the city one Christmas…

By the Three Kennedys, Doc thought, such surrender to idly drifting thoughts could only end in his own surrender to the grim reaper. He threw himself forward into the task, working shoulder to shoulder with the others. As he did, he could feel the blood begin to surge in his veins, its previous sluggish flow given further impetus by the adrenaline that his panic unleashed.

While the snow began to rise around them, that small area proscribed by the warriors and the hides they had erected became a haven of untouched, if slightly damp, grassland.

Within a short while, they had cleared a space and made a shelter that came down on three sides, with a fourth that opened in a flap. The horses were gathered beneath, and the warriors now squeezed themselves in, closing that flap to secure themselves as much as was possible from the snowstorm that still fell with relentless intensity from the darkened skies.

Isolated now from the elements, and stilled as opposed to their previous action, the war party could feel the cold of the air begin to seep into their bones. Their own body warmth seemed to rise from them with a mocking rapidity, almost taunting them as it filtered through the sagging skins that dipped above them, full already of snow.

Yet surely the snow should have acted as an insulation when gathered on the skins? Seeing the steam rise from them, Doc was able for the first time to think clearly about what had been happening.

"No. This is not right," he said, almost to himself. "Jak is right. It is weird. Does not make sense."

Although he hadn't been addressing anyone in particular with his remarks, he found that one of the warriors was willing to answer him.

"It does not have to make sense. It is a test. The

Grandfather wishes to see if we are the worthy ones, so he makes play with the elements to see if we rise to the challenge. Only if we can make our way through these tests are we the ones who can gain the knowledge and insight we need."

"Must be better way than freezing ass off," Jak muttered.

Doc kept his own counsel. He had seen too much of the ways of man and nature in his time to deny outright the existence of any spiritual dimension. Whether this was the work of Wakan Tanka or any lesser spirits didn't concern him. It was the empirical truth of it that caused him any concern he may feel.

The weather could be manipulated, but even if it was, then there were certain basic facts of nature that couldn't be denied. Even to hasten a change in a weather pattern would mean changes in pressure that Jak had previously referred to as the smell of the air. These had been noticeable by their absence. Then again there was the way in which their body heat had risen and ascended through the roof of hide above their heads, despite the heavy snow that weighed it down and should—under any normal circumstance—have made a blanket to keep in that very heat.

When nature misbehaved it was one thing. When she broke any of her own rules, it was highly suspicious.

So it was that Doc was less than surprised when the temperature began to rise suddenly and the light through the skins that surrounded them on all sides became that much brighter.

"Well, this is all very interesting, is it not?" he murmured to himself as he pulled the hide flap to one side and stepped out into the scrub grass.

The sky above was ochre-tinged blue once more. The sun beating down, the heat relentless. Casting a gaze around him, Doc couldn't help but notice that not only had the snows evaporated with an alarming quickness, there was also little sign of any of the ground around them being in the slightest damp.

He turned and took a step back, so that he could see the roof of the shelter. It still sagged, but now only from a looseness in pinning, rather than from a weight of snow.

As Jak, the warriors and the horses also came out into the light, Doc noticed something else.

Where they had all been wet from the snow moments before, they were now dry, only the salt marks of their dried sweat giving any indications of damp.

Doc fingered experimentally the heavy material of his frock coat. It should be sodden, having been soaked by the snows.

It was bone dry.

"I wonder…" he murmured to himself.

Chapter Eighteen

"I see it, but you know I don't think I can quite believe it," Mildred muttered softly.

"I dunno about believing in it," J.B. countered, "but I'll tell you this much—if they turn our way, we are really in trouble."

Ahead of the Armorer and Mildred, shimmering in the haze of heat thrown up by the evaporating rains, rode a group of Otoe warriors, proud and resplendent on their horses. In full decoration, ready for war, they moved across the horizon, seemingly oblivious to the small party of their tribesmen who stood some small distance from them.

"Where they come from?" Little Tree asked. "We're the chosen ones. Wait…" he added to Mildred and J.B., as he turned to answer the questions that poured from the rest of the warriors. On emerging from the cave in the wake of Mildred and J.B., they had been brought up short by the sight they beheld and were now in a state of confusion. They spoke poor English, which was why Little Tree was the main point of communication between themselves and the chosen ones. As with many of the tribe, the necessity had been absent, so now this kind of delay in communication was hitting Mildred and J.B. as a potential problem.

Turning away from the procession in front of them, they could see Little Tree arguing with the others. It didn't take a grasp of their language to understand that he was being bombarded with questions to which he had no answers. He looked at Mildred and J.B., his face a mask of confusion.

"How can this be? We were chosen. The idea was for a small party. What could have changed—"

"I don't think these men have anything to do with us," Mildred said softly. "Take a better look. Tell the others to do it."

Relaying the instructions, Little Tree looked as confused as the other warriors. Yet they did as he requested, and as they watched the warriors pass in the distance their confusion took on a different hue.

"They are Otoe, but they are not of us," he said wonderingly.

Mildred shook her head. "Their decoration is different. Not much, but enough. I'm not sure where they've come from, but they're not from your people."

"Then who—" he began.

She cut him short: "Only one way to find out."

Passing on the order, Little Tree and the rest of the warriors joined Mildred and J.B. in mounting their horses and setting off in pursuit of the war party that now preceded them.

It was only after they had been riding for a while that J.B. turned to Mildred, a puzzled expression on his face.

"You notice anything about the land?"

She followed his gaze. As she took in the land over which they now rode, it was a few moments before it registered with her exactly what he was talking about. When it did become clear, she began to wonder about the wisdom of following the war party in front of them.

For the ground around them, which had been so distorted and churned by the floods, then baked hard into ruts and ridges that threatened to slow their progress, had flattened out and gone from rocklike ridges to the same powdery and dusty layer of topsoil on hard-packed earth that it had been before the rains started to fall.

How was that possible?

The sound of battle, faint strains growing as the warriors in front of them speeded up, reached their ears and made them wary now of what they rode toward.

"Better get your boys ready," J.B. said. "It looks like it might be time to fight for that destiny you talked about."

"FIREBLAST AND FUCK. Where the hell did they come from?" Ryan breathed, awestruck by the tribal gathering that raced across his field of vision. There had been little indication, as the dust storm abated, that this was in the reckoning. In their shelter, there had been no sound penetrating the storm and then—more significantly—the stillness that followed. No notion that such a large party was approaching from distance. It was almost as though they had sprung, fully formed and close by, as soon as Ryan had chosen to leave the shelter.

He wasn't sure—it was so quick, almost too much so to register—but it seemed as though the massed war party had been silent when he first saw them. Like a mass of horse flesh and humanity, moving at speed, mouths open in roar, and yet silent like ghosts. And then, before this had time to fully sink in, the sound kicked in. A deafening clatter of hooves, yelling voices, clashing metal on metal of axes and knives.

There were at least two separate forces within the melee that had formed in front of him. He could tell this from the warpaint and markings that decorated the warriors. One section of the battling forces he could identify as Dakota Sioux as they were similar to—though not exactly the same as—the warriors with which he and Krysty were traveling.

The others he could not identify with any such assurance. They had decoration, warpaint and markings that singled them out as different, yet as he watched it seemed as though there was more than one tribe in opposition. He had no idea who these other tribes might be, but the fact that there were two of them got his mind racing.

Three tribes. Three pairs of chosen ones. Could it be that Mildred, Doc, J.B. and Jak were nearby?

One thing he could say for certain: whoever these warriors were, they were not real in the sense that the men who now stood at his shoulder were real. Krysty had joined the warriors of their party as they emerged from the shelter, and was also casting an eye over the battle unfolding in front of them.

"I don't recognize any of the Sioux in there," she murmured.

"They're not from this tribe," Ryan returned softly. "There's some seriously weird shit going on here. There's either more than one tribe of Sioux around here, or—"

"Or these warriors aren't for real," she said, shaking her head.

"What does your doomie sense tell you?" Ryan questioned.

Krysty shrugged, then bit her lip. "There's something going on here that's dangerous, but I just don't get it off these guys," she said, indicating the battle in front of them. "We need to be triple red, but not about this."

As if to emphasize this point, one of the warriors watching with them said, "Who are these men who claim to be us? Their warpaint is not the same."

"Mebbe they're what your people used to be like," Krysty said to him. Then, when he looked puzzled, added, "Mebbe we're not seeing what's happening now. Mebbe it's what did happen."

The warrior's face brightened with understanding and joy. "You mean that the Grandfather is showing us the great battles of the past so that we may understand the way ahead?"

"Yeah. Something like that," Krysty said. The warrior turned to tell his fellows of this great sign, while Ryan shot Krysty a questioning glance. She shrugged once again. "It may be a replaying of something from the past. That doesn't mean that it's some great spirit trying to tell us something. Just means that there's something out there playing weird shit games with us."

"So we need to keep it triple red and real frosty."

"You can say that again."

STILL TRYING TO COME to terms with the sudden cessation and disappearance of snow, Jak and Doc led their war party in the direction that had been laid out for them by the shaman before they had left the Pawnee settlement. That strange things were happening as they journeyed farther into the areas surrounding the promised land was something to which they would just have to adjust; yet despite this, none of them—whether expecting the spirits to play tricks, or perhaps something more malevolent—were quite prepared for what came next.

The flat grasslands on which they had been traveling began to slowly give way to a landscape that was even sparser, yet more uneven. Ridges and hillocks of earth, tufted with spiky grasses of many colors, began to slow their progress and also to provide shelter for creatures that they could barely glimpse as they raised their heads above the levels of the ground before darting into hiding. Strange chattering sounds echoed from ridge to ridge, almost as if the creatures were talking to one another.

"Jak, what are these creatures?" Doc asked in an undertone. He didn't wish to be overheard, as he could already see that the noises made by the creatures were unsettling the warriors who rode with them, and he had no desire to add to this dread.

"Not seen before," Jak said, with an almost imperceptible shake of the head. "Not ever," he added for emphasis. "Weird shit muties some kind."

"Perhaps," Doc said cautiously, mindful of the thoughts he was forming about the region in which they traveled. "If they are, we should be careful of what else may be here."

"If not?" Jak questioned. Unspoken was the further question of what they might be, if not muties.

"If not, we should not be surprised about what may happen," Doc mused. "I mean, really not surprised."

Jak's brow furrowed. He figured that Doc had some crazy bastard idea that was so crazy that he was wary of discussing it. But that didn't mean that it wouldn't be right…

While the two men murmured to each other in low tones, the war party had made its way into the middle of a trail that snaked between low hills and ridges that now ran almost unbroken for a distance of about half a mile. It was bright daylight, but despite this the atmosphere as they rode between the ridges dipped like the trail, so that it seemed that the party were riding into a sludge of despondency. This was not helped by the alien nature of the spiky grasses that seemed to loom out of the ground and angle toward the trail, as though narrowing the path until it was almost claustrophobic. Although the warriors still rode tall on their horses, their unease was betrayed by the flickering of their eyes as they uneasily surveyed the banks that rose around them.

The chattering of the concealed creatures was also

enough to stir anxiety in even the most courageous of men. Seeming to echo and rebound from bank to bank, it had a mocking edge, almost breaking into nervous, hyena-like laughter at times. A laugh with an equally anxious note that both mirrored and mocked the men who rode along the narrow passage. Jak and Doc could see that the warriors were holding their nerve, but only just.

What happened next blew that pretence away.

Along the length of the banking, both before and behind the mounted war party, animals began to raise their heads, so that it seemed to Jak and Doc that within the space of a minute there were eyes boring into them from all directions. Some of the animal heads were clearly visible, while others were partially obscured by the grasses, which seemed to wave their multicolored blades and fronds in a manner that seemed a little short of malevolent.

The heads that now peered at them from differing degrees of cover were both surprising and yet not, at the same time. Surprising as they were unlike animals that either Jak or Doc could ever recall seeing, both on their travels across the continent, and also in the time that they had spent in the company of the Pawnee. And yet this was also the very thing that made them no surprise at all. For, since they had been ensconced with that tribe, they had seen many strange mutations and variations that seemed to occur just the once.

So the sharp, rodent noses and dark glittering eyes of some; the full muzzles and piebald markings of others; and yet again the rounded skulls, equally round and searching eyes, and drooping, thick whiskers of others came as no real surprise.

What was disturbing, though, was the manner in which the faces now beheld them. There was an intelligence in those gazes that went beyond any ideas of animal instinct and cunning. It was a gaze that, odd as it seemed to even contemplate, betrayed an ability for rationality and logical thought that was human. Looking at some of the animals, even more human than many of the people that he had met in his time in this place, Doc paused. It was a thought that he tried to dismiss from his mind with alacrity, as he realized that this very notion made sense of the chattering voices that had followed them for some time.

If the idea of animals evolving language could be said to make sense.

"Jak, do not take anything we see or hear as being a thing of solid reality," he cautioned under his breath.

The albino youth shook his head. "Won't. Not feel any more right than snow. But you get them to do same." He indicated the warriors riding ahead and abreast of them.

Doc nodded. "We should, perhaps, be watching them more than these phantoms that beset us."

Jak shot him a strange look. Doc wasn't sure if the albino teen had truly grasped his meaning, but any further attempt to explain was cut short by the sudden voice from his left.

"You think we won't hurt you if you pretend we don't exist?"

Doc whirled to face the sound. A creature with raccoon markings on a face that betrayed more than a trace of rat and dog in its strange shape looked him squarely in the eye.

"Do you address me?" he asked, aware even as he spoke of how absurd he must sound.

"If you wish," the creature said. "If, in the country of the blind the one-eyed man is king, then in the kingdom of the mad only he who is not sane can make sense of what is happening around."

"You talk in a very similar manner to myself," Doc mused to the creature. He was aware that he had lagged behind the warriors, who rode on ahead, seemingly intent of passing through this point as swiftly as was possible. Jak was midway between the two, turning his mount to face Doc, a puzzled expression fleetingly crossing his otherwise blank visage as he wondered why Doc had dropped behind them.

"Perhaps that is because it is an idiom that you will easily understand," the creature replied. If not for the fact that its facial muscles weren't constructed for such an act, Doc could have sworn that it was smiling at him. No, more: mocking him.

An insect, like a dragonfly but with the wings and markings of a red admiral butterfly, fluttered in the space between them.

"You tell him. You got him on the run, and he don't know what's real and what ain't," it squeaked in a high-pitched and belligerent tone.

"The very crux of the matter," Doc murmured. Panic—the fear that he was losing his tenuous grip on

sanity at a time when he may most need it—poked ten-
tacled fingers of doubt into his mind. Quelling this fear,
he tried to reason with the creature, and thus, he suspected, with himself. He continued. "If you were real,
you would be a most unusual type of mutie. One the like
of which I have not yet seen."

"I could be," the creature said slyly.

Doc allowed himself a small smile. "Indeed. That
would not be entirely beyond the bounds of possibility.
And yet what, I ask myself, are the chances of such a
creature not only being able to speak, but to do so in
tones that are not so far removed from mine. I am no
egotist, but I doubt that such a manner of speech is prev-
alent anywhere in a land such as this."

"True," the creature said to him, "but is it also not a
possibility that I am a mimic, and like a bird such as—
say—the parrot, I am able to assimilate the styles of
those who I encounter?"

Doc gave a short, barking laugh. "But the parrot is
not a bird heard often on these shores, I would wager.
How would you know of such a thing? And again, such
mimics are just that—they do not have the intelligence
and ability to think constructively that would enable
speech such as yours, unless…"

"He's talking from his ass," buzzed the insect.
"You got him on the ropes. Cogent argument ain't his
suit."

"Indeed not," Doc muttered. "I would say that a
kind of insanity is closer to the mark. And perhaps that
is what this is—even if you are a real creature, stand-

ing watching, then the words are not yours but from my own head."

"Now you're getting it," the creature urged. "You're almost there, Dr. Tanner." There was an edge to its voice as it uttered his name that made his blood run cold.

Doc turned and looked ahead, to where the warriors were still riding through the passage. Other animals were peering from the grasses and over the edge of the banks. He could hear the chattering, whispering voices that he had been hearing for some time, and he realized why they had been making something that only approximated to sense; something that was on the edge of comprehensible, yet not quite.

"Jak, don't listen, whatever it seems to be saying," Doc yelled as he could see the albino teen become entranced and intrigued by what a creature with the build of a bear and the face of a rat was saying to him. Doc could not hear the voice from this distance, as it spoke— as did the creature talking to him—with a soft, almost whispering tone. He realized why they did this.

Beyond, he could see creatures of varying hues and builds leaning farther out from the banks, whispering in those sibilant, seductive tones. The warriors—despite their best efforts to ignore the distractions and continue without stopping—found themselves intrigued by whatever it was that was being muttered and murmured to them. Their progress became halting.

Doc had no doubt that the creatures were speaking to them in the tongue of the Pawnee. Just as he had no doubt that the creature talking to Jak would use the same truncated version of the language that had become so identifiable with the albino.

"Very clever, Dr. Tanner. Clever, but not quick. You were never that fast, were you. A pity…"

He whirled so that he was facing the raccoon-faced creature once again. Its eyes were large and reflective: so much so that he was sure he could see himself in the orb of its iris. He was fish-eyed and distorted, but there was no disguising the look of horror on his face, even in such a bizarre mirror.

"He's got it, he's got it," the insect mocked as it buzzed around his head. He swatted at it and missed. "Gotta be quicker than that, you old buzzard," it cackled.

"Much quicker," the creature in front of him said, so quietly as to be almost to itself.

"No!" Doc yelled. So loud that it felt as though all the oxygen in his lungs had been expelled in one manic act, and there was little left to power his body.

Illusion? Fantasy? Mutated, hard fact? It could be any of these things, but he wasn't going to take a chance on it being something that couldn't cause real, physical harm.

Doc pulled at his horse's reins, turning it to face the warriors and Jak. He kicked his heels savagely, the only thought he gave to his steed being the desire to get the damned horse moving quicker than it ever had before. Ahead of him, beyond his fellow travelers, he could see that the bank extended on for another three or four hundred yards. They were almost at the end. That was why it happened now, obviously. Before it was too late.

"Ride, don't look, ride," he yelled hoarsely, having

hardly the breath in him to force the words out. He whipped past Jak at such a speed that his horse caused the albino's to rear. Jak wrestled with it and cursed the old man, yet he was grateful for the action, as it seemed to break an almost hypnotic hold that the creature speaking to him seemed to have established. He dug in, urging his horse to gallop after Doc as the old man headed straight into the pack of warriors, scattering and awakening them in a similar manner.

As Jak set off after Doc, he could see that the old man was focused only on reaching the end of the bank. And he was soon aware why.

The creatures, who had been observing or talking from the banks, and had seemed so placid just moments before, were now ravening maws and throaty, bloodlusted yells that sprang forward from the banks, emerging from the shelter and shade of the multicolored grass to stand and loom over the riders as they picked up speed.

Or at least, most of them seemed to stand and loom. Darkening shadows around them cut across the sky, and the air whistled and moved around Jak's head as if some of the creatures were launching themselves on the attack. He felt the air pressure move as though they brushed against him, against the horse. On the periphery of his vision he saw them dart and feint. Ahead, they seemed to move in on the warriors and on Doc, with an awkward grace that belied their strange shapes. Instinctively, Jak guided his horse around the obstacles, all the while being aware at the back of his mind that these things may not be really there. Something Doc had said, allied to the fact that they seemed to have no scent, made him sure that they were somehow illusory.

Yet could he afford to take the chance?

Like hell…

An open mouth with razor teeth in two rows appeared in front of him, sweeping up to take off his head. He ducked back and almost lost his seat on the horse, staying on its back only by straining his thigh muscles as he gripped the horse's flanks. The mouth snapped, and he saw a bearlike muzzle with orange striped markings and dark-rimmed, obsidian eyes flash past him.

Yet it had no scent, no rancid breath.

The last few yards seemed to last an age as the creatures—either real or illusion—leaped from the bank to chase after him. Ahead, he could see that Doc and the warriors were clear, and that they had come to a halt, stopped by something that they could see ahead of them, yet he couldn't.

He pulled up his horse as he leveled with them, and looked back over his shoulder. The bank was still there, but there were no grasses of many colors; no creatures, either, talking or otherwise.

And then he turned to face the others, and saw what had stopped them in their tracks.

Chapter Nineteen

"Our forefathers fight before us so that we may draw strength from their battles," cried a tribesman, falling to his knees.

There were murmurs of agreement from the other Otoe warriors as they lined up to watch the fighting as it unfolded in front of them. Even Little Tree, who had been assiduous in his desire to straddle the line between his people and the strangers who had been sent to lead them, now found himself drawn in breathless awe to the panoply of violence.

It was as though the different tribes had ridden into a valley, descending with war whoops and chanted yells to meet and clash in the basin of that valley.

Yet, as they watched, both J.B. and Mildred were sure that the terrain had been flat when they first viewed it. It was as though the landscape was molding itself to the shape dictated by the desires of the watchers.

"Someone—or something—is yanking my chain. And it is really starting to piss me off," Mildred said softly, but with emphasis.

"Guess we can worry about who or what later," J.B. mused. "The real question right now is why." And, when

Mildred shot him a questioning glance, he said, "This isn't happening for no reason. Thing that really worries me is if these boys take it into their heads to stop looking, and start fighting."

"They couldn't do any harm," Mildred replied. "They'd be fighting ghosts. Besides which, you told them to ready themselves for battle yourself, John."

"Could still do each other damage," J.B. said. "And it always pays to be triple red. Don't think they're for real now, but they might well have been from a distance." Then, indicating to the far side of the conflagration, he added, "Besides which, that sure isn't an illusion. Not unless whatever's behind this knows more than we even think it does."

"HOLD YOUR POSITIONS," Ryan yelled. "Don't move in on the fight. We need to find out who or what we're up against before we charge." His words were urgent, as he could see the desire to fight grow in the men gathered around Krysty and himself.

One of the warriors turned to Ryan, angry. "These are our people. Our ancestors. They have been returned to this world so that they can help us."

"How do you figure that?" Krysty snapped.

"Woman, do not talk of things you do not understand," another of the warriors countered. "Things that you, too, do not understand, One-eye," he added. "The ways of the white-eyes do not allow for the spirits and the ways in which they talk to us. This is our time. You have led us here, but we have been picked for our courage. Now is the time to show that."

Ryan wanted to tell them that the battle that raged before them may not be real. He wanted to explain about the hallucinations that he and Krysty had seen in their travels, and how the mind could be tricked. But even as this flitted across his consciousness, he knew that it would be fruitless. These people had been isolated for generations, looking back to ways that preceded the tech that might be causing the weird shit they had encountered. They would never believe him. Thinking about it, he wondered why they should.

"Ryan…" Krysty began as the warriors mounted their steeds and rode toward the battle at a gallop, whooping like the phantoms who danced in front of them in the ballet of combat.

The one-eyed man shrugged. "Nothing we can do to stop them, Krysty. The only thing we can do is try to see that they don't get themselves too deep in shit."

She watched him mount and start toward the fast receding posse of warriors. He stopped, turning his horse back toward her. She had a sinking feeling in her gut, and her hair crawled close to her nape; yet she knew she couldn't leave Ryan to deal with this on his own. Swinging herself up onto the back of her own steed, she urged it forward. Even as she approached Ryan, she could feel herself having to raise her voice to be heard above the clamor, distant though it still was.

"Better keep it frosty, lover. More than them, for sure."

Ryan flashed her a grin. "Ever known it any other way?"

"THIS MORE WEIRD SHIT like talking bears?" Jak breathed to Doc.

The old man cast a wary eye over the warriors before taking in the vista that confronted him.

"I fear it may well be, young Jak. Whoever or whatever has power in this region is gifted in the manipulation of reality, as they have already amply proved. Whatever is within the region of the prophecy wishes very much to keep its secrets well guarded."

Jak looked at Doc and shook his head. "Lots words, most not matter. Yes or no all asked."

"If only it were that simple. I cannot be sure even of myself, let alone of anything else," Doc told him.

"Be sure of me, Doc. Keep it frosty," Jak said simply.

For all his own verbosity, Doc appreciated the youth's directness. Jak was uncomplicated, and Doc suspected that his own propensity to think and analyze too much would only confuse matters. Trust the young man's instincts.

"The truth is, I am not sure if they are real," Doc said, indicating the three warring tribes who were coming together in a valley below them. "I suspect that there is no valley, only flat plains like those we have traveled. I also suspect that these warriors are illusory. However, I also fear that will count for nothing with our friends."

Jak followed Doc's outstretched hand. The warriors of the Pawnee were rapt in concentration, following the unfolding battle and muttering excitedly to one another in their own tongue.

"Not gonna stop 'em, are we?" he murmured.

Sadly, Doc shook his head. "I fear the most we can do is keep close."

The warriors stopped taking among themselves, their attention taken by a section of the battle where Pawnee warriors were coming under siege from a group of Otoe. Unable to stand idly by while their fellows—albeit ones who may be nothing more than wisps of light—were attacked, they set themselves on a course to intercept.

"Wait!" Doc cried.

"No time," returned one of the warriors, sparing the briefest glance backward. "The Grandfather calls us to act for our destiny."

Before the words could even be lost in the heat and sound of battle, he had turned back and followed his fellow warriors into the melee. There was little Doc or Jak could do except follow.

DUST SWIRLED AROUND THEM, rising up the flanks of the horses, sticking to their sweaty pelts, changing white and piebald into a dusty brown that made it hard to distinguish one from the other. The men atop them also became a screaming, whirling mass of indistinguishable flesh. Sweat and blood made their battle colors run, so that the individual tribal markings became more and more blurred and indistinct, running the heaving mass into something amorphous.

Into the valley, they were now too close to use bow and arrow. Instead, fighting was hand-to-hand, grappling one another from horses to roll under the hooves, exchanging blows and ducking to avoid the feet of the frightened animals. Axes and knives scored flesh, cut to the bone, caused warriors to tumble from their horses screeching in agony.

And yet…

As the three war parties rode into the valley from their separate vantage points, they were all aware of these things: there was no smell of sweat, blood, fear and chilling, which they would have expected. For an area that was seemingly so densely packed with humanity, there was no rise in air temperature as they rode through. And again, if they had descended into a valley they would expect their horses to dip at an angle commensurate with the valley walls, forcing them to adjust their balance. Yet they had ridden straight, their sense of balance telling them that they were on the flat, even though their vision told them something else entirely.

As they moved among the warring factions, it soon became apparent that this was not a real battle. Blows that were aimed toward them, seemingly, by those who came to greet them rose and fell, cutting through without any effect. Similarly, the returned blows by the war party warriors, acting in what they believed to be self-defense, fell on empty air, despite all appearances to the contrary. That only served to unbalance the war parties, both literally and metaphorically.

The Pawnee, the Otoe and the Dakota Sioux moved across the floor of the valley, uncertain as to whether the ground beneath their feet was as it seemed, or was simply flat grassland plains. They struck at phantoms, uncertain as to whether they were real or imagined.

It was only when they caught sight of one another that they were able to define the difference between the imagined and the corporeal.

The flesh-and-blood warriors were somehow more solid than the phantoms that raged around them. Although these seemed at first glance to be solid enough, there was a translucent quality to them that made the denser mass of the real warriors appear to show through the bodies of those around them, so that from a distance it was as though there were three groups of ghosts who moved through the battling throng.

More than that, the real groups could also be defined by the strangers who moved with them. The Pawnee and Dakota Sioux were taken by surprise; the Otoe party not so. They had been forewarned. It had been Doc and Jak, on the far side of what appeared as a valley, who J.B. had seen from a distance and pointed out to Mildred before the war party had begun to move.

Although, at the back of each of their minds, the separated friends had hoped and suspected from the moment that it had been revealed to them that the other messengers from Wakan Tanka would be their missing companions, nonetheless to see them advancing on each other through a battle that didn't, and couldn't, touch them was an experience that none had really expected.

As the three tribes sighted one another, the warriors realizing that here was a real and living enemy, so the strangers decreed by fate or the spirits to lead them to the promised land were forgotten. Each knew that to fulfill the prophecy they had to be the only tribe to reach the sacred place and gain possession of the secrets and the power that would enable them to become triumphant.

In the face of such knowledge, all caution was forgotten. With wild yells that sounded loud above the clamor around them, ignoring the phantoms that fought on unseeing around them, the three parties of warriors charged for one another. In the midst of the ghost battle, to use a bow would beg defeat. Only hand-to-hand, ensuring that a real flesh-and-blood enemy was in your grip, would satisfy.

And yet, despite the fact that the real warriors seemed just that little more solid than the spirit forms around them, still it was hard when at full gallop to determine what was real and what was false. In the midst of such movement, it was too easy to lose sight of the enemy, and find oneself wheeling around to try to grapple with a warrior who was as air when a fist passed through him.

In the whirl of real and unreal, it was hard to keep a focus on who was the enemy, who was friend, and who really existed.

Ryan tried to keep his eye firmly on J.B. and Mildred, as they seemed to wheel the closest to him, the Otoe war party being keenest to engage with the Sioux, but it was difficult to remember who exactly the enemy might be. Particularly when one of the small groups of warring phantoms broke off as he galloped past them, stopping to turn and face him.

"Think you can best the spirits, One-eye?" asked one of the warriors.

"The Grandfather will test you," said another.

A third feinted him, making his horse rear as he tried to pull back, to avoid any engagement; thinking even as he did so that it was absurd that these creatures from another time and place should speak to him, let alone that he should fear them causing him harm.

"Ha! Nearly got you that time." The ghost warrior laughed. "Mebbe next time."

Jak and Doc saw this happen as they tried to round up the Pawnee war party and pull them back. Having long since decided that an engagement under such mind-altering circumstances could be of no benefit, they were having problems in rounding up their warriors, whose lust for combat had now been inflamed by the knowledge that at least some of the enemy were real.

Watching Ryan draw back, Jak asked, "How we know Ryan and others real, not like rest of this shit?"

"We have no guarantees, but I would wager they are as real as us," Doc replied, adding to himself, "But of our reality I could not say, right now."

Krysty moved in on Ryan as his horse threatened to throw him. She grabbed at the reins, speaking quietly, but in an authoritative tone that could be heard even over the roar of the phantoms around them.

"Easy, lover, don't let them get to you."

"How the fireblasted hell can they be talking to me when they don't exist?" he asked in return, his tone speaking of a man desperate to keep his grip on sanity and reality.

She shook her head. "Don't question. Let's just get our boys back to the edge of this shit, then take it from there."

As a plan, it was as good as any. If they could disengage from the mayhem being played out around them, then at least they could take stock of the situation, form an overview and a plan of action.

It was a strategy that suited all three parties—or at least, those who were the nominal leaders. In their turn, Mildred and J.B. were also trying to pull the Otoe war party away from their desire to clash with the Sioux. At least they were assisted by this in Little Tree. The Otoe warrior had spent enough time getting to know the Armorer that he felt he could trust in his judgment.

Slowly, almost interminably, the three war parties began to pull away from the phantom battle that still raged around them. The Sioux were hastened by further bizarre occurrences: on three occasions, warriors were startled to find that the horses of their phantom enemies turned and chided them for their lack of courage.

Once it became an entrenched idea that the battle raging around them had no physical reality, pulling away from it proved to be easy. Ryan and Krysty, J.B. and Mildred, Jak and Doc now found it easy to round up their respective war parties and pull them back to the positions from which they had entered the fray.

Within a matter of minutes, each tribe found itself facing the other two across a valley that they now knew didn't really exist. The warring tribes between them became as shadows, and it was simple now to see that each tribe faced the others with a small, but equal, number of warriors. And for the friends who had been separated for so long, it seemed that their companions were within reach, yet infinitely out of the same. A small distance seemed to be insurmountable.

"The spirits have been testing us," one of the Sioux warriors said to Ryan, his eyes fixed on the opposing parties as he spoke. "The grandfather has tested us, and with your help—the help of his chosen messengers—we are now in a position where it is our courage, and ours alone, that will be tested against the others."

Across the divide, Mildred questioned a similar statement from one of the Otoe.

"If Wakan Tanka is giving us to you as messengers, then why has he done that to the other tribes?"

Farther still across the divide, the same question from Doc elicited a response from a Pawnee warrior.

"We three tribes have kept the old ways alive. But only one of us is pure enough of heart and courage to take the ways of our people across the lands. It will be a hard road, and what better way to prove our worthiness for that road than by besting the other tribes."

This theme was taken up, in its own manner, by a Sioux warrior who faced Ryan and Krysty.

"The spirits have tested us with things that are strange beyond imagining, and we have come through these trials. Now we face that which is real—the last obstacle to our destiny."

The meaning for each group was clear—the road to

the promised land, and a prophecy fulfilled, could only be reached at the expense of the other two tribes.

A battle was imminent.

As though the spirits had heard the words of the warriors, the valley and the battle in front of them started to fade away. Or perhaps it was just the land, and whatever controlled it, responding to the changes in their thoughts. If an intelligence was behind this, then perhaps the six friends who sat at the head of their respective war parties would need to pay heed. Right now, though, there were more pressing concerns.

The land between them reverted to the flat grassland plain that it had been before the vision of battle had formed. The three war parties could see that there was only the blank space of empty distance between them. All around was flat land, with nothing to provide shelter or a strategic point from which to hole up and mount attack or counterattack.

Nowhere to hide.

No way to delay the inevitable until the friends had worked out a way in which they could unite without becoming embroiled in combat.

There was a short pause, during which the air crackled with the tension that shot between the three war parties like ball lightning, bouncing off each in turn. A pause during which it was almost painful to draw breath, knowing that any movement could break the fragile peace that, strung between the three war parties, was like the shell of the thinnest egg, waiting to be cracked underfoot.

The moment extended to a breath that was like an infinite prayer to Wakan Tanka, each party asking the Grandfather to bless them in this moment of truth.

And then it was broken. One warrior, unable to stand the tension that built in his chest like an inflated bladder that stopped him breathing, and felt as though it would crack his ribs with the pressure, gave vent to this feeling, perhaps even to try to relieve the pressure that threatened to suffocate him.

With this, the peace was ripped apart. Spurred by the cry, the horses whinnied with excitement and fear, their eyes rolling as they bucked and broke ranks, the warriors on their backs as wild-eyed as their mounts, yelling now as loudly as they could, whipping themselves into a frenzy as they charged at one another.

The six friends, try as they each might to stay aloof from the charge, found that it was impossible. Their horses responded to the herd instinct and bolted, despite their best efforts to keep them back.

So it was that they found themselves caught up in the wild ride: before they could bring their horses under control, they had been thrust into the midst of battle. And this one was for real. The warriors from each tribe were hell-for-leather, axes and knives ready to cut, hack and slash at one another as they closed for close combat. To go face-to-face, hand-to-hand with those others who had been chosen by their respective tribes would be the only real way in which they could prove how worthy they were to gain the secrets of power for their people.

Now the dust that was kicked up was real: thick and

choking as they circled one another, with barely room to move as the arena of combat grew smaller. The warpaint on each warrior was already blurred by sweat. Now it grew slicker and more indistinct as real flesh was cut, real blood was spilled. The metallic tang of fresh blood mingled with sweat from both the warriors and their horses. Fear added an undertone to the mix, driving the warriors on as each scented defeat in his opponents.

In the middle of the fight, the friends fought defensively, rather than the following the offensive stance of the warriors. They had no wish to chill those they had ridden with, nor others with whom they had no personal fight. But at the same time, they needed to stop those warriors from harming them. All the while, they kept an awareness of their surroundings. They didn't want to be sucked into the center of the fight: to keep on the fringe was the aim, so that they may put themselves in a good position for escape at the first opportunity.

It was not long in coming. Experience in combat soon told, and while the brave but wild and unskilled tribesmen gathered in a confused melee, the six friends soon found themselves on the outer fringe of the fight, and so were able to pull themselves away from the choking clouds of dust and the scent of chilling.

It happened so suddenly that it was almost as bizarre as some of the things they had seen in the times leading up to this point: they faced each other around the fringes, as though seeing one another for the first time.

Ryan looked around for some kind of cover or shelter to which they could withdraw and regroup.

And there it lay: fringed by trees of green, orange and purple blossom, a valley that was an oasis of green in the otherwise sparse plain. Thick scrub and grasses, verdant around a stream that burbled on the center, it lay about a half mile to the east.

Ryan was sure that it hadn't been there a short time before, when he had looked around for signs of cover when the tribesmen had faced off against one another. In truth, he was almost certain that it was another illusion. But it offered some respite; and the fact that it appeared meant that the location had some significance. For whatever reason, each illusion that had appeared in front of them had been there for a purpose.

Something—someone?—was directing them to this valley of illusion. Faced with this challenge or being sucked back into the fight from which they were disentangling, it needed little thought.

At least the valley may offer some answers.

"IT's NOT REALLY THERE. You realize that, of course," Doc said. They were the first words that any of the friends had uttered since they had separated themselves from the warring tribesmen and begun to ride toward the idyllic valley.

"Yeah, I know," Ryan said simply. "But there's something that it's covering. That's how this shit works, right?"

"It would appear to be so, dear boy," Doc murmured.

The party of six rode on in silence, not even pausing to look back at the tribesmen. It was obvious that none of these would follow them to the so-called promised land until they had satisfied their honor, each by wiping out the other. At least they had the luxury of a little time until that happened. And just maybe time was all they would need.

They rode into the valley, a silence falling. Each pair figured that they would have had similar experiences leading to this point, particularly if the legends surrounding the tribes, and the way in which they lived, were similar. There would be time to discuss and compare these experiences later. For now, they had to keep alert and face the immediate future with no distractions.

Although they knew that the land was flat scrub, they had the impression of riding down a slope and into the valley. The trees hung heavily over a path that was well worn, the grass there being reduced to a bare carpet, flattened by constant use. This path took them to the brook that bubbled and flowed over a bed of stones, appearing from beneath the ground, running for several hundred yards, then disappearing once again into the ground. Rustling sounds on the canopy of leaves above them, and in the scrub, betrayed the presence of small animals and birds, although there were no visual clues as to what species may be in this vision.

Whatever powered this illusion didn't quite have the strength to paint the picture with quite so much detail, Doc mused. What, he wondered, could be at the root of this strange experience?

Ryan held up his hand, gesturing them to halt. When they had gathered, he spoke.

"If this is the place we've been looking for—or has

been looking for us—then what the hell is it? And what the fuck are we looking for?"

"Something tech, not spirits, that's for sure," J.B. said, uneasily eyeing the surrounding territory. He couldn't swear to it, but he was sure that it had changed slightly...was changing every time he turned his head and then looked back. He continued, telling them in a few brief words that were punctuated by nervous glances around, about the redoubt he had seen with Little Tree, and the maps he had brought with him.

"Makes sense," Krysty affirmed. "The Dakota Sioux had a redoubt under the caves they lived in."

"Pawnee got one, too," Jak added. "Never use it except as shelter, but there all the same."

J.B. produced the maps and charts that he and Mildred had taken from the redoubt, dismounting as he did so. The others joined him, all now looking around with mixed levels of confusion and fear.

"Changing all time," Jak murmured. "Not much, but enough. And smells fake."

"I daresay it is, lad," Doc murmured. "Whatever is producing this has only the most tenuous hold on reality. As I fear for myself," he added with a grim chuckle.

"Yeah, well, we all knew that about you," Mildred commented as she helped the Armorer to unfold the charts. As they did, she looked at the others intently. "You know the real big problem we've got right now? These charts may show us where all the redoubts in the area are, but do we actually know where we are?"

"I can work that out," J.B. replied, his eyes flickering up to the position of the sun.

"Normally I'd be with you on that, John," Mildred told him, "but how the hell can we be sure that the sun we're looking at is in the right place? How can we be sure of any accuracy in what we're seeing?"

"We can't," Ryan said, taking the chart from her, "but if we can work out what kind of redoubts they had in these parts…"

"Then mebbe we can work out what's behind this weird shit and why it's brought us here," J.B. finished.

"But why us?" Doc asked plaintively.

"Not us, Doc. The Native Americans," Mildred said quietly. "It's their legend, and we just stumbled into it." Briefly, again mindful that time was of the essence, she told them what the old seer Milled Red had said to her.

When she had finished, Jak—who had been looking around while she had been speaking—turned back to them.

"Tell you something else…looks like just us now."

The others took a moment to listen. He was right. Silence reigned where previously there had been the sounds of the battling tribesmen. The illusory valley had cut them off from the outside. Was it, they wondered, also sheltering them from those who may be outside looking in?

"Mebbe that gives us all the time we're going to need," Ryan murmured, aware that the shifting landscape was changing once more.

"Mebbe we won't need it," Krysty added. "Look."

Behind Ryan and J.B., the landscape melted into a

hazy dissolve, reassembling itself once again so that a small outcrop of bare rock was revealed. Recessed into this was a door, visible against the rock only because the camou disguising it had eroded. It was a small door, enough for two people abreast.

J.B. consulted one of the charts he held. There were few redoubts of this small size that were marked.

"Dark night," he murmured as he realized a truth that had been staring him in the face all along, "that would explain everything."

Chapter Twenty

They let the horses go, watching them wander off to pick at the grass that was real, as opposed to the abundance that seemed to grow all around. Too late to be of use, perhaps, but Jak at least realized that the animals had a firmer grasp of the real than any of the six of them. No matter: the horses would be of no use to them once they entered the redoubt.

Moving to the entrance, they could see that not only had erosion revealed the once-concealed entrance, but it had also left a residue that lay undisturbed against the door.

"No one's come out of there in a long, long while," Mildred said softly.

"Doesn't mean they haven't been happy to stay inside," Krysty countered in equally soft tones.

"Triple red, people," Ryan murmured, drawing his SIG-Sauer for what seemed like the first time in an eternity.

While the others also drew and checked their blasters—an alien feeling after the insistence of the tribes on a more ancient form of weaponry—J.B. put the maps and charts back in his bag, knowing that their use was now at an end, and racked the mini-Uzi before standing in front of the area on the wall next to the door where the concealed keypad would be.

"Not sure if I hope this is still working or not," he said as his fingers played over the rock surface, searching for the catch that would reveal the entry panel. Deft probing soon caused a section of rock to swing on a hinge, and a familiar keypad device was revealed. J.B. turned to the others. "Figure it'll be a standard code, seeing as it's not a standard entry?"

Ryan shrugged. "Only one way to find out." Then, turning to the others, "Keep it triple red."

J.B. thought about it for a moment. All redoubts had different internal codes, but the exit and entrance to the outside usually ran on a standardized code. Why that should have been, he could only guess. Maybe so that returning soldiers being pursued could effect an easy entry if panic set in? That would make sense. His own nerves were making his fingers tremble slightly as he keyed in the familiar code.

Why was he, well, scared? It wasn't like him. But there was something that was causing a tightening in his gut. His fingers hovered over the last digit of the code, and he stole a look at the others. Jak was impassive, as ever, but he could see that Mildred was anxious from the furrowing on her brow. Ryan was sweating. Krysty's hair was tight to her scalp and neck. Doc had a nervous tick in his right cheek.

"We're not so calm, here," he said. "Sure we're ready?"

"I think it's whatever's been screwing with our heads

for some time. There's nothing really to fear, other than what we've faced dozens of times," Mildred said, unable to keep the tension from her voice, which was tight and high. "As long as we remember that."

"And also that there could be something," Ryan added. "But if there is, it'll be some inbred with a blaster. And we've blown away plenty of those. Do it, J.B."

The Armorer nodded and hit the last digit. With a creak that betrayed its age, the doors to the redoubt began to retract into the rock on either side. The left-hand door squealed as though in agony as it hit a piece of rock that had slid into the groove, making them wince.

"Even if their sec cams have gone, anyone who's in there's gonna know we're here now," J.B. commented.

It was a nothing remark, and yet somehow it defused some of the tension that had run between them. At a nod from Ryan, J.B. slid into the corridor that ran behind the doors. The others fell into an all-too familiar formation, even though it seemed an age since the last time.

The corridor was fairly narrow—about two yards across—and was white-painted concrete. It extended down at an angle for about twenty yards before it became a dogleg stairwell. It was well-lit: the fluorescent tubes that ran overhead, if triggered by the door mechanism as was usual, had either been well maintained or little used.

As Ryan was the last to enter, he keyed in the code to close the door, which shuddered and squealed back into place behind them. There was little sign of life within. The corridor was dust-free, and almost below the level of their hearing, the hum of the life support system and antistatic air purifier was an omnipresent drone.

The stairwell was open, and they took it in stages, Ryan now in the lead. Each flight, down to the platform that led to a corridor level, was secured by Ryan covered by the rest of the companions. It took them time, but it was essential to be certain.

On the first level, their hearts pounded as they traversed the corridor. Again, the overhead lighting was unforgiving and revealing. No shadows for any enemy to lurk; by the same token, no place for them to hide if ambushed.

The redoubt was small by the standards of most, but that still left a number of rooms that could hide an enemy. And all doors were closed.

Each one was taken the same way: swiftly, and with a minimum of risk. Krysty and Mildred covered either side of the door while Jak entered and secured the room. Corridor covered by Ryan and Doc while J.B. scouted the next door down.

It was monotonous, but necessary. Potentially hidden enemies had to be dealt with. Yet the first level was completely empty. Sec rooms, with camera monitors that showed a completely empty redoubt, and an outside that was sparse, bare and bore no relation to the lush landscape that they had ridden into; maintenance tech rooms and an armory that were dustless, cool, and had a stillness that could only come from decades of emptiness.

The second level yielded a similar result: dorms and common rooms that were tidy and had an air of being uninhabited for some considerable time; a kitchen that had supplies in store cupboards, refrigerators and freezers that looked as though they had never been broken into; storerooms with military-issue clothing that looked as though it had never been used.

And no signs of personnel at any time. It was as though the redoubt had been kitted out, and never actually put into commission.

And yet...

The third level contained offices and tech rooms. The comps chattered gently to themselves, a background burble almost as unobtrusive as the hum of the life support system. They stayed awhile here, examining the comp readouts and screens.

"What I want to know is," Mildred said, looking around, "why this place looks like it was never lived in, when it must have been."

"How do you know it was?" Ryan queried.

Mildred shook her head, her beaded plaits shadowing her face. "Everything has led us—the tribes—here. This is the place that the prophecy leads them to. Milled Red, an elder, told me that the old legends weren't that old, that they dated back to fairly recent predark times. That's got to mean that the Native Americans knew something about this place. And to do that—"

"Someone had to live and work here, so that word could get out," Krysty finished. "Right. But how does this tie in to the tribes? They hated this shit."

Mildred frowned. "I figure we find out the answer to one, it'll tell us the answer to the other."

Jak sniffed the air. "Let's clear rest this place then come back. Smells empty, but—"

"Who would trust their senses after the last day or so," Doc finished. "Quite right, dear boy. Ryan?"

The one-eyed man nodded. "Let's do it."

Despite the fact that it was almost perfunctory, they proceeded as before. Schematics they had found on the first level told them that there was just the one level below this, and they secured it easily.

And there they found the only sign of life, mechanical or otherwise. This level consisted of a single, open-floor plan, with a number of consoles and terminals. One end of the room was taken up by the armaglass structure of a mat-trans chamber, the controlling console at a safe distance. The other end had equipment for an indeterminate means. It was also the only source of sound other than the hum and chatter they had already heard.

A high-pitched, two-tone alarm sounded. It had been audible from the bend in the stairwell as they approached, and as they entered the open level they could see that it was accompanied by a flashing blue screen.

Mildred and Krysty approached it first. After experimentally tapping a few keys and gaining no result, Krysty read out the screen to the others.

"'Sector 27. Tank leak. Condition orange. Suggested action, immediate repair, gangway 5. Leak status, low-level. Potential, blue. Survey result, hairline crack, pressure potential to rise to rupture.'"

"Any idea how long that Klaxon has been sounding?"

Mildred asked, peering over Krysty's shoulder. As she spoke, she joined Krysty in trying to access the screen, but with little result.

"So it could be recent, or that bastard could have been sounding for years," Ryan stated.

"Must be fairly recent," J.B. mused, "otherwise that crack would have given way by now, and the whole fucking thing would have blown."

"Indeed, my dear John Barrymore, but surely the more pertinent question is, what it is that would have been expelled?" Doc murmured, looking around.

"What are you looking for?" Ryan asked, momentarily puzzled as he tried to follow Doc's line of thought; something that was never easy at the best of times.

Doc fixed them with a stare. "I should have thought it obvious. Tanks, leaks, storage… I'm sure Mildred will agree with me. This only suggests one thing to those who are familiar with whitecoat thinking."

Mildred agreed. "Nerve agents. Gases. Chem weaponry. Mostly outlawed by international law before the nukecaust, but I've seen enough of what happened next to think that those kinds of things didn't matter shit. If this is a chem weapons base, then that shit leaking out could be why we were seeing things like we were dropping acid—like jolt," she added, seeing their unfamiliarity with the term. "And if the tanks are near, then there could be some residual shit that can get past even the strongest air filters."

"Hence our need to find protective masks or clothing," Doc urged. "I cannot stress the importance."

"We'll look for that shit, then try to work out how to stop this from getting worse. Otherwise there's not much chance of us getting out of here in one piece," Ryan said. Trapped in an explosion, disabled by hallucination, facing the tribesmen who waited, crazed by hallucinatory gas outside the redoubt if they didn't risk the mat-trans, even risking the mat-trans if they were contaminated in some way by the nerve agent: all that crossed his mind as he led them back up two levels to where the stores were located.

Was it imagination, or was there some residue of the gas starting to leak into the life-support system? That anxiety that he knew they had all felt since before entering—the realization of which he had seen on J.B.'s face before he hit the entry code—was now exacerbated by the sudden flickering at the corner of his eye. Figures, vague and shadowy or else clear but transparent, moved in and out of the periphery of his vision. They were not threatening, but nonetheless unnerving. Military personnel going about their business as they might have done before the nukecaust, like ghosts…like the phantoms they had seen outside on the plain. Was this how the gas worked, tapping into the unconscious, the latent psyche, and suggesting images and imaginings that were already there?

He caught Krysty looking at him, and from the briefest of acknowledgments he knew that she, too, could see these things. The quicker they found protective clothing, the better.

Thankfully, when they reached the second level and

the stores, they were able to find chem protection suits and masks easily, and donning them only took a few minutes. The filters on the masks of the suits were easy to operate, and it was only when he could see that all his people were suited and protected that Ryan was able to breathe easier.

But still, he knew, there was an imperative of time. They had to move.

Hurriedly, they returned to the level that acted as an operations base for the redoubt. There was little that Ryan could do for the moment—J.B., Jak or Doc, either, for that matter—as it was down to Krysty and Mildred to work out how the comp system would yield its secrets.

Mildred exclaimed in delight as she hit a key and a screen unrolled from the ceiling and a menu flickered into view, a visual journal made by the successive commanding officers of the redoubt. She clicked on the last entry. The image of a graying, crew-cut officer with a face that was pitted and lined came on-screen. After logging-in preliminaries, his report was brief and concise.

"December 14, 2000. Essential maintenance has been completed, and the skeleton crew is now ready to depart. If tests prove positive, then the next report I make will be when we return as a full complement in precisely twelve months' time. This will enable the last traces of the accident to evaporate. Until such time, regular maintenance visits will be made by suited technicians on a monthly basis. It is to be hoped that their reports will be positive. Of those contaminated, all mil-

itary personnel have been hospitalized. The civilian
workers have, by their transient nature, been a little
more difficult to trace—"

Mildred paused the video. "That accounts for it being
like new here," she commented. "Within weeks, the
missiles were launched. Too late to bus in a full detail
when it was nuclear winter up top."

"And this is not the first time that there has been a
leak, obviously," Doc added. "Could you find details?
If what I suspect…"

"Y'know, I think I'm with you on that, Doc…" Mildred started to search the menu for earlier entries, click-
ing on and then dismissing those that promised much
and delivered little. Eventually, however, she found
what she was looking for. The same face came up on
screen. He looked younger, yet it was less than a year
before the final entry: an indication of how tough that
year had been.

"January 30, 1999. Code Seven, day eight. There are
now eighteen personnel in the sick bay. They are responding well to treatment, but it will be some time before they are fully rehabilitated. The leaks have finally
been traced to source. Tank linings were improperly fitted, and seals had not been effective. The workers on the
original construction, who were brought in to fix the
problem, were not at fault. It transpires that documen-
tation supplied by the manufacturers was incorrectly la-
beled, leading to installation instructions that were
defective. I trust that a higher level of authority will take
the necessary punitive action.

"There has been some problem with the construction workers. I understand that the decision to employ an indigenous population was initiated partly because of employment problems in such communities. I would assume this made them an, ah, economic source of labor, as well as appeasing liberal politicians bleating about unemployment levels. I trust this will tell us something about employing unskilled labor. Experienced engineering staff would have been able to draw attention to the defective instruction much sooner.

"I also believe that an indigenous population was used because of their knowledge of the topography and weather patterns in the locale. While the safe concealment of the tanks is paramount, what has happened reveals to me—and I hope this will be officially noted—the dangers of such a practice. Rumors have begun to circulate that the tribes within the population are splitting, and believe that hallucinations induced by leakages are, in fact, divinely inspired revelations.

"The dangers of having such people running around spouting such garbage when they also have sensitive information in their possession are, I hope, obvious—"

Mildred paused the video.

"Bastards," she whispered. "Screw the workers, let them suffer. Just don't let them make a noise about it."

"Except they did, and the noise they made went on awhile lot longer than that joker could ever have thought," Krysty said quietly.

Mildred chuckled and shook her head sadly. "I guess

this is what Milled Red was trying to say to me. The whole idea of going back to the old ways, moving away from what the white-eye people were doing, came from being damaged by those very same people."

"Then why do they want to come here so much?" J.B. asked. "They don't use other redoubts, so—"

"My dear John Barrymore, they do not realize that the promised land of their prophecy is a white-eye institution," Doc said sadly. "I would guess, from the reactions of myself, and what I have heard from others as well as seen, that this foul nerve agent induces visions that are inspired by the subconscious of the subject—"

"Speak proper," Jak interjected.

Doc smiled. "My apologies. It can draw out of you that which is buried in your dreams. These poor workers, subjected to the foul gas, found themselves dreaming of a way of life that would be apart from the world that had so badly treated them. And yet, to gain the power to do this, their subconscious—"

"Told them this would be the best way to get it," Ryan finished.

"And now the leak has spread across the plain with the wind, and created the illusion that things are changing—the weather, those weird shit animals we could never catch—"

"But what about weird muties we catch? And some plants. Real enough, just never saw many of 'em," Jak queried.

Millie shrugged. "I'm no botanist or biologist, but I'm guessing a slow leak would cause particles of the gas to seep into the earth over time. God knows how that could alter DNA."

"It is, I would hazard, irrelevant now. The point is that it has happened, and if it continues there is no knowing the damage it could do. Not just to these tribes, but to the rest of the land should it spread. I am no altruist when it comes to this forsaken pesthole of a continent, but if I am not to buy the farm, then I must ensure…" He shrugged. "We all must, I think."

Mildred nodded, losing the frozen image of the old soldier as she did so, and starting to scan the comp for schematics of the redoubt and surrounding areas. "I think I'm getting this system," she said. "A layout of the tanks has to be here somewhere."

While images whipped past on the screen in front of them, a kaleidoscope of colors and shapes that made sense to Mildred, yet made the heads of some others spin, J.B. turned away. It was obvious that something was bothering him, and Doc felt compelled to ask him what was on his mind.

"It's just that—" J.B. shook his head "—this is going to sound like a crazy talking, but what if the tribes were right? What if their spirits did bring us here?"

Doc pondered for a moment. "Our arrival was a happy accident for them. If the key tenet of their prophecy was that a pair of strangers arrived to lead them to the promised land, then all we did was trigger their illusions."

"But, Doc…why two?"

"Perhaps those who were originally contaminated were led from their wilderness—the scene of the accident—by teams of military who worked in pairs? From such mundane things are legends born."

J.B. snorted. "Yeah, but how come we ended up split into pairs? That's weird. And how come it happened when the stars were aligned for their medicine men?"

"Again, I would say this to you, dear John Barrymore. Perhaps they saw the stars that way because the prophecy said they would be that way when the strangers arrived, and so the traces of nerve agent in the air altered their perception?"

"That's two huge coincidences. Even if you're right, then how come—"

Doc stayed him with a hand on his shoulder. When he spoke, it was softly and with a faraway look in his eye. "Lad, fate is a strange thing. I have seen many strange things in my time, as have you. You know what has happened to me. After all these things, could I truly say to you that there is no divine, or indeed malign, hand behind the workings of man? Perhaps there are forces that are beyond our understanding. Mayhap Wakan Tanka exists, and this is his idea of a joke. Or perhaps the way in which the universe is knitted together has a kind of music to which we can only dance, without ever recognizing the tune."

J.B. fixed Doc with a stare. "Come back, Doc, I'm losing you. What the hell are you trying to say?"

Doc paused for a moment, his eyes clouded and lost in a world of his own. Then, with no prior warning, they cleared. He beamed a dazzling smile at the Armorer.

"More things on heaven and earth, Horatio, as some

hack writer once said. I think, dear boy, all I mean is never say never. Sometimes it is best not to know, just to do."

J.B. was about to tell Doc that he was still none the wiser when Mildred's voice cut across him.

"I hate to interrupt you boys and your little knitting circle, but I think we've got what we need."

J.B. turned to see that Jak and Ryan were already with Krysty and Mildred in front of the drop-down screen. They were all looking at a three-dimensional model of the area, which Mildred was scouting around with the comp cursor. In cutaway, it revealed the locations of the tanks containing the nerve agent in regard to the redoubt. The one that was causing the leak was indicated by a flashing beacon that pinpointed the crack in detail.

"Come over here," Ryan beckoned. "I figure it's pretty clear what we've got to do."

Chapter Twenty-One

"If I had any idea that it would amount to this, I would have perhaps been a little less keen on saving this shit-hole of a land," Doc panted as he carried yet another land mine from the armory, up the flight of stairs that led to the exit corridor, and placed it on one of the two carts that stood in the corridor.

"You think hard? Wait till dig it in." Jak laughed.

"That is right, make it worse," Doc grumbled. He blinked heavily, sweat dripping down his forehead and stinging his eyes. "If only I could take this mask off for a moment."

"Don't even think about it," Ryan snapped. "We can't risk it. We need to be triple red for this."

"I know, I know," Doc sighed. "I was just venting some anger, no more no less."

"Then keep it that way," Ryan cautioned. "We ready, J.B.?"

The Armorer checked the two carts. Each was loaded with twenty land mines, two spades and four SMGs taken from the armory.

"Yeah." He nodded. "This should do it."

The four men paired up—Jak and Doc, Ryan and

J.B.—and started to haul the carts toward the redoubt exit. Loaded down, the carts were heavy, but they were easy compared to the slog of carrying the mines and trolleys up from the level of the armory. It occurred to Ryan that this redoubt had to have elevators of some kind that led to the sites where the tanks were located. But they weren't obviously marked on any schematic Mildred had found, and they didn't have the time to waste. He felt uncomfortable here, even though the anxiety caused by the nerve gas had receded. The sooner they completed this task and were on their way, the happier he would be.

As J.B. tapped in the code, and the redoubt doors slid painfully open, it became startlingly obvious how much they had been affected by the nerve gas. Even though the view from the sec monitors on the first level had given them some kind of indication, it was still shocking to see how much their perception had been altered.

The lush valley was gone. In fact, they could now see that they were not in any kind of valley at all. The land around was flat, with a few areas of scrub and spiky brown grasses fighting their way through the slowly poisoned soil. The tribesmen, whose presence had seemed to fade as they entered the now vanished valley, could be clearly seen only a short distance away. Without the nerve gas to mess with their minds, the four chem-suited men could see that the warriors were executing an absurd ballet in which they seemed to be half fighting one another, and half battling against an enemy that was unseen. The ghosts of their ancestors were invisible without the inducement of chemicals.

Perhaps that was as it had always been.

Pausing only to see if the warriors noticed them, and if they would resultantly become a threat, the four men continued on their way. It was as though they didn't exist to the mounted warriors. They didn't fit in with what the warriors could see, or wanted to see, and so became invisible.

Better that way. A couple of hundred yards from the redoubt entrance, the four men split up. Ryan gestured to Jak and Doc that they take the tanks located to the east, while J.B. and himself would take those to the west. With gestures of acknowledgment, the men hauled their carts in separate directions.

ON THE THIRD LEVEL of the redoubt, Mildred and Krysty were laboring at their own task. Gradually, Mildred had familiarized herself with the comp, and was becoming more adept at finding the information she wanted. Krysty watched her carefully, picked up the codes and entry keys to the running programs, and turned to another of the terminals, using those things she had learned to try to find the program that would give them what they wanted.

"Mildred, I think I've found it," she said quietly. The screen in front of her carried a schematic of the pipes that connected the tanks. She scrolled through several pages while Mildred watched.

"That's it, back one page," Mildred prompted. And,

when Krysty had called up the correct page, added, "That's the one. The program that troubleshoots the faults on the feed lines. Run it."

Krysty clicked on the run instruction, and the women waited impatiently as the comp ticked over, finally flashing up a message that the leak had been located and a program for sealing all tanks at source was available.

"What about the gas already in the pipe?" Krysty queried.

Mildred leaned over her and scanned the figures. "Most of it will be pulled back into the tank by the suction seal. The volume of what might remain is small. We'll have to risk that. Face it, we leave it and then what?"

Krysty shrugged. "Guess it's the only way." She hit the key that triggered the seal, and they waited while the bar appearing across the screen went from empty to full, the percentage figure above it increasing with an almost painful slowness. For both of them, it seemed bizarre to be standing, doing nothing, while the others toiled above. Yet the leakage was not directly from a tank, and no amount of physical labor could replace what the comp was doing.

Still, the relief when the program finished its run, and the tanks were sealed, was palpable.

"Step one." Krysty sighed as she closed the program.

"Now let's get the hell out of here and see if we can help them," Mildred suggested, unable to keep the itching tension from her voice.

"Way ahead of you," Krysty echoed.

IN THE HEAT OF THE SUN, the chem suits made every movement strength sapping. Although the material was light, it seemed to soak up the heat from the sun. All four men could feel their skins roast; sweat prickled and irritated as it formed pools that could not even cool. It was like being broiled alive.

And so it was a delicate balance: the sooner they laid the mines, the sooner they would be able to get some distance between themselves and the source of the chem leak, making it safe to remove the suits and breathe easily once more.

Jak, for the life of him, could not understand why the full body suits were necessary. Doc had tried to explain about the ability of the gas to be absorbed by bare skin, but to Jak it was nonsense. Surely you had to breathe it into your lungs? Still, he abided by Ryan's decision to take as little risk as possible, even though he cursed the suit with every step he took; with every shovel of earth that he moved.

Despite the heat, he and Doc had established a good rhythm. Each man was laying a series of mines around the areas where the tanks lay in their sector. The plan was simple: the tanks were in pits that had been dug and then shored with concrete. That much they had seen on the schematic. They knew the locations, even though the tanks and concrete pits were hidden from their view. However, small outcrops disguised entrances to the pits that were used for maintenance, which had been exposed over the decades since nuclear winter.

The pipelines between the redoubt and the interlinked tanks were also encased in concrete. Those, they knew, would be sealed off via the comp. The fact that one of them had split, and the gas had leaked via concrete cracked by the earth movements postnukecaust, showed that to make the tanks and their concrete coffins completely safe would be an impossibility. There would always be a lurking, ticking bomb. But if they blew the access tunnels, burying the pits, then the tribes, or whoever else discovered and tried to access the tanks, would find it impossible.

Laying mines at the maintenance exits, and at points both between and at a safe distance, ensured that they would seal the tanks as effectively as was possible.

It was a repetitive task, made only marginally easier by the monotony of rhythm. Dig to a depth of three feet, lay the mine and set the timer, fill in the hole, then move on. Ryan and J.B. had calculated that to mine all the tanks and then to mine the redoubt entrance would take two hours. An hour to get away, and then the mines could safely blow.

They were on schedule, but Jak was finding the heat was getting to him, making his muscles cramp. Looking up momentarily, he could see that Doc was slowing. He guessed that it was less cramp, and more that the work was backbreaking for the older man. Cursing to himself, he looked down and continued to dig.

Across at the locations where they were laying the mines, both Ryan and J.B. were feeling the strain. Acutely aware of the time limit he had imposed on his people, Ryan could feel the tension making the muscles at the base of skull knot, at a time when he least needed the pain and tightness.

So it was that he was relieved when he saw Mildred approach them. In the distance, he could see that Krysty was joining Doc and Jak. Both women had picked up spades on their way out of the redoubt, and both—without even a word of greeting—started to dig.

Their efforts spurred on the flagging men, who found reserves of energy both from the assistance, and also from the knowledge that if the women had joined them without fuss, then the tanks had been sealed from the comp. Bury the bastards, and cover the entrance to the redoubt so that it could never again be accessed, and they would have done all that was possible to avert disaster. All that would remain would be to get as far away as possible before the mines detonated. Ryan had opted to take the overland route rather than use the mat-trans. With the residual effects of the gas in their systems, the arduous effects of such a process might have an intensified danger that he wanted to avoid; particularly for Jak and Doc, who had always been the worst affected by previous jumps.

No one in either party spoke until the final mines had been laid around the tanks, and the two crews hauled their now lighter carts to the redoubt entrance.

"So far, so good," Ryan said shortly when they came together. He checked his wristchron. "No time to waste. Everything okay?" he asked Krysty and Mildred. When the women nodded, he said, "Let's get this done and move out."

There were four mines left, and six people to lay

them. Two were placed on each side of the outcrop that acted as cover for the redoubt entrance. Buried just below the surface so that they would crumble the rock around the doors, and cripple the already failing door mechanism, they would effectively seal as well as hide the redoubt. With Ryan and Krysty digging on one side, and J.B. and Mildred on the other, the mines were laid and then the holes filled in by Jak and Doc. It was a process that was speeded by their efficiency, and also by the adrenaline pounding through them with the knowledge that it was a job completed, and time to haul out. Leaving the carts and the spades to be buried by the hoped-for rock fall around the redoubt entrance, they turned to go.

THE VISIONS OF THE PAST had faded, and the bloodlust to destroy one another had likewise begun to recede. The warriors of the three tribes fell back, each too exhausted to go in for the chill. They were battered, bruised and cut, but their skills had been on a par with each other, so despite their own best efforts, each warrior had been unable to land a telling blow.

And now they each faced the others, realizing for the first time that the ones sent to guide them by the spirits had left them to their own battles. Breathing heavily, running with sweat and blood, they looked around as if for the first time.

Though they didn't know it, the slightest of changes in the wind direction had carried the residue of nerve gas away from them. Their perceptions of the world were now in line with what was a common reality. Re-actions no longer fuzzed by a nerve agent in their systems, the rage subsided, and the ability to perceive the landscape around them returned. There were no phantom tribes; no imagined valleys; no hidden groves.

Now there was only the reality of battered and bruised warriors clustered in a loose semicircle, too beaten to fight one another, and wondering why Wakan Tanka had deserted them in their hour of need. Where was the promised land that held the secrets of the prophecy? Where were those who had been sent to guide them?

And who were the six people in odd, bizarre costumes who were turning away from a rock?

"DARK NIGHT," J.B. breathed softly. "If they come for us…"

He did not need to finish the sentence. The others knew what he meant: the entrance to the redoubt was glaring. The mines still had enough time for detonation for the warriors to make an entry.

And the six of them were hampered by chem suits that they dare not remove.

For a few moments, disbelief hung in the air. The warriors couldn't take in what they saw; the friends couldn't believe that the warriors hadn't charged them.

And then the silence was broken by a yell of fury from Little Tree. The Otoe warrior was streaked with his own blood from ax cuts, and couldn't believe that the people he had come to trust had let him—and his tribe—

down in such a manner. Kicking his mount, he drove the steed toward them, his ax held high above his head. Those who followed in his wake needed little encouragement to follow his lead.

"Fireblast! Fan out, try to take them down and save the horses," Ryan yelled, moving as quickly as the cumbersome suit would allow him.

The six chem-suited companions moved out in a spray, putting as much distance between themselves as was possible in the brief time allowed to them, aiming to make themselves impossible to hit in one bunch. Spread the attentions of the attackers, and they may have a chance.

They were armed with their blasters and the SMGs that they had taken from the redoubt. That gave them the advantage, despite the clumsiness engendered by the chem suits and the fact that their opponents were mounted. And yet it rankled with them to have to fight the men they had traveled with, and for whom they had respect despite this attack. The tribesmen were not coldhearts who needed to be wiped out. They were noble warriors whose only crime was to be faithful to their tribe, and the ways with which they had been raised.

It was doubtful that such feelings were reciprocated. The tribesmen charged with a recklessness born of the white-hot anger of betrayal. Their only aim was revenge. It was unlikely that the significance of the rocks in front of which they had sighted their prey had struck home. Which was scant consolation as they closed with a rapidity that seemed to thrust the flaring nostrils of their mounts on the faces of their opponents before even an opening volley could be fired.

The few shots that were fired rang out over the heads of the warriors, who ducked low from their mounts as the horses passed, swooping blows from ax and knife coming close to scoring their opponents. To duck and weave from the attack meant losing balance, falling to the ground and rolling to avoid the hooves of the wheeling horses, trying to steady and straighten blasters to get shots on target.

It was of little use. The blasters were bad for close-quarters combat of the sort that the warriors preferred, and for which they used their horses well. Now the advantage went their way, the height and strength of the horses putting them in control. Their greater numbers enabled them to distract the attention of their opponents, leaving them unsure of the where the next blow would fall.

Slowed by the chem suit, and all too aware of time running out before the mines went off with his people directly in the firing line, Ryan tried to see through the fog of dust kicked up by hooves and the moving walls of horse flesh, hoping that he would find some opening to effect a shift in the balance of power.

Failing that, he needed some kind of a miracle. If ever there was a time for him to believe in the Grandfather more than these tribesmen, it was now.

Maybe it was the spirits playing one last ghost trick on the tribesmen. Or favoring the friends in their desire to keep the land safe. Or perhaps it was nothing more than the erratic weather patterns that swept across the plains, always unpredictable but made worse by the nukecaust. Whichever of these—if either—the change in wind direction that had cleared the nerve gas leak enough for the tribesmen to see their enemy now shifted the balance of power once more.

To nature, rather than to either side of humanity.

In the confusion of the previous few minutes, none had noticed that the temperature had dropped as the wind that swept away the residue of gas had started to build, to grow stronger and more insistent. None had noticed that it had grown darker as it had cooled, with clouds sweeping in on the fresh breezes. In the chem suits, it was hot no matter what; the warriors had more important things on their mind than the heat of the sun.

It was only with the first heavy drop of rain that it became obvious.

They had been caught up in storms since the time they had left the ville of Brisbane and wandered onto the plains. Dust, rain, snow...all of these had befallen them. But they had all been figments of imagination spurred by the gas. Only once had there been a real storm. The flash flood that followed in its wake was something that Ryan would not forget in a long time.

Neither would he forget the feel of real rain, as opposed to the unreal sensations of the other storms.

Now, with a chem suit to protect him from the nerve gas, he knew that what he was seeing could be nothing other than the real thing; and although the rain was not hitting his skin, the feel of the heavy droplets on the thin material of the suit was something that couldn't be faked by his mind.

He knew that he had to marshal his people and get them to high ground. Fast. The rain had already increased in intensity so that the drops were falling like a sheet of water. The ground beneath their feet was becoming treacherous, making them slide, making it difficult to keep balance. The horses fared little better. It may make the warriors less of a danger, but it meant that their careering mounts became unpredictable and a danger all of their own.

Dust, mud and water smeared the clear plastic eyepiece on the suit, leaving Ryan unsure of where the others were in relation to him, and where he was in relation to any high ground. He yelled incoherently, hoping that they would follow the sound of his voice as he moved toward the only high spot—the outcrop in which the redoubt entrance was recessed.

As he scrambled onto the rocks, and clear of the ground beneath, Ryan realized his predicament. The ground beneath was a bubbling stream of mud, in which the others were sliding and slipping as they sought to join him. He saw Doc go down, skittering as he tried to regain his footing, falling face-first so that the mud covered him from head to foot before reaching out for the relative safety of the rocks.

Relative because it kept them out of the foaming mud sea that was dismounting the warriors as their horses bucked and reared, but yet kept them trapped on what amounted to nothing more than a time bomb.

Mildred yelled something at him, but her voice was drowned by the weight of water and the sound of the rain as it ricocheted off the rocks and pounded on the head-piece of the chem suit, beating a tattoo that made all else inaudible. She was pointing down below them, gesturing toward where the nerve gas tanks were situated.

He didn't need her words to understand what she meant. It was all too obvious to him.

From the corner of his eye, he saw Jak leap from the rock and into the swirling waters. Several of the riders had been dismounted. Their steeds thrashed around, panicking and unsure of what to do. Jak grabbed one, hauled himself onto it, then beckoned to his fellows on the rock.

The warriors who were still mounted had forgotten about their erstwhile enemies, lending assistance to the men who struggled in the storm.

This was the only chance they would get. Ryan urged his people to follow Jak, gesturing as words wouldn't be heard. He leaped off the rock and into the water, executing a shallow dive. He felt himself skim the floor of the plain, yet he was able to come up and struggle to his feet. There was a riderless horse within a few yards. He grabbed at it, getting hold on the second attempt. Lungs and muscles burning with the effort, he hauled himself onto the steed, looking around.

Krysty was behind Jak, who collected her from where she landed. Doc hit the water near Ryan, and without another glance for J.B. and Mildred, he headed for the old man. Doc was impeded by the water, but still managed to struggle onto the horse. As Ryan wheeled it around, he could see that J.B. and Mildred had tamed a steed between them, and were also circling.

A moment of near panic seized Ryan as he realized he had lost all bearing. The rushing water and the sheets of rain made each direction look the same. The last thing he wanted was to guide his mount to an area that was mined.

J.B. threw out an arm, indicating a direction. Through the mists of rain, Ryan could see a distant plateau that he knew lay due east. Breathing a sigh of relief that he had gained a bearing, and thankful for the steady eye of the Armorer, Ryan spurred his mount so that it headed in the right direction.

It was agonizingly slow as the horses thrashed their way through the churning waters, fighting against the tide, the rain blowing into their faces. Ryan hoped that they had buried the mines deep enough for them to stay in position in the sludge that sucked beneath the waters.

Fireblast, he thought. It was too late to worry now. They had to get away. Would the warriors try to stop them? In the lashing rain and wind, he had lost sight of them. The only thing he could be sure of was they weren't directly ahead. Right now, that was all that mattered.

Even in the pounding of the storm, the staggered explosions of the mines, fractionally apart because of timers rendered erratic by age, still sounded deafening. The water rippled and pulsed around them, threatening to throw them, and the churning mud was pitted by stones and clods of earth thrown up by the blast. They were far enough distant not to be under threat from the large chunks of rock thrown off by the explosion, but not far enough that the smaller detritus couldn't inflict some pain.

Pain they could all ignore in their relief that they were far enough clear. Pain that did not matter. They were still alive.

Had the mines done their job? If calculations were correct, then yes. But there was no way in hell that they were going to check. All they wanted to do right now was keep on going until the storm subsided, and they could ride easy.

SOME TIME PASSED before they began to slow. The rains had ceased and the skies were once more a deep blue, tinged with ochre streaks. The heat beat down on them, and it was sweltering inside the chem suits. The silence, with no rain pounding down, was almost deafening. Only now, with the faint ringing in their ears, did they realize how loud the mines had been.

"Figure it's safe to take these damn suits off?" Mildred questioned. "I feel like a Thanksgiving turkey, trussed up like this."

"Whatever the hell that means, I'll go along with it," Krysty added.

Ryan looked at the clear skies, felt the direction of what little breeze there was as it plucked at his chem suit. "What do you say, J.B.?"

"Reckon that any gas left will have been blown or washed away by the storm," the Armorer mused. "Any weird shit starts to happen, then this time we'll know what it is, anyway." He shrugged.

"Good enough." Jak sighed, removing the headpiece of the chem suit. "Feels better," he said, taking a deep breath.

"Where do we head from here?" Mildred asked.

"We could, perhaps, head back toward the ville of Brisbane. We fared well there," Doc suggested.

J.B. chuckled. "Guess I could try to figure where it is from here, but it could be one long trek."

"'Sides which, how do we explain to Hearne how we came to lose all his jack and come back like this?" Ryan chuckled. "Might be worth running down those bastard coldhearts who got us here. And there's the tribes. They've kept themselves apart for their own reasons. Who are we to stir up shit for them?"

They traveled on for a short while, then Krysty voiced the thought that had, in some degree, passed through all their minds.

"I wonder what the three tribes will do now that they realize that there's no answer at the end of the rainbow? That it was all about white-eye chem shit. And now that they're free of hallucination, what will they think when they realize that the prophecy was based on a lie and that there is no promised land for them?"

"I think," Doc replied at length, "that they will not see it as a failure. All legend is mutable, after all. A history that predates the records we have left, certainly shows that they will adapt so that defeat comes to resemble victory. They have, after all, fought a noble battle in which they sought to follow the word of their Grandfather, the great spirit Wakan Tanka."

J.B. thought about that. "But doesn't that make him a liar and a cheat?"

"You talk like it real," Jak scoffed.

Doc, remembering his conversation with the Armorer back at the redoubt, stifled a small smile. "There used to be a saying, John Barrymore, that God works in mysterious ways, his wonders to perform. I would assume that could be said of any God. Perhaps he has been testing them by asking something that will test them, stretch them to the limit. By showing blind faith and following, even if there is no gold at the end of the rainbow, then they have proved they are worthy of their God." He sniffed. "It would not be the first time this has happened. It will not be the last."

"So just by surviving they've proved themselves," Ryan pondered. "Harsh bastard."

"Gods have a tendency to be such," Doc mused, "yet without them we are lost. Generally speaking. By surviving, you win. At least until the next test of faith. And after that, you simply work with what you have."

They rode on in silence for a while longer, each lost in his or her own thoughts.

"Why not?" Mildred said eventually, as if to herself. "It's all any of us can do."

TAKE 'EM FREE

2 action-packed novels plus a mystery bonus

NO RISK

NO OBLIGATION TO BUY